texas heat

**Center Point
Large Print**

**This Large Print Book carries the
Seal of Approval of N.A.V.H.**

texas heat

LONE STAR ★ INTRIGUE

BOOK ONE

DEBRA WHITE SMITH

CENTER POINT PUBLISHING
THORNDIKE, MAINE

This Center Point Large Print edition
is published in the year 2009 by arrangement with
Avon Inspire, an imprint of HarperCollins Publishers.

The text of this Large Print edition is unabridged.
In other aspects, this book may vary
from the original edition.
Printed in the United States of America.
Set in 16-point Times New Roman type.

ISBN: 978-1-60285-549-6

Library of Congress Cataloging-in-Publication Data

Smith, Debra White.
   Texas heat / Debra White Smith.
      p. cm.
   ISBN 978-1-60285-549-6 (library binding : alk. paper)
   1. False imprisonment--Fiction. 2. Texas--Fiction. 3. Large type books. I. Title.
   PS3569.M5178T46 2009b
   813'.54--dc22
2009019742

texas heat

CHAPTER ONE

"I'm sorry to tell you this, Charli, but I'm here to arrest you." Jack gazed down at his old flame as the sweet Texas twilight ushered in a chorus of singing crickets. A whippoorwill's whistle blended in to lend a deceptive peace to the whole countryside. The summer breeze flitted across the porch and tangled with the wind chime behind Jack while Charli gazed up at him in blank horror.

"Wh-what?" she stammered.

Jack's gut knotted worse than he'd imagined. His heart pounded harder. And his mind replayed memories he hadn't counted on. Charli had been voted homecoming queen twelve years ago at Jacksonville College. Even though Jack was five years older and a college dropout, he'd been her escort. She'd never looked more beautiful. Unless you counted now. Even in a pair of blue jean cut-offs with her hair in a ponytail and those big brown eyes like beacons of terror, Charli was still the best looking woman Jack had seen . . . since the last time he saw her in the Brookshire's grocery store nearly a week ago.

He remembered the day: Saturday. The time: 6:03 P.M. And the occasion: he'd been buying hamburger for a cookout. For one.

He'd "conveniently" stood in the line behind Charli. And this time, she'd responded to his light conversation with a warm smile and easy chitchat. He'd even gotten a giggle out of Bonnie, who was usually as cautious as her mom could be. Jack had lived dangerously and asked them to join him for the cookout. She'd shocked him by agreeing and had insisted upon bringing drinks. The evening had been simple—just two "old friends" enjoying the burgers and sunset while Bonnie made friends with Jack's blue heeler, Sam. Jack had taken great pains not to pressure Charli and hadn't even walked her to the car when her two-hour visit ended. Even though she gave him no indicator that she was romantically interested, Jack virtually floated back into his log cabin.

Since the day she drove back into town five years ago, he'd been moving toward reconciling with Charli. He'd started by opening a checking account where she worked at the Bullard Savings and Loan. Then, he advanced to "accidentally" bumping into her all over town. That first year back she'd been emotionally frigid, and Jack could barely get her to look at him, but he'd never wavered in his goal.

And just when I'm seeing some results, I get to arrest her, he groused. Even now, Jack struggled with how a woman of such integrity and charm had fallen to embezzlement. But that wasn't for him to determine.

"There's a warrant for your arrest," he explained. The faint smell of fresh-baked cookies mingled with his unexpected urge to grab Charli and secretly sweep her away to some remote place in Mexico where she'd never be found.

This wasn't easy. Not by a long shot.

"For *my* arrest?" Charli clutched at the neck of her T-shirt. "Are you *sure* it's me?" she squeaked. "There must be a mistake of some sort, Jack."

"No, it's for you," he explained. Jack rested his hand on his hip, looked down, shook his head. "I'm sorry, Charli. I've *got* to take you in."

"Mommy?" a small voice called from another room before a little girl appeared on the edge of the den. She held a sugar cookie that testified to the aroma wafting over Jack. Like her mom, she wore shorts and a loose T-shirt. Cookie dough dotted her hair. Flour streaked her cheek. If that wasn't enough to shatter a heart as hard as marble, the child's long dark hair and rosy cheeks were too much like her mother's for Jack's comfort. He didn't know if he'd ever smell sugar cookies again without getting sick.

"Can you tell me what for?" Charli rasped, her eyes pooling with liquid dread.

"Embezzlement," Jack supplied, and his gaze slid back to the child.

"Mommy!" Bonnie trotted forward and wrapped herself around her mother's leg.

"It's okay, sweetie," Charli choked out and bent to pick up her daughter. While Bonnie twined her arms and legs around Charli like a scared monkey,

9

Charli buried her face in her daughter's mass of curly hair.

The silence left Jack feeling like the criminal who needed to be arrested. He'd be far more comfortable if his former love at least had the decency to look guilty or go into a rage or even glare at him.

But she didn't. Charli lifted her watery gaze back to him and peered a hole right into his soul.

"I have no idea . . ." she said, her lips quivering.

Jack looked down. The evidence said she *did* have an idea. And a big one at that.

"You've got to believe me, Jack!" Charli insisted, her mellow Texas accent adding credibility to her claim. "You can't just take me away like this! You can't! I didn't *do* anything! And what about—what about Bonnie?"

"Mommy! Don't go!" the child wailed. "Don't let him take you!"

So much for gaining ground with Bonnie, he thought. Jack pressed his fingertips against his eyes, but no amount of pressure erased the image of mother and daughter from his mind.

Of all the bizarre situations his position had flung him into, this was the worst. He hadn't believed Charli would embezzle a dime until he'd seen the bank records. And once he was convinced, Jack had been crushed. He also knew he couldn't send one of his men to the task. He'd rather be the one—even if the job did rip him to pieces. In some crazy way, he thought his presence would ease her and maybe, just maybe, he could somehow protect her, even from the consequences of her own actions.

Of course, if the Tyler FBI realized he and Charli had a history, they wouldn't have let Jack arrest her, due to conflict of interest. But even in a small town, people forgave old relationships.

"I've got to do my job," he managed to say. "Is there someone you can call to come get . . ." He pointed to the child who should have been his. He didn't even say her name. He couldn't. Charli had always said her first daughter would be named Bonnie. Jack had naively assumed her last name would be Mansfield.

"You know my mom passed away last year," she said and coughed over a sob.

"I know," Jack said. He'd sent a massive wreath to the funeral and attended both the chapel and graveside services. That's when Charli and he had moved from a friendly hello to brief conversation. Even though Jack hadn't sent the wreath and attended the funeral to score any points, he'd taken the points and been glad to get them.

Of course, Charli didn't mention her alcoholic dad as any potential help. She didn't have to. Jack knew he'd divorced her mother and the family when Charli was ten—just like Vince Friedmont had divorced Charli before she ever gave birth to their child.

"My half sister lives in San Antonio," she groaned. "And only God knows where Vince is."

Jack had been on the verge of proposing eleven years ago when that no-count Friedmont had charmed Charli into the zombie zone. Tall and blond and lean, Vince had driven a fast sports car and worked even faster on Charli. She'd ignored Jack's warnings about Vince's character, accused him of being blinded by jealousy, and went starry-eyed over the jerk. Jack balled his fist. Even now, he wanted to punch the loser.

Then he reminded himself that he was the one arresting Charli, dragging her from the clutches of her child. And he wondered who was worse— Vince for leaving her or himself for arresting her.

Except I'm just doing my job, he reminded himself. *And the evidence indicates—*

"Is it something to do with the bank?" Charli's forehead wrinkled, and she peered up at Jack as if he were her rescuer, not the arresting officer.

"Yeah." He nodded.

"H-how much?"

"Over a hundred thousand," Jack said.

Moaning, Charli stumbled away from the door and collapsed on the couch. She cradled her child and rocked back and forth.

"Oh, God help me," she whimpered. "I knew I should have quit two years ago. Something *told* me."

As Bonnie's wailing mixed with her mother's,

Jack's belief in the evidence wavered. He'd done his share of textbook work on the psychology of criminals and had enough firsthand experience to know that most people the department arrested vowed they were innocent, sometimes in the face of a line of witnesses ten miles long. But Charli's shattered expression and clueless eyes defied any knowledge of the crime.

Jack stepped into the house, nudged the door shut. His leather holster creaked with the movement, and he wished he was wearing anything but this uniform.

Something crunched under his foot. He looked down. The sugar cookie had crumbled beneath the toe of his boot. Jack rubbed his face again. This was *not* the stuff that dreams were made of. Not at all.

More like nightmares, he thought.

He finished closing the door. The knob clicked. And Jack remembered many nights stepping into this homey living room, waiting on Charli to come out for their date. The small farmhouse had been her mom's . . . and her grandparents'. Although the place had been remodeled more than once, the stone fireplace had served three generations and always made him feel welcome.

Except now.

Either she's a good actress, or she really is innocent, he thought, and he'd never wanted anyone to be innocent more than now.

The next ten minutes jumbled into a blur for Charli. Somehow, she'd managed to call her pastor's wife, Pat Jonas, but she held no memory of dialing the number even with Pat standing in her living room trying to pry Bonnie out of her arms. No one would guess the middle-aged, ruddy woman in overalls was a pastor's wife . . . or that Bonnie could resist Pat's strong hold as long as she had.

"Mommy! Mommy! Don't go, Mommy!" Bonnie screamed and dug her fingernails into Charli's back.

She winced and tried to mumble something soothing. All that came out was a muffled cough and a whimper.

"Don't let that mean man take you!" Bonnie bellowed.

Charli felt Jack hovering by the door like some sort of a police chief dinosaur who grew larger with every minute. She pulled at Bonnie's frame, but the child only tightened her hold.

"I'll be back tomorrow, honey," Charli explained and looked to Jack for some assurance.

"There's a bondsman close," he said and nodded.

"Mark and I will take a church offering and take care of the bond," Pat assured. "Lord knows we've had our share of experience." Their son had been on the church prayer list since Charli could remember. In and out of jail, he'd finally landed in prison for extended correction.

"You've *got* to believe me, Pat," she pleaded as Pat won the tug-of-war and Bonnie released her mother. Charli stumbled to regain her balance while the child wilted against Pat and inconsolably sobbed through the surrender.

"I'm not guilty," Charli continued and pressed the heels of her hands against her temples. "I don't know what's happened. There must have been some—some mistake. I'm sure it will all be straightened out t-tomorrow and the charges will be dropped. I just can't imagine what's happened!"

"Don't worry, Charli," Pat assured, her gray eyes certain. "Neither Mark nor I believe you took *one cent.*" She shot Jack a glare that would shrivel a seven-foot cactus.

"Look," Jack said, holding up his hand, "I'm just doing my job."

Pat's defiant gaze faltered. She sighed. "I know. It's just that Charli's like—like the daughter we never had and the best volunteer in our church."

Jack held Charli's gaze. His dark eyes pleaded for her forgiveness while his Chief of Police badge apologized for nothing. Once her mom died, Charli and Jack had begun developing a distant friendship. As small as Bullard was, they'd seen each other often and had fallen into light conversation more often than not. When he asked her to his place last Saturday, Charli had spontaneously agreed. She'd been a bit lonely and dreaded going back to her empty house.

But once she was on his ranch, Charli wondered if she'd made the wisest choice. Even though Jack had kept the conversation impersonal and friendly, his guarded eyes said more than he spoke. While she didn't want to give him false hope, in the end she'd been glad she went. Those two hours had awakened her to the possibility that their "chance meetings" around town weren't always accidental.

She'd also begun to wonder if she could perhaps love again. She still hadn't answered that question and certainly wasn't going to deliberate over it with Jack carting her off to jail.

Bonnie's sniffling seized her attention. Charli reached to stroke her daughter's hair, but stopped. The best thing was to make a clean break.

"I don't guess I'll need my purse, huh?" she asked and couldn't bring herself to look higher than Jack's chin this time.

"No," he said and opened the door. "We'd just have to put it in a safe."

Jack's features were as strong and rugged as his dark eyes were haunted and lonely. He'd never married. Charli's mother made sure she knew that piece of information the day she moved back home. Now Charli wondered if his remaining single had anything to with her breaking his heart.

Head drooping, Charli walked past Jack and through the door. Before stepping into the purple twilight, she glanced back at Pat. "I just started the cookies for the bake sale tomorrow," she explained. "Would you please wrap up the ones I've already finished? It doesn't look like I'll be following through on that deal."

"Don't worry about it, Charli." Pat shook her head. "You're always taking care of everybody else. This time, you need to just let it go. It's your turn for some support. Understand?"

"Thanks." Charli stepped into the night just as she'd done dozens of times when she and Jack were dating. Except this time, they weren't dating. This time, Jack Mansfield was arresting Charli for a crime she didn't commit.

CHAPTER TWO

"Is this the part where you put the handcuffs on me?" Charli paused by the police car.

Jack reached for the back passenger door handle but then moved to the front. Still standing beside the car, he turned to Charli as he opened her door. The car's interior light cast a Picasso of angles and shadows on his features. "No handcuffs," he said with a smile that looked more like a grimace. Charli once again detected a hint of misgivings . . . along with silent despair. "Go ahead and sit in front." He waved toward the passenger seat. "Somehow, I don't think you'll try to break and run."

"Let's hope not," Charli mumbled as she slid into the vehicle, into the smell of warm coffee. The thump of Jack's closing the door finalized the inevitable.

When Jack crawled into the driver's seat and closed his door, Charli cut him a quick glance. Her initial dismay gave way to a slow burn in her brain. Even though her logical side insisted that Jack wasn't to blame, Charli's neck and face heated with the injustice of his dragging her from her child.

He cranked the vehicle, put it into reverse, and backed out of the driveway.

She snapped her seat belt with a vengeance, crossed her arms, and glared out the window. The yard lights illuminated the oil-topped road, shadowed by nine o'clock twilight. Charli strained to catch a final glance of her home as Bonnie appeared at the living room window. She pawed at the pane while tears streamed down her face. As quickly as Bonnie had appeared, Pat pulled her away and yanked the drapes shut.

Charli clamped her top lip between her teeth as a hard shiver rocked her soul and her ire increased one-hundred fold. "Bonnie has already lost a father," she accused. "And now you're taking away her mother." She whirled to face her former love. "I hope you can sleep with yourself tonight, Jack Mansfield!"

"I'm just doing my job—just like I told Pat," he growled and lifted his hand. "What did you want me to do, Charli? Send Payton after you? He's like a law-and-order robot, for cryin' out loud! Who'd you rather take you to jail? Me, or a stranger?"

"Pardon me!" The hot tears blurred her vision. "But I've never had to consider those choices!" Charli hunkered against the seat and stared straight ahead as the vehicle rolled along the dark country lane.

The acres and acres of land had once belonged to her ancestors but through the years had been sold parcel by parcel. Now cattlemen claimed most of the property. The great, silent cows meandering along the fence lines in the moonlight offered little encouragement.

Charli scrubbed at the tears while her heart tore. She thought she'd known every level of heartbreak . . . until now. When her father walked out, she'd been devastated. When Vince had proven to be everything Jack said he was, Charli had been both mortified and desolate. When her mother died of multiple myeloma, Charli didn't think she could even lift her head for weeks. But this . . . this involved the welfare of Bonnie!

Her heart quivered with the weight of the burden. *What if I'm convicted?* she thought. *How long will I stay in prison? Who will take care of Bonnie? Will she even know me when I come home?* As one question after another bombarded her soul, Charli hugged herself and swallowed the low moan that floated from her inner being.

Jack slowed for the upcoming intersection.

Dazed, Charli lifted her gaze to determine where they were and to calculate how much longer she would be free. The white chapel perched near a clump of oaks proudly bore the name Oak Grove Community Church. The full moon baptized the countryside in an aura that gave the church a surreal glow, suggesting it was a mirage of yesteryear. But Charli knew otherwise. While the church building dated back to the early twentieth century, the congregation was thriving with an up-to-date experience with God.

A movement to the right, a flash of white, caught Charli's attention, and she spotted a white-tailed deer running parallel with the car. The long-legged doe darted forward and lunged in front of the vehicle.

"Watch out!" Charli exclaimed. Jack slammed on the brakes.

With a cry, he extended his arm to brace Charli. She lunged forward, and the seat belt ate into her chest. By the time she crashed back against the seat, the deer was hopping to the other side of the road.

Once the doe was out of sight, she felt Jack's appraisal. As much as Charli tried to resist looking at him, her gaze was drawn to his anyway. The dash lights illuminated the memory that played across his features . . . a memory that barged into Charli's mind despite her mental protests.

They'd been on their way to a Jaguar basketball

game. Jack had picked her up that night in his new truck. Charli sat as close as she could without helping him drive and hung on tight as he gassed the Ford along the winding lane. They'd been carefree and falling in love, singing to the beat of a Michael W. Smith CD. They were in the bend of a long curve when a deer had dashed out in front of them. Jack slammed on his brakes and braced her with the strength of his arm while the truck fishtailed to a teeth-jarring stop.

"You okay?" he'd asked.

"Y-yes," Charli had said and then the two of them fell into a fit of nervous laughter that ended in an earth-shaking kiss.

That night, Charli knew she was falling in love. But mere weeks later, she'd met Vince. Somehow she'd been duped by a master. Charli still wasn't sure she understood what happened. And she didn't think she could ever trust her instincts again. The very thought of getting married made her want to run . . . as quickly as she wanted to run from the jail cell looming ahead.

She looked down. Jack lowered his arm.

"I'm sorry, Charli," he mumbled, "for—for everything."

Charli squeezed her upper arms and began the slow rocking she'd fallen into on her couch. She gazed out her window once again. "Do you believe I'm guilty?" she asked, barely recognizing her throaty voice.

21

"When I first heard . . . and saw the evidence . . . I was shocked. It's so convincing. I didn't want to believe it, but—"

"But you *do?*" Charli asked and searched his face for any sign he might trust her.

He slowly shook his head. "No. I don't."

The honest sorrow cloaking Jack's face reaped a low sob that racked Charli's body. "Oh, Jack," she moaned, "what am I going to do?"

"I'll help you any way I possibly can," he vowed.

Despite Jack's assuring appraisal, Charli began to feel like the victim of a spider's sticky web. She'd experienced this same sensation the night Vince came home drunk with lipstick on his ear. He'd told her it was none of her business and then crashed on the couch. Charli had sat in the living room and stared at him for hours . . . feeling trapped in a black hole known as matrimony . . . not knowing what to do, where to turn.

The longer Charli sat in the unmoving vehicle, the harder it was to breathe. A surge of prickly heat crept up Charli's body and insisted she must fight her way to freedom. With a mad whimper, she clawed for the door latch, but Jack's strong hand covered hers while his arm pressed against her once more.

"Charli, no," he said.

Dismay blurred the edges of terror, and she shoved at his arm. "Get away from me! I don't need your help!"

"Okay, okay," he said and pulled back. "Just calm down."

Panting, Charli stared into his eyes, now full of torment. A look she was all too familiar with.

Jack had been waiting for her at home after she'd stood him up to be with Vince. The second Vince pulled into the drive, Jack got out of his truck and slammed the door. He'd reminded her of a tall, lean gunslinger, ready to duel to the death. Vince had paused only long enough to let Charli out, and then he'd sped from the driveway with the screech of tires. Looking back, Charli now saw what Jack had tried to warn her about that night. Vince was a low-life coward. He wouldn't even face Jack. He left Charli to the mercy of Jack's fury . . . a very cold, silent fury that had peered at her through tormented eyes.

That night, Charli officially broke up with Jack. He'd cried. She'd gone inside, believing the breakup was for the best.

Life had gotten so complicated; now Charli had no idea what was best. She'd been in survival mode for so long, she didn't know how to do anything but cling to what was constant, unchanging, and never dare choose to change another thing. Choices were dangerous. That's why she'd gone against her gut instinct and stayed at the bank. She'd been afraid to leave.

Jack broke her gaze, gripped the steering wheel with both hands, and stared straight ahead. Finally, he put the car into drive and pressed the accelerator. At last, the country trees blurred into city lights, and the car rolled to a stop at the Bullard Police Department. She stared at the brick building, as cold and inhospitable as a morgue, and fought the instinct to run again. Her whole life she'd listened to hunters who detailed the chase—how they cornered a rabbit or deer and took its life. Never had she felt such compassion for the hunted and such disdain for the hunter.

Her door opened. Charli gazed up at Jack. As her urge to escape vanished in the face of the inevitable, she stood. Jack ushered her toward the glass entryway, opened the door, and allowed her to pass into the building first.

The place smelled of coffee and musty files. The dispatcher glanced up from her work and right into Charli's face. Charli recognized her from around town. Her name was Rose something-or-other. She was the first cousin of a gal Charli went to church with. She'd even visited church a few times.

The sight of a familiar face sent a new lump into Charli's throat and the desire to plead, "Please help me," but she didn't. Jack took her arm and nudged her to the back, where she was booked, fingerprinted, and photographed.

Finally, he said, "You're allowed one phone call."

Charli shook her head. "There's no one to call."

Jack's eyebrows flexed. "No? Are you sure?"

She nodded. "My mother's dead. My father's gone. I have no idea where he is or if he's alive. Same for my husband. My half sister is so jealous she can't stand me. Who's left?" She lifted her hand and shrugged. "My church is my family. My pastor and his wife already know what's going on. They're going to try to post bond for me."

Jack turned his face and scrubbed it with the massive hand that once enveloped hers. He grabbed a set of keys from behind the desk and said, "Sit here for a few, okay?" He pointed toward an empty chair near a desk that had needed to be replaced since 1910.

Charli slumped into the chair and lowered her head. Her hair fell forward, shielded her features, and Jack suspected she might be silently weeping.

Never had he been tempted to help someone escape. But tonight the temptation overtook him and nearly pushed him to the brink of a few rash moves that would end his career.

Lieutenant Payton's dry cough dragged Jack's attention to the nearest desk. The young officer eyed Charli and then gazed up at his chief with a question. Payton's squared shoulders, his coffee-colored skin and towering physique turned a few female heads. But Jack learned that his passion for defending justice kept him from a distracting social life. He was exactly where Jack had been ten years ago—all about law and order and black and white. Problem was, everything in life wasn't staunchly black and white. Sometimes, there were shades of gray. Presently, the gray was threatening Jack's better judgment.

Jack's gaze slid past Payton to Dan Yarborough. The blue-eyed twenty-something was as inexperienced as Payton was dedicated. He shot a wary glance toward Charli and avoided looking at Jack. After a pause that hurt, Yarborough shoved back his chair and strolled toward the coffee room.

Jack didn't have to look back at Payton to know he was still staring. The last thing Jack needed was for any of his men to suspect the chief was going soft. And Payton and Yarborough were both too observant not to sense something was up—unless Jack put on the act of the decade. He braced himself, lifted his chin, and marched toward the row of cells that housed a few other women. Most of the ladies incarcerated tonight should be exactly where they were. Charli Friedmont wasn't one of them, and Jack refused to put her in a cell with someone who drank like a street bum and was a walking profanity parrot.

He neared the last cell, where Payton had just turned the key on Sal Walker before Jack left for Charli's. Sal was a "regular" who probably needed a weekend in the local mental institution rather than jail. He'd pitied her for many years and wished she could get some long-term care. All Jack could do was make recommendations and hope her family followed through. They never did.

He always made sure Sal was placed in a cell by herself when she showed up. It helped her and the other inmates as well. A few times, Jack had wondered if she actually enjoyed spending the weekend in jail as a break from reality.

Jack inserted the key into the lock. Sal gazed up at him through stringy hair that probably hadn't been washed since Christmas. "Sorry, Sal," he said, "but I'm going to have to move you."

Minutes later, he'd settled Sal into another cell with a woman who was as silent as a mime and ushered Charli toward Sal's old cell. Of course, Jack had arranged for the sheets on the cot to be changed and made sure the chamber didn't have any leftover Sal surprises.

Now Charli walked next to him without a trace of resistance, and Jack fought to keep his spine stiff, his face impassive. Payton's presence hovered behind like some kind of an all-knowing eye, and Jack maintained an emotionless air. His face set rock hard, he stared straight ahead.

Thankfully, Charli didn't seem to notice. When Jack opened the cell, she blindly stepped in and left the faintest aroma of rose perfume and sugar cookies in her wake—just enough to mock Jack. He inwardly groaned as she neared the cot and sat on the edge.

After the lock on Charli's cell clicked into place, Jack gripped the bar and lingered long enough for

27

one last gaze. Head hanging, she hugged herself and began that blasted rocking again.

He turned and strode down the corridor that led straight to Payton and Yarborough. Gritting his teeth, Jack stomped past the officers' desks and didn't dare risk a glance at them. He passed the dispatcher's desk and targeted the hallway that would take him to his office.

"Want some more coffee?" Rose Black asked. "I'm going to make a new pot."

Jack glared at the redheaded woman who was old enough to be his mother and nosey enough to be a private eye. "No!" he barked, and sensed she was every bit as interested in Charli as Payton and Yarborough were.

"Well, exc*uuuu*se me," she mumbled under her breath.

Not bothering to apologize or even look at her, Jack stormed down the hallway, into his office. He slammed the door and attacked his desk like an angry bear sweeping aside assailants with one massive paw. The desktop clutter slammed against the wall and landed in a heap of paperwork. A half-full can of root beer, plopped atop the clutter, toppled sideways and doused the mess in warm, syrupy liquid. Jack grabbed the can, slung it into the wastebasket, and kicked the pile. He crashed into his chair, which rolled back and bumped into the wall. Jack pounded his fist against the armrest and stifled the roar erupting from his soul.

In another round of fury, he stood and kicked at the clutter again. The sticky mess slapped the wall and slid toward the floor, leaving a damp, dark trail in its wake. Only a couple of papers stayed stuck to the wall, and the sight of one of them increased Jack's temperature. He snatched it up and glared at the image that had haunted him for nearly a year. Brenda Downey's smiling face was featured beneath the word in bold black letters: MISSING. The young woman had disappeared from her country home and no one had seen one trace of her. Jack took every unsolved case personally, and the woman's photo stirred his gut now more than ever. Like Brenda Downey, Charli Friedmont was another female who'd been victimized. And the longer Jack stared at Brenda the more her features took on the nuance of Charli's.

With a frustrated growl, Jack wadded the poster into a damp ball and slammed it into the trash can. Never had he hated his job so much.

CHAPTER THREE

Charli opened her gritty eyes and glanced around the Spartan cell. The weak morning light oozed passed the barred window like a mist of doom that only heightened her confusion. Her dazed mind grappled with where she was and how she landed here. Her first concern was for Bonnie. She twisted to see if her child had crawled into bed with her during the night, but there was no dark wavy hair lying on the pillow, no pink cheeks, no long lashes resting against ivory skin. Charli swung her legs from beneath the covers; as her feet touched the cool concrete, she began the remembering. When she reached for her cell phone in the pocket of her shorts, the remembering was complete.

She was in jail. They'd taken her fingerprints and photo. Charli left her cell phone at home, in her purse. Bonnie was with Pat Jonas.

Charli had never wondered what it would be like to spend the night in jail. The possibility never even crossed her mind. Equally odd was the realization that her former college flame wandered the hallways while she sat in her cell. She still wore her shorts and T-shirt, now rumpled and tired.

After scooting her feet into her sandals, Charli stood, stretched, and wondered when the church would be able to post bond for her. She paced the short distance to the brick wall, turned, and paced back. Pat Jonas had said they were going to take up an offering.

But what if it's not enough? Charli stopped, pressed the heels of her hands against her temples. *What if they don't even come through?* A swell of tension swept her body. Every person she'd counted on in life had let her down. First her father. Then Vince. While her mother hadn't purposefully abandoned her, Charli still felt the brunt of her absence as if she'd chosen to disappear.

Maybe the church people just say *they love me,* she thought. *Maybe they won't believe I'm innocent.*

Charli collapsed on her cot, covered her face, and cried out to the only source she knew would never leave or forsake her. *Oh God!* she wailed within. *Please, please help me! I'm innocent! You know I am!*

She lowered her hands, stared through the bars, straight at a wall that was as bland as the cell. *"Who could have done this to me?"* she questioned and began the slow, mental inventory of every co-worker she knew. Someone at the bank had taken *a lot* of money and had apparently created a convincing scenario against her.

"Whoever it is, they've got to be smart," she mused and deleted three faces from her mental file. A few tellers could hardly count a stack of fifties, let alone pin embezzlement on a fellow employee.

She'd barely begun the musing when a new thought left her rigid. If the bank had pressed charges against her, then she was without a job. Not only would she have to hire a defense attorney, Charli would have no way to support herself and her child. She slipped to the floor, rested her arms on the cot, and buried her face in the blanket.

"Oh, dear God"—she breathed—"I feel like even You've forsaken me. *Please, please,* let all this be a nightmare."

Someone cleared his throat outside the cell, and

Charli raised her head to encounter the guileless blue stare of the young officer she'd seen last night. The gold bar on his shirt read Dan Yarborough. The dark circles under his eyes said he was ready to go home. He held a tray emitting an odor that held little appeal. A steaming cup suggested coffee was part of the fare, and that did entice Charli to stand while he rattled the cell lock into submission.

"Thanks," she said as he set the tray on the lone table.

"Sure," he replied and directed a glance toward her that was surprisingly sharp. In a flash, Charli remembered waiting on Dan Yarborough at the bank a couple of times in the last few months. She cringed and looked away. No telling what gossip was flying. Apparently, even the police force wasn't immune to speculation.

Jack stood at his back door, watched his blue heeler trot across the pasture and gather up the cattle for feed time. Of course, it didn't take much. Once they saw the dog they were self-propelled. Jack inherited Sam with his uncle's ranch.

He'd gotten the ranch by default. At the time, his brother Ryan had just divorced, and he didn't want the weight of a ranch on top of the pain of divorce. His other brother, Sonny, was as free spirited as they came. Like Ryan, he far preferred to take the cash inheritance and leave the farm to Jack, which suited Jack just fine. He loved the old place, right down to the fifty head of cattle, half a dozen horses, and the dog who insisted on sleeping at the foot of the bed because the crazy thing thought he was human.

Uncle Abe wanted Jack to have the place anyway. Jack moved in with the old bachelor and helped take care of him until the lung cancer got so bad he had to go to a hospice unit. His uncle had never married and never had any kids. But he'd spent more time with his sister's sons than their own father had, and his will reflected that he loved them like his own.

Now Jack possessed a small ranch that came with enough chores for three men. Given his professional obligations, he barely stayed on top, even with the help of his one hand, Bud.

Jack removed his cell phone from his blue jeans pocket, stepped onto the log cabin's porch, and settled into the aged porch swing. Its squeak reminded him of an old friend, welcoming him back. Eyeing the cloud-smeared sun creeping up the horizon, Jack tapped his cell phone. To call or not to call, that was the question. The morning breeze whispered all sorts of encouragement, and brought with it the faint scent of roses growing near the porch wall. They smelled every bit as sweet as Charli had last night.

She'd made it clear that she didn't want Jack's help at all. But that hadn't stopped him from hanging out in the office until the wee hours, just to make sure she didn't need anything . . . or ask for him. It also hadn't stopped him from wondering if he should call his brother Sonny.

If anybody could get to the bottom of Charli's case Sonny Mansfield topped the list. His private investigator track record was unmatched as far as Jack was concerned. He usually stopped at nothing—was scared of nothing. A few times, Jack wondered if the guy was going to get himself killed.

Still, Jack tapped his cell phone and deliberated. If he called Sonny, Charli would eventually find out, even if Sonny kept a low profile during the investigation. Of course, if Sonny uncovered the person who'd framed Charli, Jack was certain she'd listen and be grateful.

"I'm sure of it," he mumbled as Brenda Downey's features swam into his mind. His gut went hard, and Jack knew what he had to do. He didn't want Charli, like Brenda, to be "a case" for the police. Jack would do everything in his power to exonerate Charli . . . even if it meant risking her ire.

He pressed his brother's speed-dial number. When Sonny didn't answer and his voice mail kicked in, Jack hung up. Then, he pressed the redial button. He knew for a fact that Sonny was probably in bed, and his cell phone was on the nightstand within reach. Sonny had given Jack a distinctive ring—the theme song from the old TV show *The Dukes of Hazzard*. Jack winced. He couldn't stand that show and figured that was the reason Sonny had assigned him the tune. Despite his distaste, Jack knew Sonny would recognize the ring as his.

When the voice mail picked up a second time, he tried once more. *If he doesn't answer, I'm going over there,* he thought just before a muffled "What?" came over the line.

"Get up, you lazy dawg," Jack challenged as he kicked at a carpenter ant creeping along the porch. "I've got a case for you."

"What does it pay?" Sonny asked, his voice thick.

"Nothing. You owe me. Remember?"

His brother's sigh sounded as patient as a rabid porcupine.

A couple of years ago, Jack had bailed Sonny out when he came down with mononucleosis and hadn't been able to work for nearly a month. He'd gotten behind on his truck payment and nearly lost his vehicle. Shortly thereafter, Uncle Abe had passed away, and the three brothers received their inheritance. Sonny had offered to pay Jack back, but Jack had gone with a hunch and told him he'd need his services one day. That day had come.

"What is it?" Sonny mumbled. "Did the local Girl Scout cookie stash get robbed?"

"My, my, my, aren't we in a fine mood?" Jack groused. "Have you been drinking again?"

"Not on your life," Sonny growled. "I'm going to the bathroom. Wanta go with me or wait?"

"I'll wait," Jack replied. "That's one experience I don't want to share."

Jack lowered the phone, gazed at the cattle meandering toward the fence for their morning feed. He hoped Sonny was telling him the truth about the drinking. Periodically, he worried about his youngest brother and didn't want him repeating the mistakes Jack himself made when Charli dumped him.

Jack had fallen and fallen hard. He'd found his brother at the bottom, and the two of them had stayed drunk for weeks. Finally, Jack woke up and realized he was acting like a fool. He'd draped himself over the altar in an old country church and begged God to help him get back on his feet. He confessed everything he remembered doing during his drunken phase and asked for forgiveness for everything the booze may have blotted from his mind. Jack took no chances, held nothing back. He wanted a clean slate and threw himself upon God's mercy for all he recalled and all he had forgotten.

A miracle occurred that night. Jack walked away from the booze and never went back. He also found the strength to get back in college and finally finish his bachelor's degree in criminal justice. Unfortunately, Sonny hadn't recuperated quite so swiftly. In Jack's estimation, his journey to

God was still in progress. As for the drinking, Sonny had stopped that a few years ago after he'd almost killed himself in a one-vehicle wreck near their parents' place.

Jack had known about the wreck the second it happened. No one called him. He'd just known— like he knew the night Uncle Abe was dying. Since his childhood, Jack's mother had told him he had a special guardian angel telling him these things. Jack called it his danger sensor. While he was a long way from omniscient, sometimes he "knew in his knower" that something was wrong or that danger was lurking.

That night, Jack had been sitting in front of the TV watching a football game when he'd been immersed with an awareness that Sonny was in bad trouble. When Sonny didn't answer his cell phone, Jack sped from his apartment toward his parents' house, where Sonny still lived. He'd found his unconscious brother in a ditch beneath his wrecked pickup a quarter of a mile from home. The truck rested upside down over the ditch where Sonny lay. The pickup's flattened cab proved that Sonny was one of the rare people who was fortunate to have been thrown from his vehicle. If he'd been wearing his seat belt, he'd have been as flattened as the cab. Jack still marveled that the crash didn't kill Sonny.

Since no one else was involved, Jack had given Sonny a break. But the break came with a warning:

"If you ever do this again, I'll arrest you from your hospital bed and throw you *under* the jail."

Now Jack planted the phone back to his ear and cradled it against his shoulder. "Are you through?" he asked and began rolling up his shirtsleeve.

"Yeah," Sonny answered through a yawn. "What's the case?"

"Do you remember Charli Ellen? She's Charli Friedmont now." He switched the phone to his other ear and rolled up the other sleeve.

"Uh, yeah," Sonny said, "of course. You nearly died over her. Why wouldn't I?"

"She's been charged with embezzling a hundred grand from the bank she works for," Jack explained and eyed the sun anew.

Sonny whistled.

"She says she's innocent," Jack continued and wondered if the heat index would hit one hundred again today. Even at eight thirty, he felt the potential.

"And you want me to prove it?"

"You got it." He swiped at the beads of sweat collecting along his collar and wished for that breeze again.

"You still carrying a torch for her, man, because if—"

"Nobody said anything about any torches," Jack growled. "I just want to know if you'll see what you can find out."

"Because if you are," Sonny continued, his voice

measured, "you're a glutton for punishment. She already ripped your heart out once—"

"Look." Jack stood and stomped to the edge of the deck. "I just called to ask you to take her case."

"Ask me or *tell* me?"

"Take it any way you like," Jack shot back. "You owe me."

"So, if I don't, what-er-ya-gonna-do? Arrest me?"

"I might!" Jack frowned. Sometimes his brother could be too blasted cocky for his own good . . . or anybody else's for that matter. After Sonny stopped drinking, he got serious about life and established his detective business. He'd solved a good number of solid cases. One was even a high-profile missing person case that turned out to be murder. He'd been inundated with business ever since.

Sonny's silence left Jack imagining the squint that so reminded him of his father. "Okay," he finally said. A thump preceded the sound of a slamming door. "I'll do what you want." Sonny paused and then continued in a softer tone, "I hope you know there's always the chance I'll find out she really did it. Then what?"

"She didn't," Jack replied.

"Okay," Sonny said. "I've got some coffee to make." The sound of running water accompanied his words. "I'll call you later and see when I can meet with her."

"No deal," Jack replied and started down the porch steps.

"No what?"

"No deal," Jack repeated. "She doesn't know I'm calling you." His boots scraped against the drying grass that attested to his need to supplement the herd's diet with hay. The summer had barely started, and it was already as dry as it was hot.

Sonny's silence was punctuated by more running water. "So you want me to snoop around in secret?" he questioned.

"Right." Jack didn't bother to explain.

"Just a minute," Sonny said. "I've got another call coming in."

"Okay," Jack said and was thankful for the break.

As he approached the hay barn, he wrangled with how to keep Sonny from knowing Charli had specifically told him she didn't need his help. That would probably earn Jack a five-minute lecture. Sonny trusted women like a hound trusted weasels. Jack had been there himself. He'd been a charter member of the Bachelors Against Lying Women Association for years after Charli dumped him. But the minute she stepped back into town, Jack's resolve had melted into a desperate case of renewed desire. Now he was as hooked as he'd ever been.

He shoved open the barn door. It hit the barn with a clap when Sonny's voice came back over the line. "Listen, gotta go," he said. "I'll call you in an hour or so. You can give me the details, and we'll be good to go. I'll try to do whatever you need—no matter how crazy it is," he huffed. "Except . . ."

"Except what?"

"You're in law enforcement. Do you know how much easier this would be if I could talk to Charli first?"

"No! Absolutely not!"

Sonny's sighed. "Okay. Whatever you say. You've bailed me out enough, I guess I can do the same for you."

"Thanks," Jack replied and realized the call was disconnected. He shut the cell, dropped it into his pocket, and yanked on the first bale of hay he came to. After marching to the fence, he hurled it over and watched the cattle trot toward him for their morning portion. When he went back for the next bale, Jack glanced toward Bud's plank house. The place wasn't more than a thousand square feet, but Bud called it his castle. The hard-working veteran had been with Uncle Abe for fifteen years. Bud was as much a fixture on the place as the old barn, so Abe's will granted him a lifetime job. But even if the will hadn't provided for Bud, Jack would have kept him on. He was indispensable.

If only I could get married and have about six kids to help me, Jack thought and then imagined Bonnie riding a pony across the yard. He smiled.

41

But the smile was snatched away by the memory of her watching him escort her mom to the police car. Gritting his teeth, Jack attacked another bale, stomped to the fence, and hurled the hay toward the cattle.

The merry sound of a tooting horn snagged his attention. A shiny Escalade pulling a horse trailer rolled by, and Jack waved at his neighbor. Mary Ann Osborne was a good, Christian lady. A young widow, she claimed the plot of land next to Jack's where she raised a few cattle, mostly horses.

The passenger window whizzed down, and two boys shoved half their bodies out. "Hi, Mr. Jack!" they called in unison. One's hair was as wild as it was red. The other acted as wild as his brother's hair looked. And Jack suspected those two were capable of tying up a grown man like a pretzel. Many times he'd wondered if Mary Ann was up to the task.

"Hellooooo!" Jack responded with giant wave.

Now nine and seven, the boys watched out for their mamma like a couple of short body guards. The only male they'd let in their yard was "Mr. Jack," and he'd have been blind not to know that Mary Ann wouldn't mind if he moved a little closer. But she never did more than honk and wave . . . and bring him a few pies . . . and bake him a birthday cake . . . and send him Christmas cards that played tunes like "Winter Wonderland."

Bud dropped all sorts of wry hints about her, but

Jack ignored them. Even though the redhead was attractive enough, she wasn't Charli. She never would be.

Jack went back for more hay.

Today was *supposed* to be his day off, but he couldn't even start to fool himself about staying away. If the church posted Charli's bond, she'd undergo standard Texas procedure and be processed through the Smith County jail before being released. Someone would have to transport her from the Bullard city jail, and Jack wasn't about to leave that chore to one of his guys. He'd arrested her, and he'd see her through the whole process.

Idly, Jack wondered if the church had come up with the money yet, or if they needed any assistance. He hurled the next bale toward the munching beasts. Their familiar smell was as comforting as the hay's aroma. He rested his elbow on a fence post, rubbed at his chin, and wished the rest of his life was as comforting.

CHAPTER FOUR

When Jack opened the police car's front door for Charli, she said, "I'd rather ride in the back."

"Suit yourself," Jack said and opened the back door.

Keeping her head bent, Charli crawled inside. The call had come at ten. Oak Grove Community

Church had collected all five thousand dollars needed for her bond, and her pastor was meeting her at the Smith County jail. They'd already arranged everything with the bondsman. How they came up with all that money must be a modern-day miracle. Not even one of the church members was wealthy. Furthermore, the Jonases had already spent most of what they had on their son.

One thing was certain. Any doubts Charli had about that church loving her had vanished. The congregation came through when she had no one else. Charli would be their loyal devotee until death.

Jack settled behind the wheel. Without a word, he cranked the car, put it into gear, and then waved toward a tall black man exiting the police station. "I promise, Payton would do twenty-four-hour shifts if I let him," Jack mumbled under his breath.

As Jack began the drive to the county jail, thoughts of the officer trickled away in the light of freedom. Despite her better judgment, Charli's gaze frequently swung back to Jack. Today he was dressed in a pair of jeans and an untucked shirt, unlike last night when he'd been in his uniform. She'd overheard the dispatcher mention that he was supposed to be off today. Nevertheless, he still bore an official air that went a long way toward Charli's keeping her distance.

As he steered the vehicle along the tree-lined road, Charli refocused on the terrain. Lazy Texas pastures stretched on both sides. The ever-present cattle meandered around a pond, and Charli wished she could feel only half their nonchalance. She eyed her shorts and shirt and also longed for a shower.

Once the car pulled to a stop at the Smith County jail, she reached to open the door but found no handle. Her shoulders slumping, she waited while Jack rounded the vehicle and opened the door for her. Every time he did that, Charli felt like they were on a date, and she sensed he was having too many memories.

After he shut the door, he looked her square in the eyes, and Charli remembered the first time she'd met him. Jack had been working as a security guard at the college. He'd rounded a corner in the library, and Charli nearly bumped into him. She recalled thinking his eyes were black, but a second glance revealed they were dark, dark gray. In their depths smoldered the soul of a passionate man who just might grab life by the horns and throw it on the floor.

As many times as she told herself to look away, Charli couldn't. Jack's gaze held her as mesmerized now as it had all those years ago. Within a week after that encounter, he'd asked her out. After a month, they were a steady item. Months later, Charli suspected she was falling in love. Then, she met Vince.

Charli's mind snapped back to the present as

Jack reached into his shirt pocket, pulled out a slip of paper, and extended it to her. She took it. A glimpse at the paper assured her she shouldn't have been so weak. "Jack Mansfield" was scrawled across the top with his phone number beneath it.

"That's my cell," he said. "I keep it with me all the time." Jack patted his belt. "Except when I drop it in my pond," he added with a slight tilt of his lips. "If you need me for anything, call. Okay?"

Charli stared at the numbers until they meshed together. While passion insisted she shove the paper back into his hands, logic suggested she better keep it. Even though she did not want to depend on Jack Mansfield, her list of supporters was short. Nevertheless, Charli feared keeping it might lead him to believe she was interested in romance; and she didn't think it fair to call him if she held no intent of rekindling their old relationship.

The conflict paralyzed Charli. Finally, Jack took her arm and steered her toward the county jail. His big cowboy boots crunched along the pavement while Charli's exhausted mind spun into a dull ache.

Before they entered the building, Jack paused. "I guess I need to tell you, the bank has filed a restraining order against you."

Charli's numb mind processed the information while the earth tilted. "That doesn't surprise me," she finally said. "My only problem is accessing my account, I guess."

"Uh . . . that money is frozen until you're cleared," he explained.

"But—" Charli crinkled the slip of paper he'd given her.

Jack shook his head and said, "There's nothing I can do about it, Charli."

"I thought I was supposed to be innocent until proven guilty."

"Yeah, but once there's enough evidence to arrest you . . ." His gaze shifted.

Charli gripped her throat and thanked God she'd never moved the last of her mother's money from the bank in Jacksonville. She only had a few hundred in her Bullard account. While she'd miss it, at least she still had the ten thousand at the other bank. The first thing Monday morning, she'd cash in that CD and put the money in the fireproof safe hidden in her closet wall. Charli decided she'd rather take the chance on storing ten thousand dollars at her home than having that money discovered and frozen as well.

Jack rested against the fender of his Chevy truck, crossed his arms, glanced at his watch, and swiped another layer of sweat off his forehead. He figured he'd mopped off at least half a gallon of the stuff. He eyed the patch of shade he'd pulled his truck under. It was just big enough to give him and his truck some relief. He couldn't imagine having to endure the direct sunshine that blazed down on his brother's modest brick home. The house claimed a lot on Lynch Street, not far from downtown Bullard. Sonny was as proud of it as he would have been a mansion.

He'd told Jack he'd meet him thirty minutes ago. Twice, Jack had tried to call him and got his voice mail. He pulled his cell phone from his belt and jabbed at the speed-dial number again. But before he could hit the send button, a hard, country tune pulsed up the roadway.

Squinting, Jack looked up. A new Chevy pickup neared; and the closer it got the louder "Sweet Home Alabama" thumped.

" 'Bout time," Jack complained and snapped his phone shut. "I've been waiting so long I'm nearly petrified." He picked up his cowboy hat resting on the truck's hood and slid it on. Then he retrieved the manila envelope that had been lying beneath the hat, folded it, and inserted it into his hip pocket. The contents detailed everything he knew about the Charli Friedmont case.

Sonny whipped his pickup into the driveway, slid out, slammed the door, and waved at Jack like he had no clue he was late.

Jack strode toward his younger sibling and for once decided to let the tardiness slide. The only thing Sonny had ever been punctual for was his basketball games. His six feet three height and the

48

drive to win had gotten him a free ride through college. When he failed to make the pros after repeated tries, Sonny hit rock bottom . . . exactly where Jack had joined him when Charli married Vince.

"Come on in," Sonny said and motioned Jack to follow him onto the front porch where a drooping fern gasped for water. Sonny wore the usual—a floppy pair of gym shorts, a tank top, and high-top sneakers.

Their paternal grandmother had been Swedish, and the gene attacked Sonny with a vengeance. With his carefree tangle of blond hair and pale gray eyes, no one would ever guess the guy was an investigator. He looked more like a full-time beach bum. Of course, Jack figured his appearance and offbeat personality played to his brother's advantage.

Jack strolled up the steps. The living room's cool temperature sent a chilly blast to every pore. Jack inhaled the refrigerated air, and his perspiring body sagged.

The living room was as cluttered as a flea market. A pile of unfolded clothes claimed the recliner. Newspapers were strewn along the couch. A bag of unfinished popcorn graced the coffee table . . . along with an inch of dust. The place was worse than Jack's before his housekeeper came, and that was bad. *Really bad.*

"This place is a disgrace to society." Intending to

sit down, Jack moved to the couch and shoved a newspaper aside, only to uncover a six-pack of sodas.

"I love you too," Sonny said and slapped Jack's hat off his head.

"Hey!" Jack complained and caught it before it hit the floor. "Watch it with the hat, will ya?"

"Ah man! There they are!" Sonny exclaimed and grabbed the six-pack. "I've been looking for these guys for, like, two days."

"What is it?" Jack asked.

"Carbonated fruit juice. It's better for you than sodas, but still gives you a fizz. Want one?"

Jack grimaced. "What happened to the root beer?" he asked and wondered how his brother who was on the verge of being an alcoholic ten years ago could have turned into such a health nut. A time or two Jack had even wondered if the health food tendencies were a cover.

"Swearing off," Sonny quipped. "But I think I've got a leftover or two in the fridge. Come on." He motioned Jack toward the hallway that led to the kitchen. "We'll get some ice in here and take it to my office."

"Works." When Jack stepped into the kitchen, he eyed the pile of dishes in the sink. He wondered if the bottom layer might be growing mold. While he wasn't exactly a domestic genius, Jack did fairly well when he wasn't tending the cows or running the tractor. Sonny, on the other hand, needed domestic therapy. If the guy ever got married, Jack hoped his wife was a Martha Stewart clone.

And heaven help her if she is, he thought.

Jack reached for one of the foam cups on the counter and went for the ice dispenser in the fridge's door. He felt like the disposable cup was a safe choice, considering he wasn't in the mood for typhoid fever. He was eyeing the pan of used cooking oil sitting on the stove top, wondering exactly how old it was, when Sonny shoved a can of root beer at him.

He took it and followed his brother back down the hallway, into a tiny room crammed tight with a computer, a copy machine, and a number of books spread over a desk in the far corner. The opposite corner held a collection of dirty gym socks. Oddly, this room smelled like some kind of tropical concoction. Jack spotted the source, a deodorizer plugged into a wall socket beneath the window. With a shrug, Jack decided against figuring that one out.

"Come on in. Have a seat." Sonny motioned toward the chair near the book-laden desk. He took the chair by the computer.

Jack plopped into his seat, poured his root beer, downed half the foamy liquid and waited while it wove an icy path to his eager stomach. He shivered and decided coming close to a heat stroke was worth the reward.

Sonny picked up his own cup and gulped the carbonated juice. Jack figured all the guy needed was some bean sprouts growing out his ears.

He opened the top desk drawer, pulled out two Almond Joy candy bars, and said, "Want one?"

"Uh, no." Jack shook his head. "Coconut does bad things to my digestive track."

"Spare me the details." Sonny dropped the extra candy bar back into the drawer and opened his wrapper. He took a bite, then washed it down with the carbonated fruit juice.

"Excuse me, but I'm seeing a serious oxymoron here," Jack said through a chuckle.

"Oxymoron?" Sonny squawked. "What's that? Someone who's eight times worse than a regular moron?"

"Nooooo," Jack drawled. "That would be an octamoron, you moron," he teased. "Actually, it's a contradiction—like when someone drinks fruit juice because it's better for you than soda and then eats a candy bar. Sorry, but I'm having trouble computing, here."

"So don't compute!" Sonny crammed the last bite of candy into his mouth, wadded the wrapper, and tossed it at the corner trash can. "Two points!" he cheered.

An irritated meow floated from near the table where Jack sat. That's when he noticed a cat curled up in a pet bed. Three half-grown kittens squirmed, stretched, and settled back into their sleep. The mother cat glared at Jack awhile and then closed her eyes.

"What's the deal with the cats?" he asked and pointed toward them.

"Oh, the cats," Sonny said. "You mean I didn't tell you?"

"No." Jack shook his head.

"She showed up on my back steps about two weeks ago, starving to death. I made the mistake of feeding her one morning and got the whole family by that night. They moved in the next day, and now she owns the place." Sonny offered a jaunty grin. "I just live here."

"How old are the kittens?"

"I'm guessing about six months. They're pretty big, but still not full grown. Want one?"

"No!" Jack exclaimed. "Are you kidding? Sam would eat it alive."

Sonny picked up a pen and dismissed the cats. "Now, tell me where Charli works."

"Bullard Savings and Loan," Jack supplied and pulled the manila envelope from his hip pocket. When Sonny reached for the envelope, Jack held it up and said, "And this is strictly between you and me. Right?"

"Roger," Sonny said with a nod.

"Not only will Charli come unglued, I could get into serious trouble with my job. This has conflict of interest written all over it."

"Right." Sonny pressed his lips together, took

the envelope, and nodded. "But like I already said, this would be *soooo* much easier if I could just talk with her. Are you sure she'd be upset? I mean, we're talking about a free investigation, here."

Jack rubbed his face. "I know. I know," he agreed. "But for now, let's just keep it incognito, okay? If things change, I'll let you know. I just don't want to—"

Sonny lifted his hand. "Say no more. I fully understand everything. You're putting your head on a train track for a woman who ripped out your heart—and liver and kidneys." He pried open the envelope's brads, lifted the tab.

"I just finished a case for a psychiatrist," Sonny quipped. "Supposed to be the best in Tyler." He slipped the documents out. "I'll set you up an appointment for next week if you like." His grin revealed the chipped front tooth he'd been blessed with when Jack hit him in the mouth with a baseball on his fourteenth birthday.

Jack narrowed his eyes and thought about a repeat.

"You can have the time after *my* appointment," Sonny said. "I don't know which one of us is crazier. You for getting involved in this." He wiggled the documents. "Or me for agreeing to take the case."

Jack rolled his eyes. "When it comes to crazy, I'll always vote for you," he teased.

"I still say you need to go after that next-door

neighbor chick. She's just your type. Knows about cows and horses and stuff, like you." Sonny pointed at his brother. "You two have a lot in common. You could talk about cow patties."

Jack narrowed his eyes. "Don't be dragging up my neighbor. I'm not interested."

"You're crazy. You're blind. She thinks you're hot, man. And she's not so bad herself." Sonny bobbed his head from side to side. "At your age, she's the best thing you're going to find. Most women have already been married and divorced, and then you've got an ex with the kid shuffle to deal with. But she's a widow—and a good lookin' one at that."

"I already said," Jack insisted, "I'm *not interested*." *She's not Charli,* he thought and didn't bother to tell his brother he'd tried a dozen times to conjure up a severe case of attraction to Mary Ann Osborne. He'd never gotten beyond a deep appreciation for her pecan pie. She'd certainly kept him supplied the last year.

"Why don't you manage your own love life?" Jack added. "You need all the help you can get. You've done nothing but strike out for years."

"Now he drags up my past." Sonny plopped the documents on his desk. "Next thing you know, you'll be dragging me to church and tying me to the altar."

"It's a thought." Jack removed his hat, placed it atop the books, and didn't push his luck. He'd been trying to get Sonny in church forever and had scored a big, fat zero. All Jack knew to do was pray for his brother while he harassed him from time to time. So far, the plan didn't seem to be working.

His cell phone thumped out the theme song from the *Lone Ranger*, and Jack said, "That's Ryan," before pulling the phone from his belt.

"Wonder what that ol' goat's up to," Sonny mumbled. "He borrowed my laptop two days ago and promised to have it back by now. Find out what's up with that."

"Will do," Jack said before flipping open the phone. "Ryan, my man," he said with a fond cadence. "What's up?"

"I'm at your place," Ryan said. "That's what's up. Where are you?"

"I'm over at Sonny's," Jack said, "trying to straighten him out."

"Full-time job, right?"

"Right," Jack agreed.

Sonny narrowed his eyes. "Whatever he's saying, I didn't do it."

"It's my weekend with Sean. I remembered you said you were off today, and I thought maybe we could ride a horse and fish or something. I bought my own bait and everything."

"Laptop," Sonny said and pointed at the phone.

"Shelly with you?" Jack asked and leaned back in his chair.

"Yeah, in my dreams," Ryan replied.

The whole family knew Ryan had wanted to reconcile with his ex-wife for months now and had gotten nowhere. "I'm still praying," Jack encouraged.

"Thanks," Ryan replied. "At least she's still not dating anyone. That's the only hope I have."

"'Course not, man." Jack chuckled. "After you, everyone else is a step down."

"Yeah, yeah, yeah," Ryan replied. "Listen, are you going to be home soon, then?"

"No. But Bud's there," Jack said and tapped his finger against the table. "He'll get you saddled up, and you know all my fishing gear's in the barn. Bud's got a key to the house, and there's enough bottled water in the fridge for an army. Help yourself to everything."

"You sure?"

"'Course," Jack injected. "And tell Sean his Uncle Jack says hi, and I hope he catches Godzilla."

"Godzilla?" Ryan asked.

"Yeah. It's a catfish I lost last week. The thing had to have weighed"—he turned down the corners of his mouth—"I don't know—thirty pounds."

"Yeah, right," Ryan shot back. "I'm smelling a serious exaggeration here."

"If I'm lyin', I'm dyin'," Jack said through a broad grin.

"He's lyin', Ryan!" Sonny crowed toward the

phone. "I was with him! It was a solid five-pounder!"

Ryan whistled. "Five pounds isn't bad at all."

"I promise, it topped thirty," Jack declared. "Sonny's the one who's lying. He's just jealous because all he could catch were microscopic shiners."

"Oh, get outa here!" Sonny protested and waved aside Jack's claims while Ryan and Jack both laughed out loud.

"Hey, there's some guy here who seems to think you've got his laptop," Jack said.

"Right," Ryan agreed. "It's here in my truck. Tell him I'll bring it over this evening—after we leave your place."

"Will do," Jack agreed. "And have fun fishing. If you catch quite a few, hang around, and we'll have a fish fry tonight. I might even bring Sonny over." Jack fondly punched his brother in the arm.

"In that case, you better stop by the meat market and buy some fish. There's *no way* we can catch enough to fill up that guy."

"Good idea," Jack agreed. "Let's plan on it."

CHAPTER FIVE

"Mom, are you sure you don't want me to help you inside?" Sigmund asked.

"Yes, I'm sure," she snapped. "How many times do I have to tell you, I'm sure?" Her brown eyes sparked while her glare brought back memories of the bruising blows she'd called childhood discipline. As usual, she smelled like Oil of Olay, and her thin gray hair was pulled into a prim bun. She wore a freshly starched pantsuit and a pair of 1960s rhinestone earrings.

"I might have a little arthritis, but I can do my own shopping," she snapped. "You stay put and mind your own business. I'll be back in ten minutes."

"Okay, Mom." Sigmund sighed and watched his mother slip from the vehicle to the parking lot. She pressed down on her cane, made it around the opened door, and gave it a weak shove. The door clicked shut. Cane in hand, Maggie Harlings got her stride and trudged toward the tiny dress shop.

Sigmund eyed her until she made it through the glass door, and then he idly observed the interior of the 1980 Cutlass Supreme. Many times he'd tried to get his mother to sell the vehicle, but she'd refused just as staunchly as she refused assistance in walking. Maggie Harlings adored her car and insisted upon keeping it, even though she could no longer drive. So every Saturday morning, Sigmund grudgingly drove her to downtown Bullard, where she puttered about for her odds and ends. If not for the allowance she forked over every month, Sigmund would have ditched her years ago.

Soon, the mid-morning heat engulfed him, and Sigmund opened the car and stepped into the fresher air. He brushed his hand along the front of his pleated golfing shorts and thought about the rendezvous with Margarita this afternoon. Last month, he'd moved Margarita from Guatemala to Tyler, only twenty minutes north of Bullard. The exotic beauty was now close enough for Sigmund to enjoy . . . and much less expensive. She'd even secured a job as a hostess in an upscale restaurant. Sigmund's only concern was that some other man might see her and want her bad enough to do whatever it took to get her. His one hope was that the gifts he lavished upon her were enough to keep her attached. So far, she hadn't wavered.

Sigmund shut the car door and leaned against it. He idly observed the intersection where cars rolled to a halt, waiting for the light to turn. A used-up Chrysler pulled into the line of cars and Sigmund's attention rested on a forlorn brunette sitting in the passenger seat.

He straightened. At this angle, the woman resembled Charli Friedmont. Sigmund leaned forward, hardened his stare. *There is no way that can be Charli,* he thought. This gal looked haggard, worn down—not fresh and perky like the Charli he knew. But the longer he observed her, the more convinced Sigmund was that the bedraggled brunette really was Charli Friedmont.

"How did she get out of jail so soon?" he whispered as a quiver shook him to his core.

Spinning toward the store, Sigmund marched to

the door, whipped it open, and entered the building. The cool air sent a shiver up his spine and only heightened his icy resolve. He spotted his mother at the checkout booth. She was slipping her pocketbook into her purse and taking the bag from the clerk when he grabbed her arm and leaned down to her ear.

"I've had an emergency," he hissed. "I've *got* to go."

Her doubtful gaze heated to anger. "You've gone pale," she accused with a "How dare you?" twist to her mouth.

Doesn't surprise me, he thought and urged her toward the door.

"I'm moving, I'm moving," she snapped and jerked her arm from his grip.

Sigmund maneuvered around a rack of belts and opened the door for her. She hobbled out and cast a glance behind. "Good thing I was through," she groused.

"Come on, Mom," Sigmund breathed. "Just come on. I've got to get you home."

"Home?" She waved her cane. "But I'm not through shopping!"

"Too bad. I've got to go," he urged and attempted to nudge her forward.

Her response was to move all the slower and shoot him a defiant glare.

Sigmund's pulse banged in his temples as he waited for her to hobble toward the car. Finally, he opened the door, pushed her inside, and slammed it.

Rounding the vehicle, Sigmund wondered what his mother would think if she knew about all his extracurricular activities. *As mean as she is,* he thought, *the old broad would probably tattoo MUR-DERER on my forehead and turn me in!*

Charli hurried up the steps of the farmhouse and fumbled with the screen door latch while Pastor Jonas lumbered behind at a slower pace. Bonnie's melodious laughter wove a spell around Charli that heightened her struggle to enter her own home. Somehow, the door latch had become an unknown enigma that defied her abilities.

"Here," Pastor Jonas said from behind. "Let me help you, dear."

She stepped aside, hugged herself, and strained to see if she might spot Bonnie through the drapes' tiny opening.

"It's locked," Pastor Jonas mumbled and pounded on the aluminum door with his beefy hand.

"Oh!" Charli said. "No wonder it wouldn't open."

The doorknob jiggled, Pat pulled open the inner door, and Bonnie pressed herself against the screen. "Mommy! Mommy!" she hollered and jumped up and down.

"Hi, baby," Charli said and bent to Bonnie's level.

The second the outer door popped open, Bonnie jumped into Charli's arms and wrapped herself around her mom like a baby monkey. "Mommy! Mommy! I missed you!"

"I missed you too, sweetheart . . . more than you can ever know." Charli buried her nose into Bonnie's disheveled hair and inhaled the smells of cookie dough and the slight tinge of the rose-scented body spray Charli had let her use last night. Apparently, Pat hadn't gotten around to giving Bonnie a bath. When Bonnie pulled away, Charli spotted traces of the cookie dough in her curls. She'd been in the middle of trying to get it out last night when Jack rang the doorbell.

Her eyes burned, and she wondered who'd be there to wash Bonnie's hair if she went to prison. Swallowing hard, Charli stepped into the house and prayed for the thousandth time that that wouldn't happen.

"It's so good to see you," Pat breathed and laid her hand on Charli's shoulder.

"It's good to be home." Charli pivoted to face her surrogate parents. Pastor Jonas stood six feet tall, and he tipped the scales at two sixty, according to Pat. His flushed cheeks and labored breathing concerned Charli anew. Now in his sixties, Charli didn't figure he needed the stress of a jailbird church member. Both Pat's and his modest clothing along with their thoroughly used vehicle attested that they had little reserve revenue. Charli didn't even want to ask how much they'd contributed to her bond.

"I—I don't know how in the world you raised the money for my bond," Charli began and scrambled for the rest of her thoughts while Bonnie wiggled in her arms.

"Mommy! Look!" She shimmied down Charli, broke free, and darted to the table. "Look, Mommy!" Bonnie held up a piece of paper with macaroni glued all over it. "I made it for you!"

"That's wonderful, Bonnie!" Charli knelt beside her daughter and accepted the gift. "It's so pretty. You're a little artist, aren't you?"

"Yes." Bonnie bobbed her head up and down. "I am! It's a picture of the moon. See!" She pointed to a macaroni circle at the top of the paper. "And of me in my bed." Bonnie moved her finger to the mass of brown yarn glued atop another array of macaroni. "That's my hair," she explained.

"Wonderful!"

"It's of me last night. When I was in my bed, I prayed that you'd come home today, and you *did!*" Bonnie hurled herself at Charli, wrapped her arms around her, and cried, "Please don't let that mean man take you away again, Mommy! I missed you *so bad!*" She pulled away, stomped her foot. "I *hate him!*"

"Oh, Bonnie," Charli sighed. "Please don't hate him. Jesus doesn't want us to hate anyone."

"But I do! I do!" Bonnie bellowed. "And I had

the most awfulest dream about him!" She covered her face with her hands and began to shake.

"Bonnie?" Pat knelt beside Bonnie while Charli's eyes blurred. "It's okay, honey. Remember? It was only a dream, and Granny Pat was there. He's not coming back to get your mamma. We prayed that God would take care of all of that. We've got to trust him now."

Charli made eye contact with Pat over Bonnie. Helplessly, Charli shook her head and wondered if she'd find herself in a child psychologist's office before all this was over. Pat's weathered face settled into a worried frown while she stroked Bonnie's hair and made a few more soothing noises.

After laying the artwork on the end table, Charli gathered her daughter close, picked her up, and moved to the corner where an ancient rocking chair offered the perfect medicine. When Charli lowered herself into the chair, it squeaked with her weight. The rocker had supported three generations of mothers who comforted their daughters. Charli held many memories of her mom soothing a scraped knee or rocking her to sleep. Today, she could almost feel her mom's presence as she stroked Bonnie's back, and her stiff body relaxed with the motion.

"Pat and I are going to bring dinner to you this evening," Pastor Jonas said.

Charli looked up at the couple, now hovering

only feet away. "You have been so good to me," she said. "I don't know how I'll ever repay you. I know you sacrificed to pull together the bond money. The whole congregation—"

"No." Pat vehemently shook her head.

Pastor Jonas jabbed her with his elbow and cut her a look that was unusually stern for the gentle minister.

Pat looked down and toyed with the button on the front of her overalls.

"Well," the pastor rubbed his palms together as Charli glanced from one to the other, "I guess we'll be going now," he said with forced cheerfulness. "We've got the bake sale to tend to this afternoon. Then, like I said, we'll bring dinner over tonight. A few ladies in the church offered to help, and I'm sure they'll bring you enough food to feed an army."

Pat cut Charli a cautious look and hustled toward the door. With her hand on the knob, she paused. "If you haven't already figured it out, Bonnie didn't have a good night. She's probably as tired as you look. I'm sure the two of you need to take a nap. We'll get out of your way and see you tonight about six. Okay?"

Charli's exhausted mind spun with the undercurrent of meaning that she couldn't seem to grasp. Apparently, the church had some help in scraping together her bail money—help the Jonases didn't care to reveal.

Bonnie lifted her head and twisted to sit in Charli's lap. "Don't go, Granny Pat!" she wailed. "Please, don't go. I'm afraid he'll come back like he did this morning!"

Pastor Jonas's eyes widened before he rubbed his forehead and shook his head.

"I *told* you she saw him!" Pat whispered like Charli couldn't hear. "She's smarter than you give her credit for."

Charli stopped rocking. "Did you see Jack Mansfield this morning?" she asked as her mind grappled with the clues that leaked out bit by bit.

The balding minister pulled his car keys from his pocket and rattled them. "Yes," he finally sighed.

"We might as well tell her." Pat lifted her hand and allowed it to drop back at her side. "She's going to figure it out anyway."

"Well, go ahead, then," Pastor Jonas said with a defeated nod. "You might as well spill all the beans. You've already spilled half of them."

"Oh, *please!*" Pat protested. "I only spilled *one* bean. Bonnie spilled the other part. And I *told* you not to answer that knock until I got her out of the living room anyway."

"I thought you *were* out," he defended.

Charli was so mesmerized by the sight of her pastor and wife in a tiff that she nearly forgot the issue at hand. Likewise, Bonnie had grown strangely quiet as she observed the couple.

Huffing, Pat turned to Charli, "We weren't supposed to tell you this. He made us *promise!*"

"So much for *that!*" Pastor Jonas exclaimed.

"The church only came up with fifteen hundred dollars of your bail money," Pat rushed. "*He* covered the rest. He came over this morning and asked how much we lacked and just handed over the cash. Just like that." She snapped her fingers.

Charli's numb mind stopped the spin as she encountered reality. The weight of her sleepless night dragged her shoulders into a slump. She tried to speak, but could only clutch Bonnie all the closer. The little girl rested her head on her mother's shoulder.

"I saw that mean man this morning," she whimpered. "I don't ever want to see him again."

"After he left, I was *so sorry* I said what I did to him last night," Pat continued. "I really think he was just doing his job and was as torn up about all of it as we were. He was the nicest, most polite thing I've ever seen this morning. Do you know, he even invited our children's group out to his ranch sometime. He said his neighbor might even provide a petting zoo."

"Charli," Pastor Jonas stepped toward her, "I don't know what went on between you two or when. I'm not even going to ask." He shook his head. "I don't need to know. But I know a good man when I see one. And I'd wager my last meal that he loves you more than you could ever know."

She held her pastor's sincere gaze and mutely shook her head.

"Mark!" Pat gasped. "That is none of your—Let's just go," she said, "before you stick your foot in it again!"

The two fumbled their way outside, and the door clapped shut on the beginning of another verbal exchange. The Jonases had come to Oak Grove Community Church right after Charli moved back home. In the five years she'd known them, Charli had never seen them even exasperated with each other. She eyed Bonnie, who slumped against her chest. The couple was probably as exhausted as she and her daughter were. And they still had the bake sale.

"Sweetie," Charli began and wondered why she felt the need to explain about Jack, "that mean man isn't as mean as you think he is. He's the one who paid for mamma to get out of jail."

"But he's the one who *took* you," she insisted.

"Yes, but he was just doing his job. None of this is his fault." Charli pushed at a strand of hair that had fallen into her eyes.

"I still *hate* him," Bonnie vowed.

"Please, don't hate him," Charli soothed and relived the months she'd struggled against hating Vince. "You're too young to start hating, honey."

Bonnie's measured breathing was her only response.

Charli closed her eyes and began the rocking all

over again as the new information about Jack rotated through her mind. The weight of what he'd done left her in a state of stunned disbelief. He'd apparently told the Jonases not to tell Charli he donated the money. That meant his motives had to be pure. The gift had no strings attached. He wouldn't even be expecting a thank-you.

She propped her head against the back of the chair and was so overtaken by drowsiness that thoughts of Jack's generosity became nothing but a comforting blur that was no rival for sleep. Soon, her dosing mind meandered along the pathway of illogical thoughts about sugar cookies under her jail-cell bed and Jack tossing hundred-dollar bills through the barred window.

Charli jumped, opened her eyes, and fought to orient herself. The pair of antique lamps on the end tables meant she was home. The motor oil sitting near one lamp reminded her that the Taurus was a quart low, and she needed to add the oil to the engine.

Her gaze darted around the room while she recalled something was wrong and tried to remember what it was. The crumpled sugar cookie by the front door drew her attention. Like a relic of terror, the crumbs from last night jolted her to full remembrance of her plight.

I've been arrested for embezzlement.
I have no job.
I have to hire a lawyer.

A good lawyer costs a lot of money.
I have no job.
No one will hire me.

After her mother's long fight with cancer, most of her savings were eaten up. Once Charli paid for the funeral out of her mom's modest life insurance, she was left with that lone CD at the bank in Jacksonville—a mere ten grand. That one measly CD would merely start the defense process, and Charli would need money to live on as well. The few hundred she'd sacrificed to save was now seized assets.

Swallowing a groan, she was at least thankful the CD was still in her mother's name and would not be frozen. Since Charli had power of attorney, she could cash it in with no problem. Planning a trip to the bank first thing Monday, she shifted in the rocking chair and realized she was holding Bonnie. Her numb arm tingled against the child's weight. Bonnie's mouth was opened; her eyes closed. With a yawn, Charli wondered how long she'd been asleep. The clock on the mantel indicated only fifteen minutes had lapsed.

Gingerly, she stood and cradled Bonnie close. After bestowing a kiss upon her forehead, she walked into her daughter's bedroom, decorated with a Hello Kitty motif and strewn with Strawberry Shortcake toys. Charli bent over the rumpled twin bed and gently laid her daughter in the center. Bonnie twisted, muttered something

71

about macaroni, and flopped her arm across her pillow.

Charli held her breath and waited. When she was convinced her daughter was sound asleep, she stepped into the hallway and stopped short of shutting the door. Leaning against the wall, Charli tilted her head back, closed her eyes, and prayed, "Oh, dear God, what do I do? Please show me."

That slip of paper in her pocket floated through her thoughts. Jack Mansfield told her to call if she needed him. He'd already helped her more than she could ever repay. Charli dug the slip from her pocket and unfolded it. This morning she'd debated about whether or not she should keep the number. But in the light of hard reality, Charli understood that she was in an awful predicament that could ruin her life.

This is not a time for pride, she thought. *I've got Bonnie to think about.* She walked back into the living room, picked up her cell phone from the coffee table, and eyed Jack's number.

I've got to call him, she thought. *I don't have a choice. The church only scraped together fifteen hundred dollars. They've done all they can do.*

Her mother's savings wasn't going to go a long way toward ensuring her freedom.

"I could sell the house." She gazed around the room at three generations of memories . . . her grandmother's landscape paintings, her mother's crocheting, the mantel her grandfather carved.

"No." Charli shook her head. "This is all we have."

She pressed the numbers and waited while the phone rang. Jack Mansfield picked up on the third ring.

"Hello, Jack?" Charli rasped.

"Charli?" he said. "Is something wrong? Are you okay?"

"Uh, y-yeah, I'm okay." She collapsed in the corner of the couch. "Listen, you said to call you if I—if I decided I needed help?"

"Yeah?"

"Well . . ." She swallowed at the lump in her throat, but it only enlarged. "I—I think I'm going to need . . . well, you know . . . um, h-help," she admitted and wadded the crocheted scarf on the couch's armrest.

"Are you sure?" he asked.

"Yes. I don't—don't have anyone else."

CHAPTER SIX

Jack held the cell phone to his ear and gazed at his brother.

"You look like I've morphed into a space alien or something, man," Sonny said. "What gives?"

"It's Charli," Jack mouthed.

"Charli Friedmont?" Sonny hissed back.

Jack nodded. "I gave you my number because I wanted you to know I'm here for you, Charli," he

73

said and fought to hide the shock in his voice. "And I'm not asking *anything* in return."

Her sigh quivered across the line, and Jack had never wanted to take her in his arms more than now. He would lay himself out for her. Whatever she needed. Whenever she needed it. He was there. All the way there. And if she ever wanted him to be her man, then Jack would be *more* than there.

"I—I hate to have to ask you, especially after—after—all you've done."

Jack stood, paced to the doorway, and tried to comprehend her implications. Vaguely, he began to wonder if the Jonases had somehow leaked information about his donation.

"The Jonases told me what—what you did this morning," she finally blurted.

"Oh." Jack leaned against the doorjamb and crossed his legs at the ankle. "Well, that's interesting," he drawled. "They promised me—"

"They didn't mean to," Charli rushed. "It just kinda leaked out a little and then Bonnie mentioned seeing you this morning. I pieced it together."

"I guess she's having nightmares about me by now, huh?"

"Well . . ." Charli hedged.

Jack rubbed at his chin. "And what about you? Did you have nightmares about me?" He strode back to his chair, sat down, and hoped she didn't affirm what he dreaded.

"No," Charli said. "I barely slept."

In the past month he recalled praying about God working a miracle with Charli so he could move closer. Somehow, Jack couldn't peg this fiasco as a miracle.

He eyed Sonny, now poring over the papers.

"Do you remember my brother, Sonny?" Jack asked.

"Yes," she replied. "The basketball brother, right?"

"Right." Jack nodded and picked up his root beer. "He's a private eye now. Did you know?" He downed the last swallow.

"No. I stay so busy with Bonnie, I don't keep up much," she admitted.

"Well, he's agreed to help with your case," Jack said and set the cup on the table.

Sonny looked up. Eager interest intensified his eyes.

"I think he'll take your case at no charge if you're game," Jack stated.

"Really?" she gasped.

"Yes, really," Jack assured. "Would you be willing to talk with him?"

Sonny leaned closer.

"Absolutely," she agreed. "When can I meet him?"

"Today. Could you meet now?"

"Now?" Charli repeated.

"Yes, as in, *now*," Jack said through a smile.

"Well . . . Bonnie's asleep and . . ."

"Can we come to your place?"

"Maybe," she hedged. "It's just that if Bonnie sees you again . . ."

Jack sighed. "Maybe it would help if we stressed that I'm there to help."

"Maybe," Charli agreed through a yawn.

Jack's attention landed on the cats again, and he blurted, "What if I brought her a kitten?"

"A kitten?" Charli echoed like he'd spoken Greek.

"Yeah. Sonny's got a few."

"Two," his brother hissed and held up his index and middle fingers. "Offer her two."

"Maybe you'd rather have two," Jack suggested.

"Two?"

"Yeah, that way they won't cry all night. They'll have each other."

"I can send some cat chow," Sonny said.

"Sonny's offering to send cat chow."

"Well . . ." Charli began. "Bonnie's been wanting a dog. But she likes cats too, and maybe a couple of kittens would be just as much fun. It might help her like you a little as well."

Jack smiled. "That's the whole point."

"They're great about using their litter box," Sonny continued.

"Sonny says the cats are using their litter box too," Jack repeated.

"Well, okay," Charli said. "Go ahead and bring me two. I prefer girls. They're more gentle."

"Okay." Jack stood, leaned over the table, and eyed the cats. "Do you have a preference on color? Wait." He looked at Sonny. "How many girls are there?"

"Two. I wanted to keep the tom."

"All right, that works, then. There's only two girls anyway," he said.

"Tell her we'll go by the store and pick up a new bag of cat chow and a litter box and some cat litter. My compliments," Sonny said.

"Sonny's saying he's going to cover the cat litter and box too," Jack repeated.

"Thanks," Charli breathed. "I think this is a good idea. The kittens should keep Bonnie distracted, so maybe she won't worry about everything else."

"Yeah," Jack agreed.

"Well, uh, I guess I'll put the coffeepot on," Charli finally said. "How long will it be before you're here?"

He checked his watch. "Give us thirty minutes tops," he assured.

"Um, could you make that an hour?" she requested. "I just thought—I haven't had a shower yet."

"Sure. No prob."

"And Jack?"

"Yeah."

"Thanks for everything."

He smiled as his heart melted into a warm puddle. "You bet, Charli," he replied and reaped a pointed stare from his brother, the skeptic. Jack winked and said, "The only thing I ask is that you don't spread the word that I've helped you at all. I'm not sure how this would look on my next evaluation."

"Right," she assured. "I understand."

"After today, I'll probably just turn you loose with Sonny and try to keep a low profile. Okay?"

"Yes, that's fine," she agreed, and Jack wished she hadn't sounded so relieved. "Oh, and Jack?"

"Yes?"

"Please just call me on my cell when you drive up. That's the number I called you on. I'll have it on vibrate. That way, you don't have to ring the doorbell and take the chance of waking up Bonnie."

"Sure," Jack agreed.

Charli stopped questioning the wisdom of that phone call when she hung up. Her mother used to say there was no sense grieving over a decision once it was made. Whether she wanted him in her life or not, Jack Mansfield was in. The only thing scarier was the trial she was facing.

By the time her phone vibrated in her pocket, Charli had showered, changed into fresh clothes, percolated eight cups of coffee, and even discovered the sugar cookies from last night. Pat had placed all twelve of them on a covered plate in the microwave. When she'd made them for the bake

78

sale, Charli never imagined she'd be serving them to Jack Mansfield in less than twenty-four hours. Leaving the cookies on the dining table, she hurried to the front door and opened it.

Together, the two tall men would have been overpowering, except each held a kitten and a Wal-Mart bag. The half-grown cats were identical: coal black with golden eyes. Their pitiful meows revealed pointed teeth that looked as sharp as needles.

Charli's smile wobbled. She hoped she didn't regret this decision. The kittens would be just one more detail to manage if she did wind up in prison. She opened the screen door.

"Hi, Charli," Jack said. "You remember my brother, Sonny?"

"Yes, of course." She nodded as the two men filed in. "It's good to see you again." Charli closed the door and then extended her hand to Sonny. He set down his bag, and Charli noticed a small leather case under his arm while they shook hands.

"Why don't we just take the cats and their stuff to the kitchen?" Charli picked up the bag Sonny had set down. "I can give them some food and water and fix their litter box and then shut the doors on them until Bonnie wakes up. That way, we can talk."

"Sounds like a plan," Jack said with an encouraging smile.

Charli looked away. "I've got coffee and cookies. We can have them in here once the cats are squared away." She pointed toward the dining table on the room's north end.

Within ten minutes, the cats were settled. Charli poured the men hot coffee and then served them the sugar cookies. With her own cup full of the dark liquid, Charli settled in her chair and studied Sonny's leather case sitting on the dining table near Jack's hat. She picked up her coffee, took a sip, cleared her throat.

"I . . . I don't know where to start now," she stammered and eyed Jack.

"Right. I think Sonny has a few questions for you," Jack said.

"Yeah," Sonny agreed.

Charli shifted her gaze to Jack's brother. The guy looked like he'd blend into the masses, but his light gray eyes glistened with sharp intelligence. "Jack gave me all the information he had." Sonny lifted his brows. "And to tell you the truth, it really looks bad for you."

"Yeah," Charli picked up a cookie from her saucer, pinched at it, "so I've been told." She glanced at Jack again and wished she'd quit doing that, but didn't seem to be able to stop.

"What I need from you now is a list of people you work with." Sonny snapped open his case, rifled around inside, and pulled out a pen and a pad.

"Okay." Charli set her coffee and cookie on the table, leaned back, rested her head on the chair, and stared at the ceiling fan's lazy spin. "I've already been thinking about this," she said. "So many of them are my friends, I really don't know where to start."

"Well, *some*body's not your friend," Jack insisted. "Don't hold back."

"I know." Charli cut him another glance and darted her gaze back to the fan. As much as she needed to concentrate on the case, Jack's presence threw her into a new realm of memories that would not be denied.

Charli didn't want to relive that night in his uncle's barn when Jack first kissed her, but she relived it anyway. His uncle Abe had invited the singles group from Jack's church for a fall party in his barn. They'd bobbed for apples, roasted hot dogs, enjoyed a hayride, and then a guest fiddler inspired a few to square dance.

When everyone left, Jack's uncle had mysteriously disappeared. With a mischievous grin, Jack had held an apple over her head and said, "in the fall, apples work like mistletoe at Christmas."

Before Charli even had a chance to giggle, Jack had her in a lip lock that spun the barn and left her dreaming of more.

Charli's stomach fluttered. She scrunched her toes in her sandals and decided she must have spent one too many nights in jail. Her desperate state was setting her up to be more vulnerable . . . and reminiscent . . . than was healthy.

Sonny cleared his throat.

She stiffened, stood, walked to the window, and kept her back to Jack. Charli opened the drapes and gazed across the blacktopped road to the pond nestled beneath a clump of pines. "Do you know any good lawyers?" she asked. "What am I going to do about a lawyer?"

"With Sonny on our side," Jack stated, "you can go with a court-appointed attorney. You won't have to pay anything that way." The sound of boots on the hardwood floor neared as did his voice. "But hopefully, Sonny will get to the bottom of this before you even have to go there." He rested his hand on her shoulder. "Don't worry, Charli," he said, his voice a low caress.

She stepped away and tried to tell herself his touch didn't faze her, but her lame insistence meant zilch to her overwrought nerves.

CHAPTER SEVEN

Jack was almost certain he'd seen all kinds of memories stirring Charli's eyes . . . even more strongly than last week at the cookout. Of course, he'd stored his own classic memories and took them out one by one during long, lonely nights. The last year had been the worst. The memories coupled with what-might-have-beens had eaten him up. They were like ghosts of the past that strangely kept him warm at night but filled him with sorrow.

For now, she'd moved away from his touch, and Jack didn't miss the cue. He'd overstepped his boundaries. He glanced toward his brother whose attention was all for Charli. Sonny's expression wasn't anything Jack expected. When he caught Jack watching him, Sonny rolled his eyes and mouthed, "Y'all got it bad."

I wish it really was y'all, Jack thought.

"The people I work with . . ." Charli began and turned to face Sonny. "Would it help if I made a list for you and put their positions?"

"Yes." Sonny nodded. "How many are there?"

"All together, about twenty-five."

Sonny quirked his brow. "That narrows it down nicely."

"First, let's narrow the list to those who have access to the bank's accounting," Jack suggested, and the captive kittens meowed their approval.

Sonny tapped his fingers against the table. "For all we know, it might be the bank president."

"Mr. James?" Charli gasped. "I can't imagine."

"Exactly." Sonny's sage nod drove home his point. "No one usually *does* imagine."

Charli moved back to her chair, rested her elbows on the table, and covered her face with her hands. "I can't believe I didn't quit two years ago," she said, her words muffled. "I promise, I had this strong feeling that I should quit. I didn't know why. It just wouldn't go away. And did I?" Charli lowered her hands. "No!"

She hunched forward, hugged herself. "I was too afraid to change jobs. I was terrified another place might not pay as much or treat me as good. And I was scared to death I'd make the bank mad if I quit. So—so I stayed like some—some insecure adolescent." She balled her fists in her lap and gazed into space.

The dark circles under her eyes made Jack want to hold her close until she fell to sleep in his arms. He settled for sitting back down and turning his mind to relieving her problems.

Sonny passed Charli a pad and pen. "Here," he said. "As you make the list, try to think of anything that anyone has done or said in the last year or two that might look suspicious now."

"*Anything,* Charli," Jack said.

Charli bent over the tablet and started making her list.

Jack gazed out the window, past Sonny's pickup and into the bank of clouds stacked along the horizon. Thoughts of Mary Ann Osborne floated through his mind. Maybe Sonny was right about his giving their relationship a try. She liked him. A lot. She was safe—sure. If they got married, she'd respect him. Love him. And even if Jack didn't love her at first, maybe the love would come—especially if there was a baby or two. Jack was certain that if he pushed the right buttons they could probably be married by Christmas. Their land would be joined as one farm. Her boys already worshiped him. The whole community—even crusty old Bud—would agree it was a sensible match.

Maybe that's what I need at my age, Jack thought. *Sensible.* At thirty-seven he was running out of time to keep acting like a carefree young buck. If he was going to settle down and have a family, the time was now. His doubts were mounting about Charli's availability. Mary Ann was as good as his . . . all he had to do was ask.

He dragged his gaze back to Charli. Head bent, lips pursed, she scribbled on that tablet like she was mad at it. Charli's hair hung loosely around her shoulders in a feathery, soft veil. She wore no makeup, which only heightened her vulnerability. Jack's heart pounded in rhythm with her panic. He lost all semblance of sensible . . . couldn't even remember his neighbor's name.

The kittens' cries floated from the kitchen with a renewed vengeance. Charli lifted her head. Footsteps trotted down the hallway. A door slammed.

"Bonnie's up." Charli laid her tablet on the table and stood. "Sounds like she's making a pit stop." She motioned toward the kitchen. "Come on. I've got a plan."

Jack stood and glanced toward Sonny who mumbled, "Now what's on?"

Shrugging, Jack said, "I'm just along for the ride."

Jack entered the kitchen with Sonny on his heels. Charli scooped up both kittens and placed them in Jack's hands. "Here," she said. "We'll just call you Cat Claus."

"Cat claws?" Jack questioned.

"Yeah, first cousin to Santa Claus." Charli's grin bordered on flirtatious.

Sonny laughed out loud. "I love it," he exclaimed.

"You would," Jack said and rolled his eyes.

"Just wait here," Charli admonished and exited the kitchen through the swinging door leading into the hallway.

Jack and Sonny studied each other.

"What do we do now?" Sonny asked.

"I guess we just stand here and see what happens," Jack drawled and eyed the squirming felines. He'd never been a cat person much, mainly because most of them lived indoors. He much preferred an outside dog to an inside cat. He connected more with dogs anyway, and didn't enjoy the maintenance of a full-time inside animal.

"I guess Charli's going to bring Bonnie in here and show her what a great guy you are . . . Cat Claus," Sonny teased.

"Haven't you heard? A little kitten goes a long way," Jack predicted and shifted the felines to the crook of his arm.

"If the devil showed up at the front door holding a kitten, would you like him?" Sonny lifted his brows.

"Now you're calling me the devil?" Jack scratched their ears and both of them thanked him with some playful bites.

"If the shoe fits." Sonny leaned forward and tapped one kitten on the nose.

"Remind me to punch you later," Jack mumbled.

"Come on in the kitchen," Charli encouraged. "Uncle Jack's got something for you."

"That mean man?" Bonnie's uneasy voice echoed from outside the swinging door.

"He's not mean, Bonnie," Charli said as the door squeaked open to reveal Charli holding her daughter close. "See. He brought you some new friends."

Jack lifted the kittens and smiled.

Bonnie's horrified gaze locked onto Jack's face. He braced himself for the worst. And then, one of the kittens yowled.

The child's attention darted to Jack's hands. Her eyes widened. "Kittens!" she gasped. "You brought me kittens!" Her starry eyes shifted back to Jack. She gazed at her mother as her mouth fell open in a gaping smile. "Mamma! We have kittens!" she exclaimed.

"Yes, I know," Charli crooned. "Jack brought them to you."

"Uncle Jack brought the kitty cats just for you,"

he affirmed. "I'm your friend, and I'm here to help your mamma." The kittens squirmed like two earthworms on a hook.

"Your kitties want to play," he said and was rewarded with Bonnie's wriggling from her mother's hold and hurrying toward him. Jack knelt and lifted the cats toward the child. She stopped mere feet away and gazed at Jack like she was having some serious doubts.

"See, Bonnie," Charli crooned and knelt beside her daughter, "*he's* the one who brought you the kittens. He's here to help us," she repeated. "He's not going to take me away ever again."

Bonnie reached for her cats, grabbed them, and clutched them to her chest like she wasn't so certain Jack wouldn't take them away like he had her mother. Their back feet hung to her navel and together they looked nearly half as big as Bonnie.

"Can you tell Jack thank you for the kittens?" Charli encouraged.

The child eyed Jack and finally said, "Thank you," in a tiny voice.

"You're welcome," Jack replied and felt as if he'd scored at least half a point.

Someone cleared his throat from the doorway. Jack swiveled to face his brother. Arms crossed, the guy leaned against the doorjamb like the Jolly Green Giant—except he wasn't quite green.

"Do I get an introduction here?" Sonny asked.

"Uh, yeah." Jack motioned toward his brother.

"Bonnie, this is my brother, Sonny. His mamma cat is the one that made the kittens."

Bonnie eyed Sonny like she wasn't sure whether she should dislike him or not.

"Hi, darlin'," Sonny said and drew near. He squatted beside Bonnie and scratched one of the kitten's ears. "I'm glad you got the kitties. Their mamma is very nice. I'm sure they'll give you lots and lots of love."

Bonnie sniffled and nearly smiled.

Jack frowned while Sonny cut him a glance that said, "Two points." The guy had a way with children and women that blew Jack's mind.

"I bought some string for them in the store," Sonny said. "Want me to show you how the kitties like to chase it? They go jumping-*crazy* over string."

"Okay," Bonnie said.

Jack groaned inside as Sonny came close to gloating.

"It's in the bag on the cabinet," Sonny said.

Jack stood and reached into the bag to retrieve a skein of red yarn that Sonny had insisted upon buying.

Crossing her arms, Charli leaned against the counter. Her white T-shirt only accented her pallid cheeks. She was looking more and more exhausted by the minute, and Jack couldn't talk himself out of feeling at least like he was partly to blame. As many times as he told himself he was just doing his job last night, Jack still detested the whole mess.

He concentrated on pulling out a long strand of yarn while Sonny helped Bonnie put down the kittens.

"If this works, Sonny," Charli said, "I'll let you entertain her while I finish my list . . . and be indebted to you for life," she added.

"Hey! What about me?" Jack rested his palm against his chest. "I'm the one who suggested the cats."

"Maybe you can entertain Charli, then." Sonny's under-the-breath comment sent a rush of disbelief up Jack. His eyes widening, he gazed at his brother, wondering if he'd misunderstood what the guy said. But Sonny's grimace and widened eyes confirmed he'd really put his foot in his mouth and had no idea how to get it out.

Charli's face went an unearthly shade of red, and Jack hadn't ever wanted to slug his brother so much.

The embarrassment crashed when Bonnie pulled the yarn from Jack's hands. She hurried straight back to Sonny and thrust the yarn into his hands.

"Oh, good!" Sonny exclaimed like this was the first time he'd seen the skein. "You found the yarn!" He extended the end to Bonnie and said, "You hold the end and walk that way." Sonny pointed toward the doorway. "We need to make a nice, long string."

Bonnie obeyed without question; but not

watching where she was going, she bumped into Jack.

"Woops!" he said.

The child gazed up at him with a cross between awe and uncertainty. Jack smiled, tousled her hair, and stepped next to Charli who'd taken the kittens out of Bonnie and Sonny's path. The felines had now started batting at each other.

"Do you have a pair of scissors?" Sonny asked.

"Sure," Charli said and passed the cats to Jack without a glance.

Jack caressed the kittens' satin fur and secretively observed Charli while she opened a cabinet and obtained the scissors. Keeping her head bent, she passed the scissors to Sonny, who cut the string.

"There!" Sonny exclaimed and handed the scissors back to Charli. "We're all set."

Bonnie shoved the yarn at her mom and hurried to Sonny's side.

"Okay, Jack, put them down," he said.

Bending, Jack placed the kittens on the floor while Sonny tossed the red string at them. The cats both pounced like they were great mouse slayers and this was a big one.

Squealing, Bonnie clapped her hands.

"You do it," Sonny said and passed the yarn to Bonnie.

She grabbed it and put her whole body into throwing the string toward the cats like a championship fisherman. One kitten fell to its side and pawed at the red temptation while the other sprang straight up in the air, arched her back, and began a sideways dance that sent Bonnie into hysterics.

Sonny and Jack both laughed outright, but Charli's tap on his arm interrupted Jack's mirth. Unfortunately, she wasn't laughing. Her eyes were as serious as a fifth-grade teacher who'd just found the culprit who put a frog in her desk.

"We need to talk." Charli jerked her head toward the living room.

"Okay," Jack said under his breath. He followed Charli into the living room and wasn't certain whether he was the culprit or the frog. Either way, he didn't figure the next few minutes would be good.

CHAPTER EIGHT

She closed the swinging door behind them, paced past the dining table, and fumbled with nothing. "Why—why did Sonny just say what he did?" she stammered.

"I have no idea," Jack said and lifted both hands. "I wanted to cut his tongue out but figured it wouldn't look good in front of Bonnie. Should I go do it anyway?" He placed his hands on his hips while Bonnie's delighted laughter floated from the kitchen.

"Look, I'm sorry," Jack said and shook his head.

Charli rubbed her forehead. "Jack, I appreciate your help more than you can know, but I want to make sure you and everybody understand that—"

"I understand," Jack growled.

"I just don't want you to get hurt again." She held his gaze, and the sincerity of her intent glowed from her soul. "I don't know whether or not I could ever love again. I wonder if maybe that part of me is . . . is . . . broken." Giant tears pooled in the corners of her eyes.

Jack didn't know what to say. He wanted to hold her close and run at the same time. Finally, he reverted to the principle Uncle Abe lived by: untainted honesty.

"I don't want to get hurt either, Charli," he admitted. "You nearly killed me."

"I know." She focused on his boots, doubled her fists at her side. "I'm *really* sorry, Jack." Charli shook her head from side to side and piteously observed him again. "I was so young I didn't even know *what* I wanted. I don't even know why I did what I did. I've wondered about it a thousand times," she rushed.

Moving to the nearest dining chair, she gripped the top and continued. "And now you're helping me and I don't know what to do or what to think or . . . or . . . and then Sonny said what he did and now . . ." She waved her hand toward the kitchen. "And you arrested me and I might go to prison and—"

93

"It's okay," Jack soothed and neared. Laying his hand on hers, he said, "I'll tell Sonny to stop his wisecracks or *die,* okay?"

She barely nodded.

"And you can be certain I won't put any moves on you *at all,* Charli. You said you wanted help, and I have no strings attached. I'll do everything I can to help you and once charges have been dropped, I'll disappear. Understand?"

"All right, Jack," Charli said, her lips trembling. "What would I ever do without you?" She wrapped both her hands around his and hung on as if she was drowning and he was her only chance at survival. Her big dark eyes immersed him in anxiety and bewilderment and the plea that insisted she desperately needed him.

Reeling with the effect, Jack braced himself while instinct urged him to pull her into his arms. Somehow, he held on to a few scraps of common sense and restrained himself. Lightly patting the back of her hand, Jack mumbled some *there-there*s and a few other things he was sure didn't make one lick of sense.

Charli hung her head, and her hair swung forward like a curtain that blocked his view. "You're the only real help I've got," she rushed, "and I feel so bad about how it all is. I don't want to use you."

Disengaging his hands from hers, Jack forced himself to a breathing pattern that his lungs protested. The cat celebration continued in the kitchen while the living room took on a tense silence that ushered in Charli's stiffening her shoulders.

Slowly, Charli raised her head and gazed into his face. With tears trickling from the corners of her eyes, she looked as helpless as Bonnie. But the red pall creeping up her neck suggested the under-standing of a full-grown woman. They were standing close. Really close. And Jack now saw that he wasn't the only one who was sensing the old chemistry.

While Jack waited for who-knew-what, his neighbor's name barged into his mind with full impact: *Mary Ann Osborne.*

She's safe, he reminded himself. *Uncomplicated.*

"There she goes again!" Sonny's exclamation preceded the nudge against the swinging door.

Bonnie's laughter accompanied Charli's moving to the other side of the room. Her fingers trem-bling, she wiped at her tears and then resumed her grip on that dining chair. "I'm sorry . . . I . . ." she croaked.

"You're scared. You need support, that's all," Jack said, his voice flat despite his thumping pulse.

"I guess." She stared at the bowl of fruit on the table.

"Look, I'll tell Sonny to put a sock in it," he stated. "You won't have to worry about his big mouth anymore."

"Look at that!" Sonny exclaimed.

"She got it!" Bonnie rejoiced.

"It's okay," Charli said, glancing toward the kitchen. "I'd forgive him of anything right now. I didn't think I'd ever hear her laugh like that again."

"Do you have any root beer?" Jack asked.

"Excuse me?" Charli blinked.

"Root beer. I need some. Got any?"

"No . . . the best I can offer is a bottle of carbonated fruit juice." Charli rubbed at her cheek with the back of her hand. "The doctor says that's better for Bonnie than sodas."

What is the deal *with all these people?* he thought.

"I get it at that new organic grocery store in town," she continued.

"Yeah, I guess my brother's shopping there too," he said. "Whatever you have is fine. As long as it's got fizz. It's better than nothing." Jack sank into the chair. *I guess everybody's gone fruit-juice nutso,* he thought as she turned to retrieve the drink.

He watched her sway into the kitchen. Her hips were a little more round than they'd been in college; her face a bit fuller. Other than that, she looked like the same Charli. Problem was, she *wasn't* the same Charli, and Jack wondered if he'd lost his mind to ever offer her help. Vince Friedmont had really done a number on her, and she was as emotionally disturbed as all-get-out.

Yeah, and she *did a number on* you, a jaded voice

96

insisted while he fleetingly wondered if the old Charli had died forever.

This time, he'd have to take every measure to protect his heart . . . and liver . . . and kidneys. And that started by keeping his distance yet being close enough to help.

I need some insulation, he thought, *like that insulated hunting suit that keeps me warm on the deer lease.*

When Charli handed him the juice, Jack decided Mary Ann Osborne was insulation material, and he should call her the second he got home. While he didn't want to use her any more than Charli wanted to use him, Jack was determined to once and for all give the woman a chance . . . and hopefully expunge Charli Friedmont from his blood forever.

Sigmund Harlings trolled by Charli Friedmont's country home and eyed the new Chevrolet pickup sitting in the driveway. Slowing, he pulled a pen and notepad from his shirt pocket, jotted down the license plate number, and tucked it in his pocket for later reference.

He gassed his mother's sedan and continued cruising down the country lane. Earlier, when he dropped his mother off, he calmed her by promising to drive her beloved car for the rest of the weekend. She often asked him to babysit the vehicle, just to keep it in shape. Most of the time, Sigmund squirmed out of the request. He far preferred his Lincoln and didn't like the idea of being seen in an old Cutlass—even one in mint condition.

But Sigmund's offer had nothing to do with pleasing his mother and everything to do with his own needs. If he was going to cruise Charli's neighborhood, he needed to do it in a car other than his own. Charli might recognize his flashy, blue Lincoln and wonder what he was doing in her neck of the woods.

The Cutlass purred forward for a quarter of a mile before Sigmund steered the vehicle around a bend in the road. He took one last glance at Charli's yard before the turn blocked it from sight. Sigmund pulled to the side of the road, waited a few minutes, and then turned around. When he was maneuvering the curve again, he spotted the pickup backing from Charli's drive. Braking, he slowed the vehicle to a crawl and hoped the driver didn't notice him.

From this distance, it appeared two people were sitting in the truck. Sigmund itched to know if the person in the passenger seat was Charli. He didn't dare get close enough to see until the truck was nearing Brookshire's. That's when Sigmund realized the passenger was another man—someone who filled up his side and wore a cowboy hat.

When the driver pulled onto Lynch Street, Sigmund steered into the Brookshire's parking lot, across the street from Sonny's home. He parked at a good vantage but didn't turn off the engine. With the air conditioner blasting his perspiring face, Sigmund watched the truck roll into the driveway of one of the small, brick homes that lined the road.

The pickup halted. The passenger door opened, and the big man slid out. When he pushed his hat up on his forehead, Sigmund's eyes widened.

"Jack Mansfield," he growled and wondered what the chief of police had been doing at Charli's house.

He eyed the tall blond man with the chief and recalled seeing him around, as anyone would in such a small town. But Sigmund couldn't put a name with the face.

A slow panic began to heat Sigmund's gut as his mind tumbled with possibilities. *Maybe it involves the investigation,* he finally decided. *Maybe Mansfield was questioning Charli.* But the logical musings did nothing to slow his frantic pulse.

What if she already knew the chief? What if they're friends? he worried. The fact that Jack wasn't wearing his uniform underscored this assumption. Sigmund gripped the steering wheel and tried to calm his erratic breathing, but that only resulted in his growing dizzy. *I've never seen her with Mansfield before. How could she know him?*

"No!" Sigmund barked and pounded his fist against the steering wheel. "He was just questioning her. He *had* to be!"

As the two men entered the home, Sigmund steered the Cutlass from the parking lot and by the house. The number 200 in brass claimed the front door. He committed the address to memory and planned to consult the police department's online database that listed residents by their street names and numbers. After last year's murder, Sigmund had been given all sorts of perks from his friend on the force. They would certainly come in handy now.

CHAPTER NINE

Charli jolted awake. Some foreign noise had assaulted her sleep and demanded her attention. Her first thought was for Bonnie. Prepared to dash to her room, Charli sat up and saw Bonnie's outline beneath the covers beside her. Her crawling in bed with Charli happened more often than not, and it was easier for Charli to go along with it than expend the energy to break the pattern.

To insure that she wasn't seeing things, Charli laid her hand on the covers. Sure enough, Bonnie's form proved real. Charlie gingerly uncovered Bonnie's head. The moonlight squeezing through the blinds cast glowing slices across her face. Bonnie's eyelashes rested against her cheeks in a relaxed sleep that left Charli grateful. The kittens had been such good therapy. She didn't know how she could ever thank Sonny . . . and Jack.

The thump erupted again. Charli jumped. Her heart pummeled her ribs as her mind raced with the fear that had ridden her until she went to sleep.

Whoever framed her did *not* want to go to prison. If that person discovered Charli had a good detective on the case, they just might come after her. Once Sonny had secured her list, he said he was going to do a battery of background screens and then open up a new checking account at Bullard Savings and Loan. He hadn't gone into detail, but Charli could imagine what kind of snooping he'd do around the bank when no one was looking. From that premise, she'd been overcome by the terror of his getting caught and discovered as her investigator.

Another thump preceded a crash. Shaking, Charli lunged to her door, closed it, and twisted the knob lock. She stumbled toward her computer desk, picked up the chair, and hurried for the door. Tilting it, Charli shoved the back under the knob.

Then she remembered the hammer still sitting on her dresser. She'd left it there last week after climbing on top of the roof to nail down a few loose shingles. Charli snatched up the hammer.

Her cell phone was next. She dove for it on the nightstand and pressed the speed-dial number she'd programmed to Jack's cell. His sleepy "Hello, Charli?" came over the line on the first ring. "Are you all right?"

"J-Jack . . . someone—someone's in the house. I—I—"

"Where are you?" he demanded, his voice now crisp.

"In my bedroom—with the door locked." She gripped the hammer all the harder.

"Stay put. Wait. Can you get out the window?"

Charli looked toward the lone window along the west wall. "Yes," she said.

"And you're sure somebody's there?"

"Yes . . . I think . . . there's been bumping . . . and a crash. Oh, Jack," Charli collapsed onto the bed and pulled up her feet, "what if it's the person who framed me?"

"I'm coming over there now," Jack said. "I'm going to lay the phone down for about half a minute while I throw on some clothes. Just don't hang up."

"Okay," Charli agreed and focused on her door. The seconds dragged into forever while she waited for Jack's voice back on the line.

Finally, he said, "Still there?"

"Here." Charli nodded.

"I'm stepping outside now," he informed. "I should be there in seven or so minutes. You stay in your room unless you have to leave. You're safer locked in there than out in the yard where he can—"

Charli's hand tightened on the phone, and she curled her toes.

"Never mind," Jack said. "Just stay put. Where's Bonnie?" he asked without a breath.

"She's here with me. She crawled in bed with me after I went to sleep."

"Good. I'm getting in my patrol car now. I'm going to call for backup—"

"Do you have to?" Charli asked.

"Uh, yeah," Jack replied. "If he's armed or there's more than one, I want some backup."

"Please spare me the details," Charlie rushed. "Just do what you have to do and get over here."

She held on while the sound of a cranking engine floated over the line. Next came Jack's voice as he called the dispatcher on his radio and informed her of the emergency. "Still there, Charli?" Jack finally asked.

"Yes," Charli rasped.

"I'm on my way now. Just hang in there. Any more noises?"

"N-no."

She placed the hammer on the nightstand, and her gaze darted around the room while she strained for any new sounds. Charli imagined Jack's path from his house to hers. The place was east of Bullard and not far from her family's estate. Even though Jack wasn't officially in her neighborhood, the path between them only involved a couple of turns—a left onto highway 69 and a right onto Charli's county road.

"I'm on your road now," Jack finally said.

"Good. I'm so glad," Charli breathed. For the first time, she thought to check her digital clock. Four fifty-five glowed from the nightstand. Her eyes gritty, Charli wondered if she'd ever get another good night's sleep.

"I'm only about two minutes out now," Jack said. "Any more noise?"

"No."

"Hold tight."

"I'm holding," Charli said and eased her legs down. Fleetingly, she hoped the intruder was a mere burglar who'd gotten what he wanted and left. The thought encouraged Charli to the point of an anxious giggle. She never imagined herself relieved over being robbed.

That's when the computer chair beneath the knob creaked. Charli dug her fingers into the covers. Her spine went rigid.

"Oh my word, Jack," she whispered, "I think he's trying to turn my knob."

"Stay calm," he barked.

The chair creaked again. As if influenced by an unseen force, it swiveled from the door and crashed to the floor.

Charli's scream would not be subdued.

Bonnie bolted upright and released a screech of her own while climbing on top of Charli.

"Charli! Charli!" Jack's holler mingled with Bonnie's sobs. "I'm driving up now. There's a crew not far behind me. Just hold tight. I'm not waiting on them. God help us, Charli! I'm going to just kick in the front door and deal with it."

"There's a—a—key under the big rock in the—in the flower bed," Charli stammered while her focus remained fixed upon the doorknob.

"Mommy! Mommy!" Bonnie screamed. "Please don't go! Don't let him take you!"

Nausea creeping up her throat, Charli clung to her daughter but lacked the capacity to verbally comfort her. The front door's thud affected her like a slap. Charli yelped and reaped a wail from Bonnie.

After a pause that spanned to scary, footsteps pounded the hallway and stopped outside Charli's door. A soft knock preceded Jack's, "Charli?"

"Y-yes?" she said.

"Everything's fine," he said, a smile lacing his words. "Open the door will ya?"

Frowning, Charli swung her legs out and somehow stood while Bonnie wrapped her body around her mom's. Jack's muffled voice filtered through the door as Charli fumbled with the lock. "Call off Payton, Rose. I've got it covered."

Charli opened the door to see Jack with his cell phone in one hand and a kitten in the other. He closed the phone and extended the cat. "Behold, your murderer," he said through an indulgent grin. "I found this one by the front door."

Her shoulders drooping, she stared at the half-grown cat while Bonnie twisted to face Jack and then stiffened. The last time Jack Mansfield had come in the night, he'd taken Charli with him.

"Don't worry, Bonnie," Charli crooned. "Uncle Jack just came this time to help us again. Mamma heard something. Uncle Jack came over to protect us. That's all. See . . . it wasn't a booger bear after all. It was just your kitty-cat."

She eyed the computer chair, now on its back. "I guess that thing just fell on its own, then."

"Most likely," Jack said with a nod. "You probably didn't get a good wedge on it." He lifted the kitten. "You might want to put these little ladies in the utility room at night. It looks like they broke one of your lamps."

"Oh, no," Charli gasped and started down the hallway. "They were my grandmother's. That must have been the crash I heard."

She stepped into the living room and blinked against the ceiling fan's bright light. The lamp closest to her lay broken on the hardwood floor.

"Oh, no," she groaned again.

Another lamp hung on the edge of the couch. A silk plant lay on its side in the corner.

"Looks like they went a climbin'," Jack said and didn't hide his chuckle.

"And look at the fruit basket!" Charli fretted. Once in the middle of the dining table, it now rested upside down near the toppled plant. Peaches and apples were strewn all the way to the couch.

The other golden-eyed kitten was perched on the

back of the sofa like she was ready to pounce on the defeated lamp all over again.

"Looks like you got yourself a couple of wild women." Jack scratched the neck of the one he held and laughed again.

"I guess so," Charli mused and noticed a tear in the lampshade. "I guess one of them attacked the lampshade and rode it to the floor." She deposited Bonnie on the couch before bending to pick up the pieces.

"These lamps are seventy years old," she mourned. "But I'd way rather have a broken lamp than be murdered by a stalker."

"Yeah, that *would* kinda put a bummer on things, wouldn't it?" Jack drawled.

"Right," she agreed and didn't stop her snicker. "I know when I've been murdered before it really ruined my day."

"I agree," Jack said and shifted the kitten to Bonnie's lap. "And besides all that, it's just *rude* when people kill you."

"Not very neighborly either," Charli added and shifted her attention to the lamp. All humor vanished. Her eyes stinging, Charli laid the large pieces on the end table and resisted the temptation to sit down and cry. Her heirloom was now like everything else in her life—shattered.

"Maybe you can glue it back together." Jack's strong hand appeared near Charli's as he knelt beside her. "At least it's still in big pieces."

"Yeah, maybe," Charli said and noticed the plastic container of motor oil lying wedged between the end table's leg and the wall. She pulled the oil loose, set it back on the table, and reminded herself to put it in her car tomorrow.

Charli refocused on the broken lamp. The pieces blurred while she resisted the sniffles.

He's going to think I'm nothing but a crybaby, she thought.

Bonnie giggled, and Charli glanced up. Her daughter held both cats in her lap, and they were trying to chew each other's ears off. She noticed the other lamp now safely on the end table and was thankful Jack had put it back.

"What did you name your kittens, Bonnie?" Jack asked.

"Sugar and Spice," Bonnie said and came closer to a smile for Jack than she had yet.

"Which one's which?"

"This one's Sugar, see?" She picked up one of the cats and pointed at her chest. "She's got a white spot right here. That's a sugar spot."

"Oh, I see," Jack crooned and reached to scratch the cat's ear. For once the child didn't shrink away.

Charli was strangely relieved that Bonnie seemed to be acclimating to Jack. Given the investigation, he was going to be in their lives, and she didn't want her daughter terrorized every time she saw him. After stacking the final lamp pieces on the table, Charli stood and tugged the neck of her satin pajamas to a more modest angle. Her matching house robe called her name, and Charli planned to put it on as soon as possible.

"Bonnie, do you want to help me get the kittens into the utility room?" Jack asked.

"Do we have to?" Bonnie whined.

"Afraid so," Charli injected.

"It would have been awful if the lamp had fallen on one of them," Jack explained. "If they're in the utility room, they're safe."

"Okay," Bonnie agreed without a hitch.

For the first time, Charli noticed how haggard Jack appeared. His hair was mussed, and the dark circles under his eyes looked like he hadn't slept in a week. Fleetingly, Charli wondered if he'd slept much the night before last either.

When Bonnie slid from the couch, Charli slipped to her bedroom and put on the house robe. By the time she stepped into the kitchen, Jack and Bonnie were entering the utility room. Bonnie had one cat under each arm, and Jack held their food dishes.

"Now," Jack was saying, "this is better for you and your mom and them too. They won't scare you and they won't hurt themselves."

"Okay, Sugar and Spice," Bonnie said. "You stay in here tonight. I'll leave the light on for you."

Jack glanced toward Charli. "Is that all right?"

She nodded as Bonnie closed the door. "There," the child said and wiped her hands together like

Charli had seen Pat Jonas do when she was digging in one of her flower beds.

When Jack chuckled, Bonnie hurried for her mother.

On a sigh, Charli scooped her up and said, "Thanks so much, Jack. I have a feeling that before this is over, I'll be indebted to you for life."

Jack scratched at his whiskers and smiled a bit. "I'm here to serve," he said and wondered if God had some sort of a twisted sense of humor. A month ago, Jack had lain awake many nights, begging him to bring Charli back into his life. Well, she was back, all right, but on strange terms. She admitted needing Jack, but he figured he'd have to take a hike when the needing was over.

Now, here she stood in a black house robe that made her pale skin look like that of some translucent goddess. Her hair, a tousled mass of waves, invited him to tangle his fingers in their curls. And Jack decided his best bet was to leave as soon as possible. Otherwise, she'd be slapping him into next week.

He strolled toward the living room and wagered she'd follow. "I guess since I've braved those criminals, li'l lady, I'll be moseyin' on back to the corral." Jack made a straight line for the door and paused with his hand on the knob.

Still holding Bonnie, Charli stopped in the middle of the living room. The child lifted her head

110

and looked at Jack with brown eyes as big as pancakes.

"Bye-bye, little girl," Jack said with a wink.

Bonnie didn't even blink.

"Thanks again." Charli's dubious eyes hinted that she'd really rather him stay.

What do you want me to do, he thought, *camp on your couch until sunup?* Yawning, Jack scratched the top of his head and realized he never put on his hat. The adrenaline rush was off, and his eyes were threatening to shut on the spot.

"I'm going to go to sleep standing up if I don't get out of here," he admitted.

"Would you please just double-check around the house?" Charli snagged her strawberry lip between her teeth.

Jack swallowed and pulled at the neck of his T-shirt.

"You know . . . just in case," she added.

"Sure." He glanced away and reminded himself he'd arranged a dinner date with Mary Ann tonight.

Jack stepped onto the porch and barely avoided being dive-bombed by a June bug. With the screen door closed, he glanced back at Charli and Bonnie. "I'll take a look around and call you before I leave."

"Okay, thanks again," Charli called, and now her tone communicated what her eyes had been saying. *Please don't leave . . . oh, please, please, please.*

As he rushed off the porch, Jack's mind insinuated all sorts of things about how convenient it would be if they were married and he *could* spend the night . . . except not on the couch. He rounded the house's corner. Once the shadows enveloped him as thoroughly as did the scent of pinesap, he gave himself a verbal slap.

"Stop it!" he commanded under his breath. "It ain't gonna happen! Just stop doing that to yourself!"

Mary Ann, Mary Ann, Mary Ann, he thought as he crunched through the pine needles and rounded the back of the house. Jack scanned the moon-washed yard that stretched to a pasture, set off by a barbed wire fence. Slipping his hand in his pocket he scrutinized the whole area and recalled the phone call to Ms. Osborne. Mary Ann had been so delighted with his request for a date she'd stammered her acceptance and then giggled like a teenager.

Jack planned to take her to a country steak house north of Tyler that offered horse-drawn wagon rides. He'd wear his best jeans, new boots, and the black hat reserved for special occasions. Maybe all of it would work together to make him forget this emotional-suicide fixation he had with a gal who was about as attainable as the Mona Lisa.

The ever-present crickets cheered Jack on while he strode across the back and rounded the house on the other side. As he'd suspected, there were no signs of any intruder—unless you counted a lone possum that scampered from near the well house into the woods.

Once he settled in his car, he called Charli. When her voice came over the line, Jack's sleepy mind finally recognized the reality of the clues. Charli didn't want Jack to stay because he was Jack but because she was terrified someone might start stalking her. She was simply clinging to the closest symbol of protection, and that happened to be Jack. If Sonny were here, *he'd* be the one she didn't want to leave.

"The coast is clear," he encouraged. "Go on back to bed."

"Roger that," she said.

"Oh, and by the way," Jack snapped his door shut, "I *did* rip out Sonny's tongue at my house last night. My other brother, Ryan, helped me after our fish fry. We actually fried his tongue and fed it to the buzzards. Just thought I'd let you know."

"Oh, good," Charli breathed. "I really don't think he needs it anyway. Do you?"

"Uh-uh," Jack said, his lips quirking. "He's way better off without it. Or at least, I am anyway." He inserted his key into the ignition and turned it. The vehicle purred to full attention.

Charli's low chuckle nearly made Jack purr as eagerly as the engine.

CHAPTER TEN

Sigmund Harlings remembered. After badgering his mind for over a day, he finally remembered. He'd accessed the police database yesterday and discovered the home at 200 Lynch Street belonged to Sonny Mansfield. He deduced Sonny must be Jack's brother or cousin. On the heels of that deduction, his mind began indistinctive whispering about the name Sonny Mansfield and why it seemed familiar.

The whispering chose Sunday morning to become comprehendible, and Sigmund was almost certain why he recognized the name. The certainty sent a nauseous wave through his gut, a clammy film to his palms. He needed to verify his assumption, and his overwrought nerves demanded immediate knowledge.

Glancing to one side and then the other, he eased from the church pew. His wife, Dianne, looked up like he was crazy for standing in the middle of the sermon. Her bright pink lips puckered like some caricature of a southern prude who's been shocked into fanning herself with her lace fan and saying, "Well, I never!" but Dianne spent more time "I never-ing" him than not.

Sigmund had long ago stopped expecting her to understand him. He also never imagined she would suspect he was having an affair. The more he left her alone, the happier Dianne was. She'd far rather spend hours at her church craft shows than put any energy into their marriage. That used to bother Sigmund. Now he was thrilled.

He didn't bother to offer a reason for his departure. It was none of her business. She'd probably assume he was making a trip to the men's room. So let it be.

Sigmund strode through the foyer and hurried across the humid parking lot, straight to his Town Car. As he slid into the driver's seat and slammed the door, the scent of new leather mingled with the smell of the recent rain. Sigmund reached to his side, beneath the seat, and pulled out the phone book. He'd started carrying the book in his car years ago when he got his cell phone and had been repeatedly glad of the foresight. Never had the book been more handy.

He flipped the yellow pages opened to Private Investigators. Running his finger down the page, Sigmund stopped when he came to the name, Sonny Mansfield.

He yanked at his necktie while his mind went into a frenetic whirl. This confirmed the worst was happening. Somehow, Charli Friedmont had connections Sigmund never counted on. She must have hired Sonny Mansfield to investigate the embezzlement. Sonny was closely related to the police chief. That meant Jack Mansfield might somehow be involved in trying to exonerate Charli.

Sigmund let the phone book fall into his lap. He gazed at the white cross steeple that once meant something to him; what, he couldn't remember. The magnitude of what he was facing blotted out all moral concerns—both past and present. Last year when his secretary, Brenda Downey, discovered too much and threatened to reveal all, she'd come up missing. Her disappearance had been a mystery no one had solved—especially when Sigmund's contact in the force compromised evidence. Sigmund hadn't planned to murder Brenda the night he'd stepped into her house, but she'd pushed him into a blind fury. When he came to his senses, his hands were like a vice on her neck, and her eyes were fixed in the blank stare of death.

Sigmund had sat with the body for an hour, not knowing what to do. Finally, he decided to bury Brenda on his mom's land. Once he'd stuffed Brenda in his trunk, Sigmund had taken the time to clean anything he'd touched in her home. When he righted the end table overturned in the struggle, he'd discovered the stash of cocaine hidden in the drawer's cavity and the evidence that Brenda had been dealing the stuff for a police officer. He'd taken the cocaine and evidence, and that information was all he needed to insure he was never arrested for the crime.

He'd buried Brenda deep in the woods behind his mother's place and now wondered if he should add Charli Friedmont to the hidden grave.

Sigmund rested his forehead against the steering wheel and squeezed his eyes tight as the memory of that late-night journey into the woods presented a possible solution for Charli Friedmont. If she mysteriously disappeared, that might up the investigation. But if his "friend" on the force understood he must cover evidence or risk being uncovered himself, then Sigmund could get away with killing Charli just as easily as he had Brenda. Murdering Charli would shift focus from the embezzlement to her disappearance; and while his contact covered evidence, Sigmund would have time to quietly slip out of town and never return.

I'll change my name, he thought, *and arrange for a fake passport. Margarita and I could go back to her family in Guatemala.* Once the distraction over Charli's disappearance subsided, Sigmund would be long gone. Even if they discovered he was behind the embezzlement, they'd never find him.

He fleetingly thought about simply taking Margarita and leaving town now, without killing Charli. But an insatiable need to end her life swelled up within and sent a driving passion through his soul that heated his face. Charli's investigation was threatening Sigmund as much as Brenda had, and he *hated* women who threatened him. They reminded him too much of his mother.

A hard lump started in his stomach and pushed up his throat as he recalled the night his mom threw salt in his eyes and locked him in a dark closet for hours. He'd wailed until she finally let him out, but she mocked him for crying. That was the last time Sigmund ever remembered crying.

The lump threatened to erupt into a groan, but Sigmund swallowed it back. The longer he thought about Charli Friedmont, the more he hated her as much as he'd hated his mother that night. "How dare you threaten me," he growled.

Sigmund lifted his head from the steering wheel, spread open his hands, and gazed at his palms. These hands had already taken the life of one woman. Killing another wasn't that far of a stretch. Margarita was worth every sacrifice—even *human* sacrifice.

Jack stepped aside and allowed Mary Ann to enter the grocery store before him. They'd just spent the last two hours together, first at dinner, and then on a horse-drawn wagon ride. Mary Ann's eyes had glistened when she saw the rustic wagon awaiting them, and Jack had been mighty pleased with himself. The driver gave them a slow tour of the rolling acres that belonged to the family who owned the steak house. The end of the tour involved passing the family estate—a pillared mansion that dated back to the early twentieth century. The whole experience created quite a memory and left both Jack and Mary Ann hungry for the dessert they'd declined in the restaurant.

Now they were invading Brookshire's with the sole intent of purchasing one of those sinful cheesecakes that Jack resisted three days ago. While he wasn't overweight by any means, he was definitely healthy. The closer he got to forty, the more he had to cut back at the table, or live with the consequences. But tonight, he'd decided to repent of his bothersome carb-counting habit.

"Here they are," Mary Ann said and hurried to the end of the deli's open case. "Look, here's the one I was talking about. It's got four different kinds of cheesecake—strawberry, blueberry, chocolate turtle, and plain."

"Oh, man!" Jack exclaimed. "I'll take one of each."

Mary Ann beamed up at him like he was the King of England and she was ready to kiss his ring . . . or him. She'd acted a little disappointed after the wagon ride. Jack hadn't understood why until now. He hadn't even held her hand, let alone kissed her. Now Jack realized Mary Ann had expected a little more action than he was ready for.

Nevertheless, he admitted that her red hair and blue eyes probably turned more heads than not. And in that western-style sundress and a pair of snakeskin boots that nearly matched his, she looked like some chick-next-door who was as friendly as she was attractive. Except, Mary Ann *was* the girl next door. He also figured there were a line of young bucks from twenty-five to forty willing to kiss her thirty-year-old lips on the first date. Bullard was a small town and good-looking young widows were a rare find—especially one who owned a twenty-acre horse ranch. But to his knowledge, Jack was the first man she'd gone out with since a tractor flipped on her husband and killed him. Zane had been a good neighbor to Uncle Abe, and his tragic death disturbed Jack.

Now I'm on a date with Zane's wife, he thought and felt a teeny bit like a scoundrel until he shook himself. *Zane's dead,* Jack affirmed. *And Mary Ann's lonely. So am I, for all that matter.*

He reached for her hand.

"Are you sure this one's okay?" She peered up as he twined his fingers with hers, and a blushing smile flushed her peaches-and-cream cheeks. "I—I don't want to be the one to do all the choosing. If you'd really rather have another one—"

"No." Jack shook his head and squeezed her hand. "This is the one I counted on. Let's get it out to my place before I eat half of it on the spot."

Tonight, he'd prayed that he could fall in love with Mary Ann Osborne. He repeated the prayer every time he caught himself wishing he was with Charli instead. Refusing to dwell upon Ms. Friedmont or how inviting she'd been at four A.M., Jack scooped up the cheesecake and tugged Mary Ann toward the checkout.

Nevertheless, thoughts of Charli reminded him of the suggestion he'd spontaneously made to Pat and Mark Jonas when he paid Charli's bond. Mrs. Jonas had called this afternoon and inquired again about the possibility of the church children coming to his ranch for a tour and perhaps a ride on a horse. Jack had mentioned that Mary Ann also had a few rabbits and goats. That plus a gentle calf or two would provide an ample petting zoo. Jack wondered what possessed him to make the offer and chalked it up to trying to improve his image. After all, Pat Jonas hadn't exactly been thrilled with him when he hauled Charli off Friday night. While the offer had been sincere, Jack hadn't expected her to take him up on it so soon. When she called today, she'd asked if Tuesday night was open. Now Jack was feeling the pressure of having offered Mary Ann's animals without first consulting her.

"You do still have the rabbits and goats, don't you?" he asked as they emerged from the deli.

"Yes, why?" she questioned.

"Well, a local church wants to bring their children's group out to the ranch, and I mentioned my neighbor might be willing to put some of her animals in a petting zoo. They're talking about coming Tuesday night. I know it's a last-minute request. I had no idea they'd take me up on it at all—let alone so soon. You wouldn't even have to come. I'd be glad to pick up a few goats and rabbits and then bring them back. You know with Bud around they'd be taken care of."

"I'd be delighted to come and bring them," Mary Ann enthused. "I think that's *so* thoughtful of you." She tightened her fingers around his hand, and Jack couldn't stop his ego from swelling just a tad. But then, what normal guy wouldn't be boosted with an attractive lady looking at him like he was the hero of the hour.

"Uh, just to be honest," he insisted, "I didn't put much thought into it. It was kind of a spontaneous offer."

"Oh, no! I'm not going to let you go all humble on me. It *was thoughtful!* Do you mind if the boys come with me?"

"No, of course not. They're always welcome," Jack insisted and beamed into her eyes.

As they emerged from the deli, he glanced down an aisle to his right and spotted a familiar little girl sitting in a cart's child seat. At first, Jack thought he'd imagined how much she looked like Bonnie Friedmont until she met his gaze. She lowered her lollipop and observed him with those big-as-pancake eyes. Then, Bonnie nearly smiled at Jack for the second time.

His eyes widened, and he shifted his focus to Charli. Like Bonnie, she was dressed in a dress and sandals. Jack figured she'd just gotten out of Sunday-night church. Normally, he would have too, except he'd made an exception this evening. With her back to Jack, Charli gazed at a shelf and appeared to have no idea he was present.

Pulling his hat lower, he forgot all about the petting zoo and sped to the first cashier he came to. Thankfully, there was no line.

"Hey, why the hurry?" Mary Ann teased. "You're about to drag me flat."

"Uh . . ." Jack plopped the cheesecake onto the moving merchandise belt and said, "I'm a growing boy! I'm ready for my cheesecake." His smile felt strained, but Mary Ann didn't seem to notice.

Before pulling his billfold from his jeans pocket, Jack glanced toward Charli's aisle and saw no signs of her. He did *not* want Charli to see him with Mary Ann; he'd figure out the reason later. But for now, Jack couldn't exit soon enough.

Once the cheesecake was bagged, he grabbed it and strode toward the exit. Jack had no thoughts for holding Mary Ann's hand, but she inserted her fingers into the crook of his arm anyway. Jack tried to grin down at her, but had trouble making it look sincere considering he was short of breath. His normal breathing didn't return until he was steering his truck from the parking lot. At last glance, he noticed Charli's well-used Taurus sitting near the store's entrance, and he wondered if she'd ever owned a brand-new vehicle, let alone an Escalade.

Charli walked down the aisle of bottled drinks and searched until she spotted a display of root beer. She'd turned down this aisle on a hunch that lead her to the beverage Jack requested yesterday. Charli eyed the bottles and wondered if she should purchase one.

If he ever comes back to my house, he'll be glad I have some, she thought and decided it was the least she could do for him. After all, he'd paid most of her bond.

When she reached for the root beer and placed it in the cart, Bonnie said, "I want Sprite, Mamma, not that."

"This isn't for you," Charli explained, "It's for—" She didn't finish.

"I want Sprite," Bonnie repeated.

"Sprite isn't good for you. The doctor says—"

"But you bought coke for you."

"It isn't for me," Charli explained and sensed someone watching her.

She glanced behind and encountered a couple of ogling cowboys near a display of Diet Coke. Charli gave them the drop-dead stare that usually took care of the problem. Then, she turned her head and marched toward the checkout.

As a single mom, Charli mastered the art of putting men in their place. Presently, none of the single guys at work—or where she used to work—wasted any time on her. Word had spread that Charli Friedmont was *not interested.* The *last* thing Charli needed was another man to tangle up her life.

She went through the whole checkout routine

without a hitch—unless you counted finally giving in to buying Bonnie a Sprite to keep her quiet. Charli didn't usually give in, but she was so tired this evening she didn't care. After her sleep was interrupted in the wee hours, Charli had lain back in bed but never went to sleep. Even though she'd taken a short nap after Sunday lunch, it had been just enough to make her groggy. Now her foggy mind was ready for a long night of uninterrupted snoozing.

Once her groceries were bagged, she pushed her cart to her Taurus and began loading them into her trunk. The effort reaped a rash of sweat along her hairline. Charli wiped away the moisture and noticed beads of sweat forming beneath Bonnie's eyes. The eight o'clock sun blasting from the horizon baked the concrete, moist from the evening shower. Rather than cooling off the area, the rain had just added humidity to heat.

When she shut the trunk and prepared to push her cart to the rack, her cell phone began to chirp like a cricket. She knew from the distinctive ring that the caller was Pat Jonas. Charli had barely answered when Pat's voice rushed over the line.

"Charli . . . you said you were going to Brookshire's. Are you still there?"

"Yes," Charli said.

"Oh, good. My sister, Leigh, and her husband were here a few minutes ago. They'd already been by your house and needed to talk to you. I told them you said you were going to Brookshire's, and they were going to try to intersect you there."

"Okaaaay," Charli drawled and tried to recall who Pat's sister was. She hated to sound rude, but she held no memory of the woman and possessed no idea why she'd be looking for her.

"I hate to steal their thunder," Pat continued, "so I won't say more."

"Well, should I *wait* for them?" Charli questioned. "I was about to leave." She scanned the parking lot in search of anyone who might resemble Pat.

"If they don't see you before you leave, just call me back and I'll tell them to go back to your house."

"Okay," Charli agreed as a low wolf whistle echoed across the parking lot. Charli spotted those two cowboys striding toward a pickup a few places down from hers. She jumped. Charli bent her head, stopped the cart near the lot's rack, lifted Bonnie from the child seat, and held her close.

The cowboys' whistling merged into crude catcalls. "Hey, cover girl, busy later?" one asked.

"What about *now?*" the other jeered. "And can you let us borrow some money?"

"Wanta double date?"

Keeping her head bent, Charli tried to make sense of their jeers while darting a glance at them. Both now leaned against the pickup bed and held beer bottles.

Great! she thought. *The perfect end to the perfect weekend. Two drunk cowboys on my trail.*

She held Bonnie close and stomped to her car. Hopefully, they'd have the sense to back off. With the lollipop in one hand and the Sprite in the other, Bonnie wound up tangling Charli's hair in the sucker and dowsing her blouse with the Sprite. But Charli didn't care. Those were minor issues compared to sexual harassment . . . or assault.

Once she unlocked the car, Charli cast a last glance over her shoulder. The two men were mere feet away. Their leering gazes suggested they were planning to put action to their attitudes. Charli plopped into the car's heat, dumped Bonnie in the passenger seat, slammed the door, and locked it seconds before one of them pressed his palm against her window.

Charli laid on her horn.

"Mommy!" Bonnie bellowed.

"Don't worry, baby," Charli exclaimed and wondered if that even meant anything to Bonnie anymore.

"Mommy, stop!" the child exclaimed.

But Charli didn't let up until an older gentleman trotted to her rescue. The two cowboys raced to their vehicle. She lifted her hand off the horn, scrambled from the car, and strained to get their license plate number: BJT 30D. Charli mentally repeated it until she had it memorized.

"They didn't hurt you, did they?" the man asked.

"No." Charli shook her head and stepped around her opened door. "They were just being obnoxious."

A plump lady wearing a pantsuit and fresh makeup strolled to the man's side. Like his wife, the man was in dress clothes, and Charli suspected they'd just come from church as she had. She thought she remembered seeing them at a multi-church Christmas celebration last year. Of course, Bullard was so small most of the population saw each other several times a year. Nonetheless, she never remembered seeing the likes of those crude men.

"Did you get their license plate number?" the lady gazed toward the truck, now turning at the next block.

Charli nodded. "Yes. I was thinking of giving it to the police." Her mind darted to Jack. She hadn't planned to call him again unless it was a dire emergency, but Charli didn't want to take the chance of the men following her or showing up again.

"I strongly suggest you do," the man said. "I also suggest turning it into the store manager and letting him know everything. You *are* Charli Friedmont, right?"

"Yes." She rested her hand atop her door's warm frame.

"You poor dear," the lady crooned and patted her hand.

Charli's fingers curled against the door as her mind fought to piece together the last few minutes.

In her fervor to get away from the cowboys, she'd dismissed the phone call from Pat, but now she began to suspect this might be Pat's sister and brother-in-law.

She gazed from the man to the woman and asked, "Are you by chance Pat Jonas's sister?"

"Yes. Pat told us you were here."

"I was just on the phone with her. She told me you were coming." Charli swiped at her bangs.

"Mommy, I want to go," Bonnie said.

Charli looked inside the car to encounter her daughter's startled gaze. She'd climbed into the driver's seat. Her sucker lay in the passenger seat. The Sprite was precariously perched on the console. And Bonnie was clinging to Charli's skirt.

"Go ahead and crawl in the backseat. I'll buckle you in," Charli encouraged.

"But it's hot back there," she complained, a stream of sweat trickling down her cheek.

"I know. I know, sweetheart. Look, everything's just fine. Go ahead and crawl back there, and I'll start the car and turn on the air conditioner. Mamma won't be long."

"Okay," Bonnie said, and for once Charli was glad she didn't have to wrangle her into the task. Bonnie twisted to climb to the back when Charli remembered the Sprite. "Wait!" she squawked and retrieved the drink before Bonnie toppled it.

"I'm sorry," she said toward the couple, only to realize they were no longer there. They'd walked to the newspaper stand and were purchasing a paper.

Odd, she thought before reaching into the car, cranking it, and turning the A.C. on high. Then, Charli opened the back door, handed the Sprite to Bonnie, and helped her into her seat belt. She'd just shut Bonnie's door when the couple arrived with a newspaper in hand.

"We were about to buy this for you when we saw the men," the gentleman said and extended it to Charli.

Her forehead wrinkling, she took the paper and read the headlines, "Local Woman Arrested for Embezzlement." Charli's mug shot claimed the front page. Her temples began to throb. The parking lot spun. The paper trembled in her hands. And those cowboys' comments now made sense. They'd called her "cover girl" and asked if they could borrow some money. In all the upheaval, she'd never thought of her arrest making headlines.

She hadn't subscribed to the paper since she had Bonnie because she never had time to read it anyway. She often joked that the red army could seize Bullard and she'd never even know about it. Presently, she regretted her lack of interest in current events.

Furthermore, something from today at church now made perfect sense. When she'd walked into her small Sunday-school class, all chatter had stopped. The teacher, a mature lady who adored

Charli, was hurriedly shoving a newspaper under her bible. Charli had interpreted the breathless pause as the normal fallout of the news of her arrest. So she'd taken the initiative, smiled, and told them she'd survived jail with all her teeth intact. The nervous chuckling that followed ushered in a good round of support and encouragement. Every one of them said they believed in her innocence. But not one of them had the heart to mention the cover story—not even the Jonases.

By this point, Charli was too numb to even cry. There didn't seem to be any end to the repercussions of her arrest. Now the whole community knew what had happened. And even though she was innocent, Charli wanted to crawl underneath her car and melt into the concrete.

"Dear?" the lady prompted. "We're sorry to have to show you this, but we convinced Pat that ignorance is not bliss in this situation. You need to know."

"Y-yes, you're—you're right," Charli stammered and lifted her attention to the lady. "Thanks for letting me know. Those—those men called me cover girl. Now I know why."

"They should be *shot,*" the man growled.

"Ross!" his wife exclaimed.

"Well, it's the truth," he snapped and reached into his hip pocket. He pulled out his billfold, flipped it open, removed a card, and extended it to Charli. "My name's Ross Lavine," he said.

She took the card and recalled seeing his name on a downtown office window. She scanned the card and read, "Attorney at Law," as he explained, "I'm an attorney."

"Oh." Charli looked into his kind, gray eyes.

"If you need my services, I'm available."

His wife elbowed him, and he added, "At no charge."

Charli gasped. "But—but *why?*"

"Because she says so." He pointed to his wife, who beamed at Charli.

"Pat called this afternoon. She's never asked us for anything—even with all her son's problems. But this time, she did. She and Mark are *worried sick.*"

"Besides," Ross added, "you remind us a little of our daughter." His gaze trailed past Charli.

"She died of a cerebral hemorrhage five years ago," Leigh explained, her eyes reddening.

"I'm *so sorry.*" Charli breathed and couldn't imagine the horror of losing Bonnie.

"I decided before we left our church tonight that I'd represent you," Ross explained. "So we went by your church to see if we could catch you. Mark and Pat told us you'd mentioned going to Brookshire's." He lifted his bushy brows.

"Yes, that's what she just told me on the phone," Charli explained.

"Mamma, let's go!" Bonnie called.

"All right, honey." Charli glanced toward her

daughter, now with the Sprite bottle turned up to her mouth.

"Thank you *so much,*" Charli said and swiveled back to the couple. "I don't know what to say."

"Try, yes," Ross encouraged.

Charli nodded and wondered what Jack knew of the man. The fact that he was Pat's brother-in-law pretty much cinched the deal. However, she also had to consider the work that Sonny was doing and how having a lawyer would affect him. As much as she wanted to immediately agree, Charli also didn't need to make a rash decision.

"I'll certainly pray about it," she said with a nod. "I can't imagine saying no," she added, "but I need time to process it all." Charli smiled her appreciation and hoped the man didn't think she was being ungrateful.

"Of course, dear," Leigh agreed. "You don't need to jump into anything. All this has got to be terribly disconcerting. Just give it some thought."

"Yes, and call me when you decide," Ross confirmed. "My office is downtown."

Charli gripped the card and watched the couple stroll away. As her eyes blurred, she shifted her gaze to the man's name and number. *Maybe God hasn't forgotten me after all,* she thought.

CHAPTER ELEVEN

Sigmund circled Charli's house, searching for the easiest way to enter. He'd tried every window with no luck. The front door was locked, as he'd assumed. And the only back entry to the house was through the cluttered garage's door. With the sun getting closer to the horizon, Sigmund decided he'd do what he hadn't wanted to do: kick in the back door. Even though that would likely bust the lock, it would be less noticeable than breaking a window. And, if Charli didn't use the back door much, she might not notice it for days.

Before slamming his foot against the door, Sigmund examined the knob and lock. The lock clearly dated to the first half of the twentieth century and required a skeleton key.

Sigmund prepared to kick the door, but realized he had yet to try the knob. He'd brought a handkerchief with him for exactly such purposes. He pulled the handkerchief from his pocket, wrapped it around the knob, and twisted. The door squeaked open.

Holding his breath, he listened. When he had checked to see if any windows were opened, he'd peered inside when possible to see if anyone might be in the house. Even though Charli's car was gone, Sigmund didn't want to take any chances.

Once he was certain no one was home, he

stepped inside. High-pitched squeaking filtered from the left. Sigmund jumped and swiveled to meet his opponent. He faced a closed door. The squeaking grew louder and began to suspiciously sound like kittens. He wrinkled his brow. When a lone paw emerged beneath the door, Sigmund sighed.

Focusing anew on his task, he nudged the door shut behind him and eased into the kitchen. Little-girl cups and artwork cluttered the counter. Photos and paintings decorated the refrigerator.

Until now, he'd been so focused on needing to get rid of Charli that he hadn't even thought about her daughter. Several around the bank had mentioned that Bonnie was five. Sigmund thought of his own daughters, Kelly and Kari. Kelly was now twenty, away in college. Kari never made it past three. She'd dashed in front of a car in a parking lot and was run over right in front of Dianne and Sigmund's eyes. Dianne had blamed him for some reason; Sigmund never understood why—except that that seemed to be the way of the women in his life. His mother had certainly blamed him for more than his share of mishaps. Even though his and Dianne's marriage had never been spectacular, it gradually died the year after Kari's funeral.

Despite the fact that he'd been forced to take Brenda's life . . . and now Charli's . . . he couldn't imagine killing any child. "No," he whispered. "I won't kill the little girl. She doesn't have to die, just the mother—and only because she's investigating. It's her own fault." He thought about the child crying for her mother as he'd cried for his the day she locked him out of the house. After a cringe, he hardened his resolve.

She'll get over it, he thought and strode through the kitchen, into the living room. *I certainly did.* His running shoes made little noise against the hardwood floors, and Sigmund decided he should wear them tonight. Pausing in the middle of the room, he gazed at every piece of furniture, noticing the basket of fruit sitting on the dining table at the room's north end. Rolling fruit made a lot of noise.

"Avoid the fruit," Sigmund mumbled.

From the living room, he emerged into the hallway that stretched behind the living room, through the middle of the house. He looked to the left, saw the kitchen. A glance to his right revealed two bedrooms.

Sigmund stepped into the first one he came to. A change of clothing lay in the middle of the unmade bed. A computer desk sat in the corner. A huge window covered in blinds claimed the west wall. Stepping over a pair of high heels, Sigmund walked toward the window. He raised the blinds, squinted against the setting sun, and twisted the ancient window's lock. He'd already wrestled a few of his mother's windows into submission and didn't plan to let this one outwit him either. Wrapping his handkerchief around the handle,

Sigmund yanked. The window slid up with no complaints and then stayed where he left it.

"The gods are smiling on me," he drawled and eyed the screen. Two token fasteners held it in place. Sigmund turned them and thus completed the task of paving the way for later entry . . . if she remembered to lock the back door and he couldn't finagle the lock with one of his mom's old skeleton keys.

Sigmund lowered the window and blinds, then scrutinized the room's every detail until the location of the bed and dresser and every other piece of furniture were blazoned upon his mind. He paced back toward the hallway and counted his steps as he went. Only about fifteen feet separated the window from the hall. He then gazed toward the kitchen and estimated the distance to be a mere twenty feet.

The house was small. That was good. More conducive to a quick entry, a quick job, and a quick exit.

Sigmund stepped to the child's room and was stricken with the smell of peanut butter. An open jar of the stuff sitting on her dresser confirmed the scent. All manner of kiddy decorations claimed the area, right down to the cat-covered comforter on the bed. He absorbed the locale of her toy boxes and noted several items lying in the middle of the floor.

He spotted a rag doll, much like the one they'd

placed in Kari's arms before they buried her. Sigmund picked it up, stroked her hair, and his face puckered into a frown that hurt. He remembered the child tumbling over him while he tickled her and her sister. She'd been a good girl. Sigmund's fingers curled into the doll. Then, he released it. She fell to her face on the floor.

"Stay out of this room," he commanded. "Just deal with the mother and get her body out."

He nodded approval of the plan and turned back toward the kitchen. The visit had been profitable and gave Sigmund exactly what he was looking for: his bearings. When he entered the house tonight, he didn't want to have to guess where anything was. Now, he knew.

Once the couple left, Charli took Mr. Lavine's advice. Holding Bonnie, she went straight back into the cool store to file a report. The chilled air hit her like a blast of ice water as she veered straight toward the manager's glassed-in office. Just as she was walking up, a lanky man was exiting. His nametag read, "Doug Brown, Manager."

No sooner had he politely inquired if he could help her than the story spilled from Charli in a breathless gush. As his lined face hardened, he wasted no time calling the store security guard.

The second the fresh-faced guard stepped into her line of vision, Charli recognized him as the blond officer who'd served her coffee yesterday morning. He'd barely stopped when she said, "Oh, it's you," and didn't know whether to smile or frown.

"Yes." His grin reminded her of a shy schoolboy, but his blue eyes held the observant edge of a man. "Something wrong?" he asked and glanced toward the manager.

Brown began rolling up his shirtsleeves. "Remember those two idiots who were on the parking lot last night?"

"Yeah," Yarborough said.

"Looks like they were at it again, and this time they were drinking."

Bonnie wiggled in Charli's arms and cried, "I want down." Charli released Bonnie, allowing her to stand close while holding her hand. Straightening, she related her story to the officer, and he nodded.

"I'll keep a watch out for them and also alert the station. You got their license plate number. If they're drinking and an officer can find them he can haul them in for DWI." He pulled his cell phone from his belt. "I think Payton's back on again tonight. *Nobody* gets away from that cat."

"Thanks so much," Charli said and never imagined she'd be grateful to one of the officers who'd held the key to her cell. But then, she was eternally grateful for all Jack was doing, and he'd been her arresting officer.

All the way home, Charli checked and double-checked her rearview mirror to make certain the men weren't following her. Pulling into her driveway, she was confident she'd shaken them for good.

Nonetheless, she still planned to phone Jack and let him know about the men as well as ask him about the lawyer. Before her trial was over, the man would probably think she was a pest.

So let it be, she thought as she climbed from the car. *Once it's all over, I'll stay out of his way.*

Getting the groceries in while dodging Bonnie was an ordeal, as usual. By the time Charli set the final bag on her counter, Bonnie had spilled her Sprite, pulled the cats out of the utility room, and accidentally let one of them outside. Charli traced down both kittens and deposited them back into the utility room until she had everything under control. When closing the utility room's door, Charli noticed the door leading to the garage was ajar.

Tilting her head, she walked to it and peered into her garage so crowded with boxes and lawn para-phernalia, there was no room for her car. When she saw nothing unusual in the mix, she closed the door and turned the ancient lock. Charli eyed the skeleton keyhole and put "replace" at the top of her to-do list next week. She'd lived in this house her whole childhood and had always possessed a high sense of safety within the walls. But now Charli didn't feel safe anywhere. She eyed the antique lock that had kept her secure her whole life and gave herself a serious reality check. The lock was the epitome of fragile and useless and would be no good against a hard blow.

Thankfully, the kittens had been in the utility room while they were gone and hadn't been able to slip out. Wondering if Bonnie had opened the door again after Charli locked it, she called, "Bonnie?" while walking back into the kitchen.

The child was now sitting in the floor with the Sprite bottle on its side. Bonnie held her sucker in one hand and a dish towel in the other. She gazed up at her mom and pragmatically said, "I spilled it again."

"Oh, Bonnie," Charli groaned and the pressure of the weekend rose within. Her volume increasing with every word, she blurted, "How could you be so—"

The child's alarmed gaze stopped Charli's spiel.

She took a deep breath, counted to ten, reached for a fresh towel on the counter, and knelt beside her daughter. "Here, let Mamma help you," she said in a calmer voice.

Bonnie's face relaxed.

"I'm sorry I got a little excited. Everybody spills stuff sometimes." She ruffled her daughter's hair.

"Yep!" Bonnie smiled and licked her lollipop. "Everybody spills stuff. You spilled the coffee this morning, and I spilled the Sprite tonight. We all spill stuff."

Charli chuckled and mopped up the final moisture. "Thanks for the reminder," she said. After dampening the towel and sponging up the sugary residue, she threw the wet cloth in the sink and said, "Come on, let's wash our hands."

With the hand washing complete, Charli set Bonnie on the counter near the groceries and said, "Before we left for church, did you open the garage door again?"

"No." Bonnie shook her head, and her ponytail swung with the movement.

"Hmmm." A pall of unease crept up Charli's spine as she gazed toward the hallway. She had caught Bonnie opening the back door more than once when they were on the verge of leaving. Charli had explained to Bonnie that the door should remain closed and locked.

She eyed her daughter. Even though Bonnie wasn't a habitual liar, chances were significant she was covering her tracks after she saw how Charli nearly lost her composure about the Sprite.

Bonnie stopped licking her sucker long enough to gaze up at Charli. "I saw Uncle Jack tonight in the store," she reported.

"Really?" Charli questioned.

"Yes." She nodded. "He was with a lady with orange hair."

"Orange hair?" she echoed and tried to conjure the image.

Bonnie nodded. "You know, like Mrs. Whatley's at church."

"Oh, that's called *red* hair," Charli said.

"No, Mommy," she insisted. "That's not *red*. It's *orange*."

"All right, all right," Charli agreed and wondered if Bonnie had simply seen someone who looked like Jack. She couldn't imagine him not saying something if he'd seen Bonnie. Jack had made a point of talking to her for a year now. Besides, Charli never recalled seeing him with any female before and decided Bonnie must have just seen someone who resembled Jack.

Before unpacking the groceries, she glanced toward the back door again and decided to put her mind totally at ease. Even though the door was probably the result of Bonnie's carelessness, she needed to double-check the house. Charli settled Bonnie in front of a *Barney* video in the living room, discreetly pulled her grandfather's cane from the brass holder by the front door and entered the hallway. After a careful examination of both her and Bonnie's rooms along with the closets and bathroom, Charli's mind rested easy.

When she slipped the cane back into the brass cylinder, Charli decided the time had come to install a childproof lock on the back door. With people framing her for embezzlement and men chasing her in the parking lot and her photo on the newspaper's front page, Charli couldn't take any chances on Bonnie's leaving the back door opened and making it too convenient for anyone to enter.

She paused at the kitchen doorway and observed Bonnie, now totally fixated upon the dancing purple dinosaur. Charli considered scolding her daughter but decided not to. The weekend had been too traumatic already. Bonnie probably held no memory of leaving the door open.

Sighing, Charli turned to her task in the kitchen. She pulled the two-liter jug of root beer from the bag and set it under the cabinet. She was shoving the crackers on the shelf when she remembered the business card she'd slipped into her skirt pocket. Pulling it out, she read the information again. A very deep sense of peace wove its way through her spirit as she considered the prospect of allowing Mr. Lavine to represent her.

Perhaps this was God's answer to her jail-cell prayer for deliverance and help. She had a private eye who was representing her for free, and now a lawyer had miraculously appeared to offer the same. She found her purse beneath the bag of eggs, dug her cell phone from it, and paused before pressing Jack's speed-dial button.

CHAPTER TWELVE

Holding a tall glass of iced tea, Jack stepped onto his porch and settled on the swing. As things turned out, Mary Ann's babysitter called her home early. The boys had poured bubbles all over the kitchen floor and began a sliding contest, and that had been too much for the sixteen-year-old sitter. When Mary Ann laughed it off and offered the kids cheesecake, Jack suspected she needed to take a firmer hand with them, but he'd stayed out of it. That was none of his business. He'd stayed long enough to eat his cheesecake and then came on home when the boys absorbed Mary Ann.

Jack squinted and gazed toward Mary Ann's place, fifteen acres and one creek away. The trees partially blocked the view of her brick home and red barn. Nonetheless, Jack was stricken with just how cozy this whole setup was.

His cell phone's ringing barged into his thoughts. After setting his tea aside, he pulled his phone from his belt and glanced at the screen. Charli's name obliterated all thoughts of Mary Ann and the cozy setup.

"Charli?" he said into the phone. "Everything okay?"

"Yes," she replied. "I'm sorry to keep being a pest—"

"You're not a pest," he said through a smile. "Like I said, I'm here if you need me."

"Well, the reason I was calling," she explained, "is because a lawyer has offered to represent me for free, and I was wondering—"

"For free?" Jack exclaimed and glanced toward Sam who trotted up the steps.

"Yes."

"Who, for cryin' out loud?"

"Ross Lavine."

"Lavine? Are you serious? Are you sure?"

"As a heart attack," Charli answered.

"I promise, Charli, you must have some sort of a guardian angel working overtime for you." Sam rested his chin on Jack's knee, and he scratched the dog's ears. "This is unbelievable."

"So, he's good?"

Jack laughed. "He's *the best!* He moved here from Houston to retire. If you can call winning every case retiring."

"He wins every case?" Charli gasped.

"Well, if he's lost one, I sure don't know about it. There's been a time or two I've hated to see him coming, if you want the truth."

"Sounds like a winner to me, then," Charli said, and Jack realized that she'd called just to ask his opinion. He sat a little straighter and eyed an eagle soaring toward the sunset—a blazing mural of golden velvet and purple satin and ribbon the color of pomegranates.

Jack stood. "Of course, you'll need to consult with Sonny, but I'm sure he and Lavine can work together."

"Right," Charli said.

A spirited breeze whisked around the house and relieved Jack of the heat creeping up his neck.

"I, um, also wanted to tell you about something

146

that happened to me tonight at Brookshire's," Charli continued. "I went there after church just to pick up a few things." She paused.

"Oh?" Jack stiffened and wondered if Bonnie had told all.

"And a couple of men were really staring at me in the store," she continued and Jack relaxed. "Then, outside, they started making crude remarks and then chased me to my car."

His knees locked. "Did they hurt you?"

"N-no," Charli explained. "They just scared me. I got in the car and laid on my horn. That's when Mr. Lavine and his wife came to help me. Anyway, I reported it to the store manager."

"Good."

"And he got the security guard. He's a police officer."

"Yarborough?"

"Yes."

"He's a good guy."

"He seemed to be," Charli said. "He told me he'd alert the police station as well. He said that officer named Payton was on duty—"

"Yeah. He is. And if he can find them he'll have them thrown *under* the jail within the hour. I'd hate to face him if I was a criminal."

"Me too," Charli agreed. "I think I remember seeing him the other night. He looked like he could be somebody's worst nightmare."

"Yeah. On a good day." Jack chuckled.

"Anyway," Charli continued, "those guys at the store were calling me cover girl and asking me if they could borrow some money."

Jack went silent. He'd seen the headlines this morning, but hoped Charli hadn't. Her next statement ended that unrealistic wish.

"That's because of the lead story in the paper," she explained.

"Yes, I saw that this morning," Jack said. "I'm really sorry. I would have liked to have stopped it, but I have no control over—"

"I know," Charli assured. "I think I've read something somewhere about freedom of the press," she added through a dry chuckle.

"Yeah." Jack shook his head. "And to tell you the truth, there have been a few times when I wished I *did* have some say in it."

"I understand," Charli said as Mary Ann's Escalade rolled up his driveway.

"Good." Jack returned Mary Ann's wave and noticed she had the boys with her. She parked her vehicle and slid out while wearing a smile that could knock the horns off a bull.

He returned the smile and hoped it didn't look stiff from this distance. As she strolled toward him and the boys raced to the porch steps, he wondered if Charli would mind that he'd been on a date. Somehow, he didn't think she'd give one flip. The only reason he was in her life was for pure necessity and nothing else.

Once the need is gone, so am I, he reminded himself and moved toward the steps.

"Are you still there?" Charli asked.

"Uh, yeah," Jack replied. "Someone just drove up to my house, and it distracted me."

"Well, I should go, then," Charli said. "Thanks for the info about Lavine."

"Any time," Jack replied.

A long pause followed. "Like I said, I just got home from Brookshire's. I bought a few things for dinner tonight. I need to get Bonnie fed."

"Of course," he stated and avoided looking Mary Ann in the eyes. Jack was beginning to feel like a two-faced womanizer, and the image rubbed him wrong. But he hadn't asked his former girlfriend to call him or his date from the evening to drive back over. He was caught in a trap on this one. Nevertheless, he didn't like the sensation that went with the trap.

"I guess I'll hear from Sonny soon, then?"

"Yes, you should. Probably tomorrow," he replied as the noisy boys charged the steps and crashed into him.

"Whoa!" Jack said while grabbing the porch railing. Sam added his gleeful barking to the din and then romped off the porch like a six-month old pup.

"Boys! Boys!" Mary Ann cried. "Stop it now! Jack, I'm *so sorry!*" She scrambled for her sons as Jack fought to keep his balance.

149

"Sounds like it's getting crazy there," Charli commented.

"Yeah." Jack laughed out loud.

Mary Ann grabbed both her sons by the arms and plunked them onto the porch swing. It danced wildly while Brett and Brad protested their mother's discipline.

"Thanks for everything," she added.

"Sure," Jack said and bid farewell.

He closed the phone, put it in his shirt pocket, crossed his arms, and watched Mary Ann shake her finger at her sons while verbally chastising them. This time, Jack repented of his thinking she should be harder on the little guys. Apparently, he'd just seen her in a soft moment earlier because this Mary Ann was a cross between Hitler and an army sergeant.

"And I want you to apologize to Mr. Jack," she ended.

The boys, now sitting still on the swing, both looked up at Jack like two juvenile delinquents. The older boy, Brett, had hair as red as Mary Ann's. His bangs hung just above his eyes. That, coupled with his freckles, made him look like he was up to all sorts of private mischief. Brad wasn't much better. His brown hair was as short as could be, but a cowlick forced a sprig cockeyed above his forehead. His shirt was as splotchy as his brother's. His skinned knee testified to who-knew-what rough and tumble antics.

Jack bit on his lower lip and tried hard not to smile. Mary Ann noticed, and narrowed her eyes in a silent message: *Don't you dare laugh.* That made the grin all the more difficult to manage.

Hands on hips, she turned back to her sons. "Boys?"

"Sorry," Brad finally mumbled.

"Sorry, Mr. Jack," Brett added.

"It's okay, guys," Jack said and let his grin go free.

Sam trotted up the steps, lowered his head and barked out an invitation. "Sam's Frisbee is behind the swing. He's asking you to come play." Jack stepped around the swing, retrieved the Frisbee, and tossed it to the middle of the yard. Sam dashed to the task, lunged into the air, and caught the Frisbee.

The boys' exclamations were followed by their eager gazes toward their mother.

"All right." She nodded. "You can go play. But no repeats, do you hear?"

They were halfway down the porch steps before Mary Ann finished.

Jack's laughter mingled with their joyous calling for Sam. The dog met them and wagged his whole body.

Inserting his hands into his jeans pockets, Jack watched the kids enjoy Sam. But a whippoorwill's call echoing across the countryside tugged his attention toward the woods. The whippoorwill always reminded Jack of the April evening he and Charli had gone on a hike in his uncle's woods with Ryan and his then girlfriend, Shelly. They'd stopped at the rocky creek, taken off their shoes, and waded in the cold water. Even though April had set record highs, the water still had the bite of winter in it. Charli had squealed and clutched at Jack when her feet sank into the stream. Once they'd taken all they could stand, both couples had climbed to a giant, flat rock where they'd sat bare-footed while a whippoorwill serenaded them.

"A penny for your thoughts." Mary Ann's sweet voice interrupted his reverie and Jack realized he'd been blankly staring across the pasture . . . at nothing.

A yawn crept up Jack's throat. As much as he tried to stifle the thing, it pried open his mouth and Jack was forced to give in. "Sorry," he said and focused on Mary Ann. "I guess I zoned-out on you, didn't I? I'm a little tired. Had an early start today." He didn't bother to tell Mary Ann he'd been rescuing Charli from two wild felines.

"It's okay. I just figure you're trying to solve a mystery or something." Mary Ann leaned against the porch railing.

"Something like that." He peered toward the woods once more. "I guess."

"I didn't just come back over so you could get knocked flat by my kids," she teased. "I think I left my purse in your truck," Mary Ann explained. "Or at least I *hope* I did. I can't find it anywhere. I was so eager to get into the house when the babysitter called, I think I pulled my keys out of my purse and just left it." She lifted both hands.

Jack smiled at her and did his best to whack himself into an awareness of how attractive red hair and translucent skin could be in a scarlet sunset. His gaze trailed to her lips, and he wondered what it would take for him to be tempted to kiss her. Right now, there was nothing of the zing that he felt with Charli . . . only a mild, male interest that he figured any buck would feel in the presence of an attractive lady. Nothing earthshaking.

"Come on," he said and pulled his keys out of his pocket while motioning Mary Ann to his truck. "I'll unlock it for you." But he'd only taken a few steps when his cell phone emitted a "ding-dong" much like a doorbell. He didn't have to look at the screen to know the caller was Sonny. Jack had assigned him the "ding-dong" because, well, he *was* one sometimes; and nothing proved it more than *The Dukes of Hazzard* distinctive ring Sonny had assigned to Jack. Turnabout was fair play . . . and fair play was as good as revenge.

"I need to take this one," Jack said through an apologetic grin. He pointed the remote lock at his pickup and pressed a button that made the vehicle chirp. "I think it involves a case. Do you mind?"

"No, not at all," Mary Ann said as her cell phone began a low-slung funk tune. "Woops! Looks like it's catching anyway." She pulled her phone from her jeans pocket and said, "It's my brother-in-law, Zeke. He's supposed to be coming over to help me with my hot-water heater. It quit."

"I could have—"

"No, no." Mary Ann waved away his offer. "That's okay. Zeke's always willing."

Jack opened the phone and took his call at the same time Mary Ann took hers. He'd turned it off on their date and wouldn't have taken the call now if not for the potential urgency. No telling what Sonny was up to.

"Hey," Jack said into the receiver and retraced his steps toward the porch.

"Hey, yourself," Sonny responded.

"What's up? Are you on the case or—"

"Just letting you know I'm going into the bank tomorrow morning to open up a checking account and scout out the scene. After that, I'm going to do some serious digging into some backgrounds."

Jack nodded. "Good," he said and eyed Mary Ann as she approached the vehicle. The setting sun *did* make her hair come to life. And she didn't look half bad in those jeans she'd changed into. *Not as good as Charli,* he thought, *but not bad either*.

"You still with me?" Sonny asked, and Jack suspected he may have just been asked a question but didn't know what.

"Still here," Jack replied through a yawn.

Sam's barking mingled with the boys' laughter

as they neared from the barn. They'd found Sam's favorite football and were tossing it back and forth while Sam jumped for it.

"I was just wondering what you were going to be doing tonight," Sonny repeated. "Thought I might come over and we can watch the Rangers. Once I jump into this case tomorrow, I'll be scarce until it's solved."

Jack yawned again. "I'm zonked," he admitted as his eyes drooped. "Charli called early this morning. She thought she had a prowler. It was just those darned cats you gave her. They rode one lamp to the floor and turned the living room upside down. I've been up since four forty-five."

The football turned end over end and crashed into the bottom porch step. Brad and Brett dashed toward the ball with Sam on their heels. The dog barked as loudly as the boys bellowed, "I got it! I got it!" while shoving at each other.

"You got company?" Sonny asked as the brothers dove for the football like two rough and tumble professionals.

"Boy! Boys!" Mary Ann hollered from the truck. "Calm down!"

"Uh, yeah. Mary Ann Osborne and her boys just came over. She left her purse in my truck. We, uh, had a date," he explained.

She slammed the truck's door, looped her purse strap over her shoulder, and hustled toward her sons, who now rolled around on the ground like two mud wrestlers. His tail wagging his whole body, Sam playfully nipped at them between yelps and pants.

"Well, well, well," Sonny drawled. "I guess you took my advice and finally asked her out. Didn't take you long, either, lover boy."

"Would you just stop it?" Jack protested and kept his focus on the fighting boys.

"Hey, I think it's great!" Sonny said. "You've been wrapped around Charli Friedmont's finger long enough, and she *knows* she's got you right where she wants you. This'll do her good."

"What do you mean?" Jack leaned against the porch post and tried to appear as casual as possible. He did *not* want Mary Ann to know his brother had brought up Charli.

"I was with both of you yesterday. I saw how you both acted. You're nothing but a whipped pup ready to fetch every time she lifts a finger, and she knows it too. I think she still thinks you've got it, but I don't think she's ever going to give the nod unless you stop groveling at her feet."

"I'm not groveling!" Jack barked and straightened.

Mary Ann, now nearing her sons, glanced toward Jack. He turned toward the house and doubled his fist.

"Maybe it's time for you to stop asking 'how high' every time she says 'jump'," Sonny advised. "Next time she calls you to rescue her, call the station and send one of your men. You're too easy."

"Easy?" Jack whispered and tried to wrap his mind around Sonny's logic.

"All I know is, some chicks have to know you just might not be there forever before they'll take the bait. Now that you and Mary Ann are an item, I don't see how it's going to hurt to let Charli know."

Jack glanced over his shoulder. Mary Ann held each boy by the arm and was hunched over them. Both covered in dirt and grass, they were more interested in kicking at each other than listening to their mother. Sam, now in possession of the football, romped in circles around them and whined for more action.

"We aren't an item," he claimed and wondered if anyone else in Mary Ann's life was thinking her sons needed a strong male figure to snap them into shape. "I've just taken her out one time. She forgot her purse. She's here to get it."

"You don't have to explain," Sonny drawled. "I'm a big boy. You'd rather spend the evening with her than me. Hey, I can handle that. If you want me to, I'll call Charli and let her know who you're with."

"That's taking it a little far. Don't you think?" Jack groused.

"Sometimes, you do what you gotta do," Sonny shot back.

"Well, you don't gotta do that."

"Okay, okay. I'm just tryin' to help," Sonny said, a smile in his voice.

"You mean, help me over a cliff?"

"Let's not jump to conclusions," Sonny teased.

"Maybe I'm speaking from experience." Jack rubbed his nose and remembered that drop into the gulley that broke it. Even twenty-five years later, Jack couldn't forget the pain . . . or the memory of Sonny and Ryan peering over the edge.

"Now he's dragging up the past," Sonny complained. "I'm outa here before you start a sermon and take up the offering."

"I only preach where it's needed," Jack claimed.

"Touché and goodbye!" Sonny shot before the line went dead.

CHAPTER THIRTEEN

Sigmund pulled the Cutlass onto Charli's road and steered the vehicle down the winding lane. His headlights sliced through the night, highlighting a cloud of bugs that splattered the windshield.

He groaned and knew he'd have to run the vehicle through the car wash. His mother would throw a fit if she got into the car next Saturday and spotted bugs all over her precious "baby." But even dealing with a mean-spirited old lady was worth a couple thousand a month.

Fortunately, Sigmund had possessed the foresight to save the allowance for years. That, plus the money he'd embezzled insured that he and Margarita would survive for many moons, even if he did ditch his job.

He glanced toward the passenger seat at the ziplock bag that held the chemical injection he needed to end Charli's life. His mother's insulin syringe held a liquid potion he'd created himself. Years ago during his deer hunting days, Sigmund and his father had laced their arrows with a white powder called succinylcholine. The muscle relaxant did dreadful things to deer. Once the arrow entered their body, they dropped within thirty seconds and stopped breathing. Of course, it didn't kill them right away. They'd twitch a bit and then go limp while their heart raced and their brain eventually shut down from lack of oxygen. All the while, their glassy eyes stared at the world they were leaving, and the deer held no power to fight the oncoming death. Sigmund never told his father, but that was the part of hunting he liked best—watching his victim suffocate. It reminded him of the time his mother shoved a pillow over his head and held him down until he nearly passed out.

Sometimes when he hovered between the dream-world and reality, Sigmund even recalled what his mind had blocked out during the murder—Brenda Downey's eyes filling with the panic of suffocation. The rush of adrenaline usually awakened him. A few times, he lay in the twilight and daydreamed of repeating the deed. Now his daydream was becoming a reality.

Tonight, he'd revisit the thrill as soon as he injected Charli Friedmont with the white powder he'd mixed with water. A syringe full would be more than sufficient. For a few minutes, her heart would race even though she couldn't breath, and Sigmund's heart would race with the excitement of the kill.

Once she was dead, Sigmund would stuff her in his trunk, just as he had Brenda. When the missing person report was filed, he'd place one threatening phone call before leaving the area. One was all it would take. And Charli's death would be covered just as Brenda's had been.

Then all Sigmund's worries would be over, and he'd be free to leave the country with Margarita. That's all that mattered.

Sigmund pressed the accelerator and hurried to the task. He planned to park on the side of the road near a bunch of oak trees across the street from Charli's place. The trees were thick enough to hide his car and close enough so that he wouldn't have to haul Charli's body far. At one A.M., no one was out on these back roads. But in case someone did drive by, he'd dressed in black pants, shoes, and a long-sleeved, black T-shirt. Sigmund would merge into the shadows just like a demon.

His pulse now beat with the adrenaline of the hunter. His fingers flexed against the steering wheel. His ragged breathing became that of a predator, ready to complete the kill.

But when Sigmund rounded the final curve and his headlights illuminated Charli's yard, he coughed over an expletive and compulsively braked the Cutlass. A police car sat in the middle of her front yard like a big bully, daring anyone to cross into Charli's territory.

Jack stood in the middle of Charli's living room, gazing down at her sleep-heavy features. He'd been awakened from a deep sleep at 12:45 by a presence in the room so strong it nearly scared him. But all fear had vanished as an urgency overtook him.

Go to Charli's. NOW!

This experience had been as vivid as his awareness that Sonny had had a wreck and, later, that his Uncle Abe was dying. He'd awakened in the middle of the night and knew he had to get to the hospital if he wanted to see his uncle alive again. The second Jack stepped into the hospital room, the nurse had been leaving to call relatives.

This time, Jack hadn't hesitated any more than he had with his uncle or Sonny. He was parking his car in her front yard and calling her cell phone before he was fully awake.

Now Jack stood in Charli's living room with her looking up at him like a sleepy-eyed hoot owl.

"I'm sorry to bother you . . . I guess," he added.

"But I was asleep and something woke me up—told me to come over here immediately. It's happened before, uh, several times. I call it my danger sensor. Are you okay? What about Bonnie?" he gazed past Charli toward the hallway.

"Bonnie's fine," Charli said through another yawn. She slipped her cell phone into her robe's pocket, tied the sash, and rubbed at her eyes. Without a word, Charli stumbled to the rocking chair and plopped therein. She placed her elbow on the armrest and propped her head in her hand.

Jack wore the same pair of jeans he'd taken off last night along with a crumpled T-shirt he'd found at the foot of his bed. He'd managed to strap on his gun belt before crawling into his car. Now his hackles rose as he pivoted around the room.

Something's wrong, he thought, *way wrong.*

"Have you seen anything out of the ordinary around here tonight?"

"Uh, no," Charli said, her voice sounding a bit stronger.

Jack stepped toward the row of windows along the east wall and glanced toward Charli. She was now blinking faster, sitting straighter. He double-checked the locks. The window on the wall behind the dining table was next. But he found it locked as tightly as the others.

"Those guys who followed you in the parking lot—"

"Haven't seen them," she stated.

His hand on his gun, Jack moved toward the kitchen. Out of the corner of his eyes, he glimpsed Charli standing. Motioning for her to sit back down, he lifted his Glock 40 from its holster. With the barrel pointing upward, Jack scoped the kitchen. When he approached the door opening onto the garage, he eyed the lock. The thing looked like it belonged to Abraham Lincoln.

"Oh, Charli," he groaned and shook his head. "This absolutely will not do."

He inserted his gun back into his holster before a final glance around the kitchen. But Jack's attention was snared, not by some clue, but by a two-liter bottle of root beer sitting on the counter. He blinked and wondered if perhaps Charli had bought it for him.

Nah, he thought and shook his head. *Don't get your hopes up. It's probably left over from a church social or something.*

Jack strode back the way he'd come and found Charli standing in the middle of the living room, her fingers tangled with her robe's sash. "I just double-checked Bonnie," she explained. "She's always crawling in bed with me. She's in my bed now. She's fine."

"Good. Are all your bedroom windows locked?"

"I haven't tried them lately, but I assume they are."

"No assuming." He shook his head. "And I didn't check the window over the kitchen sink either." Jack marched back to the kitchen with Charli on his heels. After tugging upward on the wooden handles, he said, "I don't think this puppy's been opened in decades."

"I've tried and tried but I think it's painted shut," Charli affirmed.

A faint feline cry floated from the laundry room, and Jack glanced toward the door. "Any windows in there?"

"No. Only kittens."

"Mind if I look in?"

"Please," Charli said and clutched the neck of her house robe.

Placing his boot near the doorway, Jack opened it. The smell of laundry soap met him as he scanned the utility room but only spotted a laundry basket and clutter. When he tried to shut the door, the cats climbed his leg. "Yeow," Jack exclaimed and pulled them off.

"Here," Charli offered from behind, "let me help."

He stepped aside and handed Charli the cats. She hurried into the room, dropped them both in their basket-bed, and was back in the kitchen before the door clicked shut behind her. Nodding, Charli said, "There."

"Looks like you've got it down to a fine art," Jack observed.

"Yep," she said and eased away. Jack watched her all the way to the cabinets, and then his attention landed on that root beer. "I see you've decided to get some culture." Pointing toward the soda, he hoped he didn't sound too optimistic about its presence being all for him.

Charli looked at the bottle like she'd never seen it before. "Yeah. You asked for it the other day," she commented as if the gesture were meaningless.

Nevertheless, the thought warmed Jack. Presently, he was grasping at the tiniest signs that Charli might be thinking of him . . . or planning to have him in her life.

"Thanks," he said and offered a conservative smile.

She looked down.

Clearing his throat, Jack decided to get on with the task at hand. He'd been awakened in the night for a reason. He didn't need to be resorting to a nice little social chat about root beer.

He moved toward the doorway. "Let's check your room, okay?"

"Just be quiet," Charli begged as Jack entered the hallway. "If Bonnie wakes up and sees you in there . . ."

"I'm good," Jack whispered over his shoulder before pausing at the bedroom door. He tiptoed across the room, illuminated by the lamp's soft glow. Bonnie lay in the middle of Charli's bed, and her flushed cheeks reminded Jack of two candied apples. He smiled.

When he neared the window, Jack's moment of

softness was swept aside by the task before him. His danger sensor sent a chill up his back, and Jack suspected this window wouldn't be locked like the others. He raised the blinds. Even in the limited lighting, he could see the outer screen was cocked at an angle. A quick check of the window lock revealed his assumption was correct. It was not engaged. Jack lifted the frame with the rasp of wood on wood and gradually released the handle. It held.

"Oh, my word," Charli breathed from behind. "I have *not* unlocked that window or screen."

Jack's gut tightened as he reached for the screen and secured it with the sorry-excuse-for-a-lock. Once the window was back in place, Jack turned the latch, then lowered the blinds. But the cord slipped in his unsteady fingers, and the blinds clapped against the windowsill.

Bonnie mumbled, and the sheets whispered with her movement.

Jack twisted toward the child. She shifted her head from side to side and then rolled to her side. He observed Charli. Her eyes now haunted, she motioned Jack back into the hallway and then pushed him into Bonnie's room and flipped on the light switch.

Hurrying forward, Jack stepped over a Raggedy Ann and past a jar of opened peanut butter on the dresser. Normally, the smell of peanut butter sent Jack looking for some crackers. But with his gut in knots, the smell only repulsed him. Jack focused on the window, identical to the one in the other room. Unlike the other window, this one was securely locked.

He lowered the blinds, glanced over his shoulder, and gave Charli a thumbs-up. Although her lips were unsteady, her nod was firm.

On the way past the dresser, Jack picked up the peanut butter jar, pulled out the plastic spoon, and screwed the lid back on. He dropped the spoon in the nearby wastebasket and handed the jar to Charli.

"Bet you've been wondering where that was," he quipped in an attempt to sound less alarmed then he was.

"Yeah," she agreed, and her smile was as limp as his felt.

They strode up the hallway together, and Jack followed Charli into the living room. She set the peanut butter jar on the end table, now void of the broken lamp. Hunching forward, Charli stared into space.

Jack rubbed his face and paced toward the front door, then back. Thoughts of leaving her and Bonnie alone horrified him. He could not. He would not. It wasn't even an option.

Tonight, he was on assignment from God. Let the neighbors say what they wanted. His car was going to stay parked in her front yard.

"How many neighbors do you have now?" he asked.

She looked at him like he was talking pig Latin.

"I can't remember seeing many." Jack rubbed at his gritty eyes.

"No." Charli shook her head. "Not many. You know, the usual. One about ten acres that way." She pointed north. "Another twenty-five acres that way." She pointed south. "Then, the Jacobsons live over the hill. Pretty much the same families that were here when you and I were . . ." Charli's gaze faltered.

"Well, I hate to play havoc with your reputation," Jack placed his hands on his hips, "but I drove my car over for a reason. I thought it might send a message—if you know what I mean—if it was in your yard tonight. Do you want me to sleep out there or in here?"

"In here," she rushed. "On the couch. Look." She reached for the cushions, flipped them off. "It makes into a bed. No problem about my reputation." Charli scooted the coffee table. "If I have to choose between being dead and being alive with a bad reputation, I choose life. Let the reputation fall where it may. I've already been accused of embezzlement. My reputation is smeared anyway."

"Do you think your pastor's wife would come over tonight as well?" Jack asked and lifted the table to the other side of the room. "If her car was parked out front too, then it would look less suspicious." He set down the table and straightened.

"Or better yet, maybe I could just go spend the

168

night at their house." She abandoned the task of lifting the hide-a-bed out of the sofa.

Jack leveled a stare at her. "You think Pastor Jonas is going to be big protection? With all due respect, he's like the Pillsbury Doughboy. No. I'm the one on this case." He jabbed at the center of his chest.

"Right," Charli sighed and nodded. "Besides, I really *hate* to wake them up in the middle of the night like this. I think they're still worn out from having to handle Bonnie Friday night and then the bake sale Saturday."

Jack moved beside Charli and shooed her away from the hide-a-bed. With one heave, he jerked the frame and thin mattress from the couch and flopped it to full length.

"Thanks, muscle man," Charli joked.

He lifted a brow and eyed her. She was suddenly making a monumental task of straightening the doily on the end table, and Jack couldn't stop the pleasurable smile. "Really, the bed weighs nothing compared to the bales of hay I've man-handled and the overgrown calves I've wrestled."

"That's what wrestling Bonnie feels like some days," she quipped and lifted her gaze to his. Deep appreciation and respect mingled with the humor in her eyes.

Jack tried to conjure some kind of flippant retort, but couldn't come up with a syllable. He'd barely looked at her since he stormed the place. But now, he absorbed the full impact of her appreciation and growing trust.

In the middle of all that trust, her strawberry lips beckoned as never before. And Jack wondered how many more nights he could take this without giving in to the temptation to thoroughly kiss her senseless.

The gentleman within insisted that would be taking advantage of her vulnerable state. And that gentleman beat his primitive instincts into compliance. Jack looked down.

"Bonnie said she saw you tonight in Brookshire's," Charli said, her voice light yet forced.

Jack jerked his gaze back to her.

Drawing her brows, she awaited his answer.

"She did?" he echoed.

"Yeah."

"Hmmph." He yanked the mattress straight. "Got any sheets? Or do you want me to sleep without any? I can—don't mind a bit." He eyed the crocheted throw lying on the chair next to the sofa.

Charli folded her arms. "So . . . did she?"

"Who?"

"Bonnie. Did Bonnie see you?"

Jack scratched at his stubble and searched for any way around the inevitable. Finally, he told himself there was no logical reason to hide anything from Charli. He was his own man. He owed her nothing, not even an explanation. But Jack decided to tell her anyway.

"Yeah." He nodded. "She saw me."

"Oh."

When he looked up, Charli was exiting the room. Her stiff shoulders and straight back hinted that Bonnie had also seen Mary Ann. He further wondered if she suspected that Mary Ann had come over when they were on the phone. After Sonny called, she'd only stayed about fifteen minutes— just long enough to retrieve her purse and hint that she was free next weekend. Jack hadn't arranged anything definite, but was certainly giving it some thought.

Watching Charli depart, he wondered exactly what a man should say in such a situation. By the time she got back with the bedding, Jack gave up the wondering. It was too late to try to figure that out.

After they snapped on the fitted sheet and placed the top sheet over it, Jack's groggy mind suggested that Charli Friedmont just might be jealous. She'd barely looked at him since she came back and hadn't said a word either. Furthermore, a heavy silence permeated the room.

While Jack would never claim to be a leading expert on the ways of women, he certainly wasn't daft. And Charli's stiff lips and wary expression struck him in the funniest way. Jack laughed out loud before he could even stop himself.

"What's so funny?" she challenged.

"You're jealous," he said and couldn't believe he'd just blurted what he was thinking.

Her mouth fell open. "Jealous?" she challenged.

"Well, yeah. I'm guessing Bonnie also told you I was with someone."

"She said she had orange hair, actually." Charli picked up the coverlet she'd placed in the rocker.

Jack laughed again. "I can see a child maybe thinking that."

"So, that's the reason you didn't speak to me?" Charli asked.

"Well . . ." Jack shrugged and lifted his hands. "What exactly did you expect me to do? Introduce my date to my old girlfriend? Like, that really works." He placed his hands on his hips.

"Was she the one who was driving up when I called you?"

"Hmmph! What are you? Psychic?"

"No." Charli shook her head. "I just heard a woman's voice and assumed . . ."

"She has a couple of sons," Jack supplied and wondered if she'd secretly injected him with some kind of truth serum.

"Does she know you're here now?"

"Uh, no," Jack said. "Why would she? It's the middle of the night."

She looked down and left Jack wondering what she must be thinking.

"I'm not *living* with her, Charli," he insisted. "I've still got Christian standards."

"I never said you were," she defended. "I don't

even know why I asked that. I guess I just wasn't thinking." She rubbed her temple. "It's late."

"Right." Jack squelched the voice that suggested she'd just slammed his integrity and that he had every right to give in to the irritation nibbling at his mind.

"So . . . are you going to tell her?" she asked as if the brief explanation had never happened.

"Tell her?"

"That you came here."

"Probably not," he answered. *It's none of her business,* he added to himself. *And this is none of your business.*

"Oh," Charli said again and grabbed the pillow from the rocker.

Jack spread the coverlet over the bed and wondered why he was answering such questions from a woman who had barely been in his life until he arrested her two nights ago. *This has been one bizarre weekend,* he thought, *and it's getting weirder by the minute.*

"Well, good night, then," she said and strolled toward the hallway.

"Good night," Jack replied. "I've had the weekend off," he added, "but I'm on tomorrow. I'll have to get up early and go back to my place to get ready for work."

"All right." Charli turned to face him. "If you leave about sunup, maybe none of the neighbors will notice."

"That works for me," he said and plopped onto the side of the bed. "And we're going to have to have a serious encounter with your locks tomorrow. I might send somebody out to just *deal* with it. We might as well get them to install an alarm system too. Otherwise, I'll never get any sleep."

"But I can't afford—"

Jack held up his hand. "Just don't worry about it, okay? If you insist, we'll settle up later. Otherwise, I'll count it as the price I'm paying to get some sleep. Right now, it's worth it, believe me."

"Someone was in here tonight, weren't they?" she asked.

Observing her pale cheeks, Jack deliberated whether to go ahead and scare her batty or minimize the stark truth. Finally, he decided minimizing truth wouldn't do anybody any good. Charli needed to know.

"Yeah, I think so. At least, that's what my gut's saying, and it's not usually wrong. I think somebody came in and unlocked your window from the inside so they can get in later while you're here."

"When I came home from the grocery store, the back door was ajar," she explained.

He stood. "Why didn't you *say* something when you called?"

"Because I thought Bonnie had left it open. She's done that several times here lately."

Jack stepped within inches of her, peered into her

eyes, and said, "Don't overlook anything like that anymore. Understand?"

She jumped. Her eyes widened, and she gazed up at him like she didn't know whether to run or thank him for being her very own guardian angel sent directly from heaven. As if that weren't enough, a huge tear pooled in the corner of her eye and trickled down her cheek.

Sighing, Jack rubbed his eyes, then his face. "Sorry," he mumbled. "I didn't mean to bark at you. I guess this is all just starting to wear on me."

"I'm scared," she whimpered. Hunching forward, Charli rubbed her upper arms, and Jack couldn't resist resting his hand on her shoulder.

"It's all going to be okay," he soothed and wished he sounded more assuring.

Again, she gazed up at him, but this time she leaned into his touch. And the invitation was too much for Jack to ignore.

No matter how much his internal gentleman insisted he not respond, Jack ignored that guy and accepted her offer. His arms slipped around Charli, and she clung to him like he was her last link to sanity.

"I am *so, so* scared," she repeated.

"I know . . . I know," Jack crooned. "But it's all going to be okay. It really is. We're going to get through all this. Remember, God's got protection on his agenda. He woke me up and dragged me over here, didn't He?"

"Yes, and I'm so glad you came. I almost never went to sleep tonight. I jumped at every sound. Then when you found my window opened . . ." She pulled back. "I promise Jack, I *did not* unlock that window and screen."

"I believe you," he said as his gaze trailed to her strawberry lips, too inviting to resist.

CHAPTER FOURTEEN

Even though all systems were charged, Jack moved more slowly than impulse suggested. No sense in scaring her. But when Jack lowered his head, she did nothing to stop him. Quite the contrary, her eyelids fluttered shut, and the silent encouragement increased in potency.

That only intensified the enjoyment. Her lips tasted as sweet as Jack remembered . . . and then some. The years that had heightened the longing also ripened the appreciation. Jack's mind spun with the memory of how right Charli felt in his arms. No other woman had ever come close.

Once his lips left hers, Jack trailed a row of kisses to her ear and mumbled, "Charli. Oh Charli, please tell me this isn't a dream."

The second she stiffened, Jack sensed trouble. When she backed away, he wondered if he'd been crazy to move so fast and wanted to pound his head against the wall. Not bothering to even pretend, Jack abruptly released her.

"I'm sorry," she babbled. "I shouldn't have—have—I'm really not trying to throw myself at you. I shouldn't, especially not since . . . uh, the redhead and all."

Her words affected him like a dunk in an icy pool; and the heat of their fairy-tale kiss was swept away by cold reality. Jack glowered at her a full three seconds. He didn't know what to say and finally decided he was tired of not knowing what to say. So he just didn't say anything. It was late—too late to be dicing through a dead end relationship.

"Just go to bed," he grumbled and plopped to the edge of the mattress. Jack yanked off his boots and kicked at them. Before he flopped back, he remembered to remove his gun belt. When he pulled it off, he glanced toward the hall. Charli had done exactly what he'd said. She was gone.

He didn't want to think about her another second. "Forget it all," he mumbled. "I'm just ready for some sleep."

Before he put his head on the pillow, Jack pulled the Glock 40 from his holster, laid it on the end table, and hoped he had a solid night's rest. He wasn't in the mood to shoot anybody—not that he ever was in the mood to shoot anybody. But sometimes he was more up to the task than others. And living through the kiss of the decade only to be rejected put Jack more in the mood for howling at the moon than taking down criminals.

He punched at his pillow, squeezed his eyes tight, and wished the heat in his gut would disappear. He was *way* too old to be playing adolescent games. For some reason Charli Friedmont had dumped him for a loser. Now that she'd seen what a no-good Vince was, she was still doing a relationship hokey-pokey on Jack.

Maybe Sonny was right. Maybe Jack was too easy. Too ready to drop everything every time she whimpered. Too willing to open his arms when she swayed his way. He wondered if there was value in playing a little harder to get, but the very idea made Jack groan. He'd never been one to resort to games.

Either you want to try again or you don't, he thought and flopped onto his back. *But don't give me the come hither and then shove me away. What in the world is wrong with you anyway?* he fumed.

He focused on the ceiling fan's lazy rotation. The light from the kitchen cast a faint glow into the living room, and the ceiling fan blades projected long shadows across the ceiling.

Jack sat up, swung his feet off the bed, hung his head.

Charli had had her share of hard blows in her life, and he knew they had to have taken a very deep toll.

His family wasn't exactly free of its problems. There was a valid reason he'd been closer to his mother's brother than he was to his own father.

Uncle Abe had been there for Jack when his father wasn't. He'd attended his high school football games and college graduation while Jack's dad had been too busy building his trucking empire. Jack had also realized that his father's workaholism had contributed to Sonny's drinking problem, and more recently, to his brother Ryan's divorce.

Years ago when Jack had tried to confront the family issues, his mother had defended his dad and accused Jack of being unforgiving. Somehow, she equated enabling dysfunction with forgiveness. In her world, the more you allowed people to get away with, the more forgiving you were. Her denial and twisted logic had been so blatant and hot, Jack had been struck speechless. But more often than not, Jack met people who'd prefer to dupe themselves than face the hard task of working through their issues.

He groaned and wondered if Charli could ever find freedom. Jack had already lived through the frustration of trying to make a difference with his parents, and he just didn't know if he was up to the task with Charli. If she went into the denial mode, there was no hope.

"I need to just forget Charli and go for Mary Ann," he decided. The date tonight had been nice. Comfortable. Promising. Mary Ann seemed so normal and predictable. Sweet, kindhearted. When she came back for her purse, she hadn't stayed long after Jack ended the call with Sonny. She'd simply thanked him and corralled those rowdy boys like a pro. She'd make a very good wife for someone.

"And Brett and Brad need a strong father," Jack mused.

He rested his elbows on his knees, hunched his shoulders, stared at his scattered boots, and tried to convince himself he'd be way better off with his neighbor. Even though her lips weren't nearly as enticing, Jack had yet to give them a chance.

He gazed toward the hallway and wondered who'd be guarding Charli tonight if he and Mary Ann were already married. The disturbing answer sent a ripple of unrest through him.

Jack stood and meandered toward the kitchen. That root beer was calling his name.

With a last glance toward Bonnie, Charli clicked off the lamp on her nightstand, and the shadows enveloped her like a comforting blanket. Interestingly enough, she'd left the lamp on when she went to bed at ten. Then the shadows had been terrifying. But Jack's presence had extinguished Charli's fear.

His presence had also upped her temperature. Charli walked to the window, raised the blinds, and double-checked the lock. She gazed toward the horizon where dozens of stars twinkled in the night like the glowing embers that had sprung back to life when Jack's lips touched hers. The power of that kiss had immersed Charli in stunned wonder. Wrapped in Jack's arms, she'd been consumed by the old flame that once burned bright and hot.

And that's all it was, she told herself, *the memory of the old attraction. At least that's all it was for* me.

Resting her hand against the window frame, Charli hunched forward and wondered who Jack had been with in the grocery store. He admitted it had been a date. On the phone, he'd called her his neighbor. Frowning, Charli tried to remember who lived near him.

Whoever she is, she fumed, *it's a mighty snug setup.*

Tapping her fingertips against the wooden frame, she wondered if the woman's red hair was natural or the product of some bottle. Bonnie had called it orange. If the color were bottle red, then it might have a more brassy appearance and explain Bonnie's description. Charli had always wanted auburn hair and had been tempted a few times to make the switch herself.

She fiercely balled her fist. A wild urge to shave that woman bald plunged through her before she could stop it. Jack had accused her of being jealous. The memory only heightened Charli's irritation. She curled her toes against the cool wooden floor and tightened her sash until it bit into her waist.

"I am *not jealous,*" she hissed.

But Charli's next thought only increased her ire. *I wonder if he kissed her good night?* Her mouth fell open as she realized the implications. If so, he'd kissed one woman and mere hours later kissed another.

What does he think I am? she fumed and straightened her shoulders. *Some kind of a little— little . . . hussy who sits around waiting for him to come barging in so I can just fall in his arms at a blink?*

The sound of shattering glass crashed into Charli's thoughts. She jumped and held her breath. Bonnie mumbled and twisted in the sheets.

Afraid to move, afraid not to, Charli stood in an indecisive trance and wondered if the person who'd unlocked her window had somehow gotten into the house. If so, Jack might be in combat with him. A hard tremble started in the center of her soul and spread to her fingertips. She swallowed against her tightening throat and waited.

But the only new sound was the howling of kittens and Jack's fiercely whispering, "Come back here, you little varmints!"

Charli scurried toward the doorway and peeked down the hall. Jack stood midway between her room and the kitchen with one kitten in hand while he stooped for the other.

"What are you doing?" Charli asked and stepped into the hall.

"I broke a glass," he hissed, "and when I went for the broom in the utility room they escaped and shot down the hall."

Sugar dashed from his grasp, and Charli dove to catch her. With the cat squirming in her arms, she followed Jack into the kitchen.

"Here," she said as he neared the utility room, "let me have Spice."

Jack pivoted to face her and readily released the feline to Charli's care. "I promise, these two must have belonged to Houdini!"

Charli giggled and wondered what it would be like to have Jack here every night . . . for good. "I agree. But they've really given Bonnie a lot of fun already. I'm so glad you brought them, and so is she," she chattered and tried to hide her wayward thoughts . . . or the fact that she'd considered shaving his neighbor bald. Charli stepped into the laundry room, plopped the sisters in their basket, and whisked back into the kitchen before they could escape again.

"But wait!" Jack said when she clicked the door shut. "I still need the broom." He pointed to a glass shattered near the cabinet.

"No big deal," Charli said and stepped toward a narrow closet near the pantry. "This is where I keep my broom and mop." She opened door, and the broom fell out. "Ta-da!" Charli said and lifted her hand.

"Maybe *you're* the one who's Houdini," Jack

teased and bent for the broom, which only brought him close enough to touch.

Charli's unruly mind savored the memory of their kiss and sent her into another meltdown. Whether she could ever love him or not, she now fully accepted that she and Jack Mansfield could still make the sparks fly. Even after all these years, he held the power to mess with her mind and send her into a wilting fit. Charli wondered what had possessed her when she dumped Jack for Vince Friedmont. Even after they were married, Vince hadn't affected her like Jack did with just one kiss.

Broom in hand, he straightened and said, "Do you have a dustpan?"

Charli gazed into his guarded eyes and wondered what he might be thinking . . . if that kiss was still jumbling his logic or making him wish for more. The longer she stared at him, the more Charli also needed to know if he'd kissed his neighbor. And her frazzled mind insisted that she find out. *Now!*

"Did you kiss *her* tonight too?" she blurted.

"Who?" Jack squinted.

"Your neighbor. The redhead." She bit the end of her tongue and nearly swayed with the heat that rushed her face.

Jack's brows quirked before his mouth sagged open and a thread of resentment fluttered through his haggard eyes.

Covering her mouth, Charli nearly fell into a round of apologies but couldn't get out one garbled syllable. No matter how much she wanted to know the truth, even in her zombie state she realized she'd gone too far.

He started to speak and then worked his mouth while a tense silence engulfed the kitchen. "You know, Charli," he finally said while narrowing his eyes, "that's really none of your business." He lifted his chin, stared her down, and then turned to the broken glass.

Gaping, Charli watched him sweep the shards into a neat pile. Even though she'd been on the verge of apologizing, Jack's statement and haughty attitude started a fire in her gut. She yanked the dustpan from the closet, whacked shut the door, and marched past him. Slamming the dustpan on the shelf, Charli planned a speedy exit when Jack's booming voice stopped her short.

"Charli!" he commanded.

His arresting tone overruled her desire for a fiery exit. Like a robot caught in a controlling laser, Charli turned to face him. His piercing eyes held her mesmerized as he gazed into her soul. Her hammering heart insisted he was about to kiss her again. And this time, there'd be nothing slow about it. But he didn't. He just held her captive with the power of his focus, and Charli possessed no strength to look away.

After he'd seen what he suspected, Jack looked down at the pile of shattered glass, every bit as broken as Charli. Her asking him if he'd kissed Mary Ann had made him lose it. While it *really wasn't* any of her business, Jack didn't like the idea of her thinking he was some sort of a kissing bandit who smooched on several women a night any more than he enjoyed her insinuating he and Mary Ann were living together.

Again, he wondered if Sonny had been right. Jack was swiftly becoming Charli's puppy dog on call. Even though she hadn't called him tonight, it was like she expected him to just get in line like a good little puppet while she slammed his character or any other insult she so chose to hurl at him. Sure, she'd been grateful for all his help and kept thanking him for everything from the cats to the bond money. But still, Jack wondered if their relationship—if that's what you wanted to call it—might be better served if he put up some serious boundaries.

Finally, he looked up at her. She was gazing at him like he'd morphed into some three-headed beast. And oddly, her eyes were full of tears again.

As much as Jack was tempted to give in to his softening heart, he didn't. "For your information, Charli Friedmont," he said in a measured voice, "I did *not* kiss Mary Ann tonight, and I didn't appreciate your slamming my integrity before either. I'll be the first to tell you I'm a long way from being a saint, but I can also tell you I've walked the walk ever since—" He stopped himself and decided not

186

to go there. That, too, was none of her business. "Anyway, there's no reason for you to even think about insulting me again." His fingers tightened around the broom handle.

A tear spilled onto Charli's cheek.

"Tonight was the first time I've ever even gone out with Mary Ann. I asked her out because—" Jack stopped himself again and listened to Sonny's sage advice still floating through his psyche. Gritting his teeth, Jack grabbed the dustpan and scooped the glass into it. When he straightened, Charli was gone.

Grimacing, Jack marched to the garbage can, dumped out the glass, and eyed the myriad pieces now mixed with the rubbish. Putting Charli back together was going to be as hard as piecing that glass back together. And that was something Jack was incapable of doing. She needed a miracle from God.

Oh Lord, help her, he pleaded and didn't have a clue if standing up to her had been the right thing. It could have just shattered her all the more.

When he turned back around, Jack caught sight of someone out of the corner of his eye and compulsively jumped into a defensive stance.

Charli stumbled into the wall. "It's just—just me," she rasped.

"Oh, it's you," Jack repeated and allowed his arms to relax. He glanced toward the dustpan still in hand and wondered exactly what he'd been planning to do with the thing if Charli *had* been an intruder.

"I just came back to apologize," she said, her lips trembling. "It seems I'm doing that a lot these days." Charli clutched the top of her robe. "It's late. I'm scared. And my brain isn't exactly working right. I didn't mean to slam your integrity at—at all. And you're right. It really isn't any of my business if you kissed your neighbor, *ever*." She glanced down, but not before Jack noticed a faint flicker of distaste in her eyes . . . or was that the jealousy he'd noticed earlier?

Not exactly knowing what to say, he propped the dustpan next to the trash can and went for the root beer. This time, Jack retrieved a nice, safe plastic tumbler. He filled it with ice from the freezer's door dispenser and then went for the root beer. Once the liquid foamed over the ice, Jack downed half of it. His mother told him the stuff was what had put ten pounds on him this past year. Jack still wasn't convinced and was a long way from giving it up. He licked foam from his lips and then diverted his attention to Charli, who still stood on the edge of the kitchen like some silent defendant, awaiting his sentence.

Finally, he realized he'd never accepted her apology. "It's okay," he said and wondered if Charli even realized she was jealous. "I'm sorry I was so grouchy too. It's late, like you said. We're both on edge. And everything is . . . uh . . . weird."

He poured more root beer into his cup. When the foam was at its highest, he downed some more and wished it could all be foam. Her being jealous left Jack with all sorts of mixed emotions. He was as elated as he was irritated, and Jack didn't know whether to laugh all over again or glower.

Jack sighed and downed the rest of his root beer. The fizzing liquid traced a cold trail all the way to his stomach and satisfied the urge that had sent him in here in the first place. He placed the cap back on the beverage, set his tumbler in the sink, and strolled toward the doorway. "Get some sleep, Charli," he said and tried to smile. "You look beat."

CHAPTER FIFTEEN

Jack placed the last throw pillow on the couch and followed that with the stack of bedding he set on one of the cushions. He glanced around the room. The dim morning light seeping through the curtains affirmed that he'd tidied everything back to normal, right down to the coffee table that was back in place.

He checked his watch. *A quarter till seven,* he thought. Only fifteen minutes had lapsed since he got up. He still had plenty of time to get home, shower, and make it to work by eight. But first, Jack needed a drink of water. His mouth tasted like the sludge in the bottom of Sonny's refrigerator.

Jack padded toward the kitchen in his socks. The boots, he'd put on once he exited the house. That way, he wouldn't be thumping around and wake up Charli and Bonnie.

But when he stepped into the kitchen, he found that Bonnie was already awake. She'd opened the bottom cabinet and was using the tiers as a stepladder to higher ground. Apparently, the cabinet holding the tumblers was her destination.

Jack debated what to do. If he wasn't careful, he'd scare her. She'd go into a traumatized fit, and he'd lose every inch he gained with her.

When she started slipping and the fall was imminent, he stepped forward to catch her. Hands flailing, Bonnie landed in Jack's arms with a grunt and a faint cry. She squirmed around and gazed into his eyes like she didn't know whether to shriek or smile.

Jack decided to give her a suggestion, so he smiled. "Good morning, li'l girl," he said. The faint scent of baby powder and the soft feel of rumpled hair against his arm stirred his fatherly instincts.

"G'mornin'," she replied with a what-are-you-doing-here question in her eyes.

"I spent the night on the couch, so your Mommy and you would be safe," Jack explained and set her on the counter. "Were you trying to get a cup for a drink?"

"Yes." Bonnie nodded. "I wanted some water."

"Me too," Jack admitted. "Why don't I get two cups, then. Okay?" He raised his brows and awaited her approval.

"Okay." She rubbed her sleepy eyes and then stretched the bottom of her pajama shirt that had a purple dinosaur on the front.

Even though he wasn't up on the latest kids' stuff, Jack had enough sense to match the purple dinosaur with the picture on the front cover of the book lying near a stack of mail. Sensing a serious chance to score some points, Jack filled their glasses with ice and then water.

Once they'd both downed a good portion of the cold liquid, Jack set aside his cup and reached for the book. "Is this yours?" he asked. "It matches the guy on your shirt."

Bonnie giggled and looked at her top. "Yes. He's Barney," she explained.

"Barney!" Jack exclaimed. "Is he your boyfriend?"

"No, silly." She rolled her eyes like he was seriously lacking all kinds of culture. "He's *Barney*."

"Well, I've never met him before." Jack leaned against the counter and opened the book. "Would you help me get to know him?"

"Yes." Bonnie nodded. "Here. I'll read the book to you."

"Would you?" Jack said through a smile.

"Uh, huh." Bonnie nodded. "But you'll have to sit still and listen." She pushed her tangled hair away from her face and opened the book like some sage teacher doing her students a favor.

"I can be still, and I'm a *good listener,*" Jack said with an indulgent tone he was sure would make Sonny proud.

Fully expecting Bonnie to simply tell him about each picture, Jack was shocked into a nonstop grin when the child began to read the book for real. For the next five minutes, he listened as she enunciated every word on each page. Even though some of her pronunciations weren't perfect, he couldn't fault her efforts. Some second graders couldn't read as well as she.

"Wow!" Jack said and softly clapped once she shut the book. "You did a great job! Who taught you to read like that?"

"Granny Pat," Bonnie replied without a blink. "I go see her every day, and she teaches me."

"You're very lucky to have a granny like that."

She extended the book, and Jack accepted it.

"Yes, that's what Mommy says," Bonnie agreed and reached for her water, sitting near Jack's. She gulped down the rest, lowered the tumbler, and said, "Now, it's your turn to read to me."

When Jack began opening the cover, she said, "Wait!" and rested her hand on the book. "Can you read?" her earnest eyes and puckered lips said she really wanted to know.

Jack bit his bottom lip to stop the smile. "Yes, as a matter of fact, I can," he said.

With an approving nod, she removed her hand and said, "Mommy always reads it to me in there." She pointed toward the living room and then yawned.

"Okay," Jack agreed. He placed the book back on the counter, lifted Bonnie to the floor, and followed her into the living room. When she settled in the middle of the couch, Jack stacked the throw pillows atop the bedding and snuggled into the corner.

Bonnie "helped" him turn the page and then pointed at the first word. "Start here," she said through another yawn.

"Right," Jack agreed.

She rested her head on Jack's arm and quietly listened as his deep voice wove its spell. With every page he turned, Jack glanced toward his pupil and noticed her eyes were getting heavier and heavier. When he closed the book, Bonnie was on the verge of a coma.

"Want to go crawl back in bed now?" he asked and discreetly checked his watch. It was now a quarter after seven and he'd be pressed to get to the office by eight. Furthermore, Bud would have to feed the cattle by himself.

His brother Ryan's son usually fought sleep at any time, no matter how groggy he was. Fully expecting Bonnie to protest, Jack brainstormed ways to expedite the trip to bed so he could hurry home.

But Bonnie surprised him by simply taking the book, clutching it to her chest, standing, and meandering from the living room, up the hallway.

"Okaaaaay," Jack breathed and sensed he'd just won a major battle that had nothing to do with sleep.

Sigmund Harlings extended his hand to the young couple who'd just inked a sizable loan on a new home. He forced himself to keep his smile genuine when, inside, he was gloating. This one had been a quarter-million-dollar deal. The week was peppered with similar closings, and that only upped his end-of-quarter bonus, coming this week.

Just last week the bank president, Ted James, had said, *Harlings, you know how to hook 'em and reel 'em in! There's a reason you're a VP, and I like it!*

Sigmund pumped Mrs. Lawrence's hand with even more enthusiasm, then said, "And remember, we offer discount rates on auto loans to those who have their home mortgages with us. So when you get ready for that Mercedes—"

"Get ready for?" Mr. Lawrence scoffed. "She's already taken care of *that* need."

The brunette rested her diamond-crusted hand against her chest and said, "But I might be ready for a new one soon. And when I am—"

"Come on! Come on!" Lawrence teased and pulled on his wife. "Let's get outa here before you spend every dime we have!"

Laughing, Sigmund followed the couple into the bank's entryway. He was bidding them adieu when a familiar man stepped through the glass doorway—a tall, lanky, blond man whose very sight made Sigmund's blood pressure escalate.

When Sonny Mansfield made a straight line for him, Sigmund forced himself not to run into his office and crawl under his desk.

"Excuse me," Sonny said and glanced at his name tag, "but could you please tell me who can help me open a new account?"

Mansfield's smile was as slow and easy as some teenager who didn't have anything better to do than lie in the sun. His fashionable blue jeans were as baggy as his shirt that hung past his belt. His wind-tossed hair topped the whole disguise.

But the disguise was not lost on Sigmund. He knew why the private eye was in the bank.

Sigmund pointed toward Rita Juarez and said, "She's the new-accounts manager." Then, he turned and strode straight to his office without a backward glance.

Once inside, Sigmund snapped the door shut. He gazed through the glass wall that gave him a clear view of Sonny, now settling at Rita's desk. Her coy smile suggested the blond buffoon had gotten her attention for more reasons than just a new account. Sigmund yanked on the blind cord hanging near the doorway. The wooden blinds swooshed down and covered the glass wall from floor to ceiling.

Panting, Sigmund locked his door, snapped off the lights, and inched apart two of the blinds with his forefinger and thumb.

The office grew smaller and smaller with Sigmund's every heartbeat. A cold wad of leaden terror filled his gut. He pulled at his tie, gulped for each breath, and strained for every nuance of Mansfield's expressions.

The private eye pointed a smile at Rita that would probably charm the stripes off a tiger. And Sigmund could only imagine what bank information he'd extract from the bleached blonde.

Sonny's relaxed demeanor suggested the guy was simply taking care of some business. But Sigmund wasn't fooled—not even a little bit. Sonny came in here for one reason . . . and that reason drove Sigmund from his office.

When he stepped past his secretary, he glanced toward her and mentally processed an excuse to cover his departure. But Gail took care of the excuse herself.

"You don't look so hot," she said. "You've gone pale." A prim brunette, she reminded Sigmund of his wife—a double-knit queen who couldn't feel one ounce of passion if someone put a gun to her head.

"I'm sick," Sigmund lied and rubbed at his damp neck. "Cancel all my appointments for today." He hurried past the new-accounts desk and forced himself not to look at Sonny Mansfield. However, his presence in the bank drove Sigmund to the parking lot, and to the task that had been thwarted last night.

After seeing the chief's car in Charli's front yard, Sigmund had slipped back into his room at home through the outside door. He'd paced his room until after two and then fell into an unsettled sleep. Of course, Dianne had never known he left or returned and possessed no idea he was disturbed. He hadn't shared a room with his wife in ages. She claimed he tossed all night and that his stuff got in her way. So Sigmund had gladly left her lair for the guest suite. The room featured an outside door that opened onto the back porch, near the garage. Dianne's suite was upstairs, so the setup couldn't have been more perfect for nights when Sigmund couldn't sleep—or wanted to visit Margarita.

Now, he made it to his Lincoln, clicked the remote lock, and crashed into the driver's seat. Sigmund removed his tie, slung it against the passenger door, and ripped at his shirt's top button. He dug his blunt fingernails into the steering wheel and prepared for swift action. No more slinking around during the night. That plan had failed. Given the presence of Jack Mansfield's car in Charli's driveway, Sigmund assumed they were having an affair. Therefore, breaking into her house at night was no longer an option.

"Maybe I should use a more direct approach," he mused and decided that perhaps the most creative murderers worked like the best deer hunters—during the light of day.

CHAPTER SIXTEEN

Charli lead Bonnie to Pat Jonas's front door. The simple frame home matched the church that stood only fifty yards away. Nestled at the base of a hill, the place reminded Charli of something from a Thomas Kinkade painting. All the home needed was a brook running nearby, and she was certain Kinkade himself would arrive to capture the beauty. Pat's blooming flower beds and manicured lawn testified to the reason the woman was forever wearing overalls. She claimed the yard and garden work was good therapy.

Sighing, Charli wished Pat would come to her house and have a few "therapy" sessions. But when she rang the doorbell, she chided herself for even thinking such. The Jonases had already helped her so much—too much. The last thing Charli needed to do was pine about yard work.

"You'll be right back, Mommy?" Bonnie asked and clung to Charli's hand all the tighter.

"Yes, sweetie," Charli assured. She shifted Bonnie's canvas tote to her shoulder and bent to pick up her daughter. "Just like I already told you. Mamma won't be gone long." She kissed Bonnie's cheek and gave her a tight squeeze. "I'm just going to the bank in Jacksonville and then I'm going to another appointment and then I'll be home. I won't be gone more than three or so hours."

The door swung inward as Bonnie wrapped her arms around Charli's neck. "I don't want you to go," she whined.

"It's okay, baby," Charli encouraged her. "Look. Granny Pat's right here." She pointed toward her pastor's wife as she opened the door. As usual, her overalls had dirt on the knees.

"Come on in here, you!" Pat teased. "I'm making chocolate chip cookies. Wanta help?"

Bonnie's head snapped up. She smiled at Pat and then squirmed from Charli's arms.

"Here's her bag," Charli said through a smile. "I packed her lunch, as usual, but I hope to be back by then." She checked her watch. "It's nine-thirty. I should be home by eleven-thirty or twelve."

"Take your time, dear," Pat said. "I'm used to having her all day anyway. I'll be lonely this afternoon without her."

"Thanks, Pat." Charli stepped forward for a brief hug. "I'd be sunk without you guys."

"And we'd be sunk without you," Pat assured her. After a hearty rub on the back, she pulled away and said, "Now, just go take care of your business. The sooner you meet with Ross, the sooner you'll be out of this mess."

"Okay, okay," Charli agreed and turned back to

her car. She hadn't told Bonnie that Sonny Mansfield called this morning to arrange a meeting with her lawyer because she didn't want to have to explain exactly what a lawyer was and why she needed to meet with one. Charli had been afraid Bonnie wouldn't understand and would become frightened all over again.

"Oh! I almost forgot!" Pat called.

Charli stopped near her Taurus and turned back to face Pat. Now standing on the sidewalk, she held Bonnie. "We had a children's committee meeting last night and decided to take Jack Mansfield up on his offer."

"His offer?" Charli questioned.

"Yes." Pat bobbed her head. "You know when he stopped by, uh, Saturday morning?"

"Yes."

"He mentioned he owned a small ranch and that his neighbor owns a horse ranch."

"His neighbor?" Charli repeated, and her mind conjured images of a tall, lithe redhead who'd rival Miss America. She glanced down at her broomstick skirt and Wal-Mart special sandals.

"Yes. Remember, I said something to you about it when Mark brought you home Saturday morning?"

"Uh . . ." Charli rubbed her temple and finally conjured a vague memory of Pat's mentioning something about Jack's ranch and a petting zoo.

"Anyway, the neighbor's supposed to have some rabbits and a few goats."

Charli gripped her throat. "Really?" she wheezed.

"Yes!" Pat chattered. "Wasn't it so nice of Jack to offer?"

"I wanta go to the petting zoo," Bonnie exclaimed.

"We asked him if we can come out Tuesday night," Pat continued.

"As in, tomorrow?" Charli asked.

"Yes."

"Why so soon?"

"Why not?" Pat's grin couldn't have been prouder. "It's summer. The kids are out of school. They're starting to get bored. All the moms were thinking the sooner the better. I called Jack this morning, and he's all for it."

"Uncle Jack brought me kitty cats," Bonnie exclaimed.

"He did?" Pat asked.

"He brought them Saturday," Charli explained. "They've been a good diversion."

"So . . . you've seen him some over the weekend?" Pat questioned.

Charli gazed toward the northeast Texas hills that stretched all the way to Arkansas. She hadn't mentioned Jack to Pastor Jonas or Pat, especially not since Pastor Jonas had said what he did about Jack loving Charli.

"Uncle Jack spent the night last night," Bonnie blurted.

Her mouth falling open, Charli gazed at her daughter. "Bonnie!" she croaked. "How'd you know?"

"I saw him this morning," she explained, "when I got up to go get a drink of water. He was getting out of the bed in the living room. He helped me get a drink, and we read a book."

Pat's questioning gaze shifted from Bonnie to Charli. Charli's face heated and then went cold. "He slept on the couch," she rushed. "He came over late last night because he was afraid someone had been . . ." Charli stopped and eyed her daughter, now squirming from Pat's grasp.

Pat set her down and knelt beside her. "Look, Bonnie," she said, "Pastor Jonas is in the kitchen helping me make cookies. I bet you could put some cookies in the oven now if you hurry!"

Bonnie zoomed toward the house and banged through the screen door without a backward glance.

Charli strode toward Pat, who met her halfway. "Pat, I would have never let him stay if I hadn't believed we were in danger. You've got to believe me. He slept on the couch for *protection only*." Charli lifted her hand and hoped Pat couldn't see "kiss" written all over her.

"I believe you." Pat wrapped her arms around Charli for a brief hug. "Out of the mouths of babes, huh?" she teased and pulled away.

Charli chuckled and rubbed her upper arms.

"You got that right," she agreed. "But just so you know, my bedroom window *was* unlocked and I didn't unlock it. We knew it would look bad if his car was at my house all night, but decided for safety purposes . . . we nearly called you to come over too, but didn't want to wake you. I didn't want to—to worry you," Charli stammered to a halt.

Pat huffed. "Worry me? You *should* have called me! I'd have been glad to come over. Or you could have come over here."

"I know, I know." Charli stroked her forehead. "But I was just *so scared,*" she admitted. "I'm afraid whoever framed me might try to . . ."

"Here now!" Pat gripped Charli's arms. "Don't even *talk* like that. We're going to pray for God's protection."

"Well, why didn't He protect me from being framed?" Charli blurted.

Pat blinked. "I have *no idea,*" she admitted. "Maybe he has some purpose in all this."

"If anything happens to me, Pat," Charli whispered, "will you and Pastor Jonas take Bonnie?"

"Of course!" Pat exclaimed and then vehemently shook her head. "But we're not even going to *think* like that. Do you hear?" She motioned toward Charli's car. "Just go on and take care of your business. It doesn't sound like Jack Mansfield is going to let you out of his sight long enough for anything bad to happen anyway."

Charli sighed and tried not to read too much into Pat's knowing smile.

"I guess you'll be at his ranch tomorrow night with Bonnie?" Pat asked.

"Well, I hadn't planned—"

"Of course you hadn't," Pat fussed, "but now that you know, you'll bring Bonnie, right?"

"Uh . . ." Charli examined her toenails, covered in chipped pink polish, and wondered if Jack's neighbor's manicure was as perfect as she sounded. As much as Charli wanted to shy away from the redhead, her curiosity stirred to a new level. However, she had no guarantees that this neighbor was actually the woman he'd gone out with. He probably had several neighbors with ranches or farms. For all she knew, the horse-ranch neighbor might be a man.

"Um, did Jack mention his neighbor's name?" Charli asked.

Pat gazed toward the sky, squinted, and finally said, "Mary Ann something-or-other, I think." Her candid gaze rested on Charli. "Do you know her?"

"Uh, no." Charli shook her head and recalled Jack's mentioning Mary Ann's name when he told Charli he hadn't kissed his date.

"Well, maybe it's time you do. Don't you think?" Pat lifted her brows and rested her hands on her hips.

Charli's mind was such a jumble of indecision that she didn't even try to pin a meaning on Pat's pointed expression. "I—I don't know right now." Charli pressed her fingertips between her brows. "I just don't know. If I don't go, then I guess I can let Bonnie go with you. She's probably going to have her heart set on going now." She shook her head, held her hand up, and said, "I can't think about it all right now anyway."

"Right. You've got to go take care of your business," Pat encouraged. "We can let tomorrow night take care of itself right now. But I *do* think it would do you and Bonnie both worlds of good to go."

"I'll—I'll think about it," Charli agreed and turned toward her vehicle. She opened her Taurus, gathered her skirt, and slid into the driver's seat.

No matter how hard Charli fought against images of Jack, he refused to be ignored one second more. The bustle of getting ready and managing Bonnie had given Charli ample distractions all morning. Even when she found that Jack had returned the living room to order and neatly folded the bedclothes, Charli squelched all tendencies toward being impressed. Furthermore, she'd hidden the bottle of root beer at the back of the cabinet and set his empty cup out of sight in the dishwasher. Of course, Bonnie's constant chatter and facing her first meeting with her lawyer had made blotting Jack from her mind all the easier.

But now Pat Jonas had plunged Charli into speculations that echoed with the nuance of last night, and Charli's emotions went into overdrive. She reached for her keys, still in the ignition, cranked the car, and turned the radio's volume to high. The contemporary Christian music filled her ears, but did nothing to obliterate Jack from her mind. Her temperature rising, Charli turned the air conditioner on full blast and then backed the car onto the road. When she gassed her engine, the tires squeaked. Charli winced and glanced toward the Jonases' home.

Once Charli turned onto Highway 69 and drove south, she had turned off the music and given into the Jack-party her brain was throwing. Last night, he'd come to her rescue again, rattled her senses with a kiss that would melt a glacier, and stood around in her kitchen like some domesticated, root beer-loving hunk.

Charli drummed her fingertips against the steering wheel and wondered if Pat was right. *Maybe it* is *time I meet his neighbor,* she thought.

CHAPTER SEVENTEEN

"What's up?" Payton's rich voice jarred Jack in the middle of yet another yawn.

When he shifted his attention to the erect officer, Jack realized he'd been standing by the station's front window, gazing out . . . at nothing. "Not much." He glanced away. "Whazup with you?"

"Not much," Payton replied, and the silence settling between them vibrated with the pressure of the unknown. Jack sipped his coffee and wished Payton didn't have that knowing gleam in his eyes. A few times Jack had wondered if the guy came from some kind of mystic royalty who saw all and knew all. Payton had a way of looking straight into a person's soul and sizing up more than any man wanted him to know.

"Yarborough sent me on a chase last night," Payton continued.

"Yeah." Jack squinted at the tall officer, who looked him eye to eye. He downed a swallow of his tepid coffee.

"Some guys were harassing Charli Friedmont at Brookshire's," Payton continued.

"I already know you didn't catch them. What's the point?" Jack snapped.

Payton blinked and finally glanced out the window, toward the street. "Are you thinking she's another Brenda Downey?" he asked. "Is that it? Or . . . is it something else?" Slowly, his gaze slid back to Jack and implied all sorts of personal things that were too close to the truth.

Jack's fingers pressed the coffee cup, and he thought about firing Payton on the spot. The officer had just stepped way over a line that should have never even been touched. *Maybe I've been too much like a friend to him and not enough like a boss,* Jack thought, and recalled the special interest he'd shown in the dedicated officer . . . mainly because he reminded Jack so much of himself.

He ground his teeth and fought the urge to verbally shove Payton into next week. *Not professional!* he warned himself. *Stay calm!* After a hard swallow of the bitter liquid, Jack ground out, "I don't know anybody in the office who wants another Brenda Downey," and strode across the foyer with every intention of holing up in his office and burying himself in the paperwork he was behind on. Last night's trip to Charli's only added to his sleep deprivation, and Jack didn't trust himself to hold his tongue with anyone.

"The reason I'm asking," Payton called, "is because I hate to see you fall over a woman. That's all."

Jack whipped around to face him. "Who says I'm falling?" he demanded and silently dared Payton to reply.

He didn't. His level gaze spoke more than any words could. And Jack knew that Payton somehow knew that he was behind helping Charli Friedmont . . . a little more than was acceptable for the Chief of Police. How Payton knew was anybody's guess. *Maybe he's like me and just knows in his knower,* he thought. Nevertheless, Jack wasn't about to confirm one scrap of any doubt Payton might hold.

Jack turned from the hallway, stomped into his office, and slammed the door.

Sigmund Harlings watched Charli get out of her car and walk toward the bank. He'd pulled into a street-side parking place when she drove into the lot behind the bank. The last time he'd planned an attack on Charli, the passenger seat held a syringe. Today, his briefcase held a drywall screw, electric drill, and a screwdriver.

"That's right. That's right. Good girl," he crooned as Charli sashayed toward the bank. Her long skirt couldn't hide the attractive way her slender hips swayed. Even though her features were puckered in a frown, her fluffy brunette hair softened her features and made Sigmund recall the days before he'd met Margarita. He'd toyed around more than once with making a pass at Charli Friedmont.

His gut quivered. Sigmund ground his teeth, doubled his fist, and forced himself to see her as the enemy . . . and nothing more. He had no room for appreciating her better qualities. Any appreciation could lead to softening. And that was the last thing he needed.

The second Charli stepped into the bank, Sigmund picked up the briefcase and opened his car door. Scouting the area, he stepped from the car and made certain no one noticed him. Only one pedestrian strolled along the sidewalk—a regal black lady who looked like she owned half the town and certainly had no time for him. Sigmund had never been so happy to be snubbed.

He locked his vehicle and strode directly to Charli's Taurus. Only a dozen or so cars occupied the small parking lot. Charli's car sat in the last slot on the east side, farthest from the bank. As Sigmund approached, he once again scanned the area. His task would take little time and chances were high that once he squatted by her back tire no one would even notice him. However, doing such a deed in broad daylight hadn't been in his original plans.

He mopped at the beads of perspiration forming on his upper lip. The morning was humid, as usual. The ten o'clock sunshine promised another day from Hades. But Sigmund suspected he'd be sweating if it was thirty degrees.

He rounded the car and cast a final glance over his shoulder. Only a few cars cruised the block; no pedestrians in sight. Sigmund hunkered down by the back tire where the warming concrete faintly smelled of old oil. He laid his briefcase on the pavement, clicked it open, and pulled out the portable drill and drywall screw.

Sigmund strategically placed the screw on the back of the tire, near the ground, inserted the drill into the slot, and pressed the trigger. The drill whirred but a few seconds while the screw sank deep into the tire. Once the puncture was guaranteed, Sigmund reversed the drill and removed the screw. He dropped both into his briefcase and pulled out the screwdriver.

After removing the valve stem cover, Sigmund used the screwdriver to press the center of the valve stem and watched as the tire grew flat. Even though the screw hole would have eventually leaked out the air, using the valve stem would speed up the process. Satisfied, he screwed the cover back on the stem, laid the screwdriver in his briefcase, and snapped it shut.

Gripping the briefcase handle, he stood and perused the area. A beat-up truck rolled past, but the man driving looked as rusty as the truck and didn't appear to care about anything but whether or not he had another chaw of tobacco to replace the one protruding his bottom lip.

"The joys of a small, southern town." Sigmund breathed through a satisfied snicker. *Not only do a good number of people not give a flip about what's going on right under their noses, the laws of chivalry are still in full force.* He strolled toward his Town Car and rehearsed the next step in his scheme. As soon as Charli was ready to accept the help of a chivalrous gentleman, Sigmund would be at her side . . . at her service. He patted the hidden pocket in his suit's coat and felt the money clip strategically holding a hundred-dollar bill. His generous offer of friendship and monetary support today would guarantee his welcome into her house tomorrow; and his welcome would be her death.

Charli tucked her purse under the driver's seat. She snapped her door shut, locked it, and glanced around the parking lot. No one had followed her from the bank. She'd never carried ten thousand dollars in her purse before and the whole idea made her as nervous as a long-tailed cat at a rocking chair convention. Cranking the car, she chuckled in memory of the southern cliché her mother had used often. Charli had asked for a hundred one-hundred-dollar bills. That, plus the interest the CD had earned created a bundle small enough to fit in her purse, but it was large enough to support her and Bonnie for a few months. She planned to place the money in the fireproof safe in her closet where she kept valuable documents, like the title to her car.

She turned the A.C. on high, put the vehicle into drive, and pressed the gas pedal. However, the car had rolled only a few feet when a lurching tire announced a flat. Groaning, she put the car into park and rested her head on the steering wheel.

"Why, God?" she begged. "Why a flat today—of *all days!*"

Sighing, she lifted her head and decided sitting here whining about it wasn't going to do any good. Charli got out and examined both tires on the driver's side. When they passed inspection, she rounded the car and found the back tire so flat it was sitting on the rim.

"Good grief," she muttered and squatted beside the tire. "I must have run over a nail or something." Charli hurried back to the driver's seat, retrieved her cell phone from her purse, and sat behind the wheel once more. After turning off the engine, she debated who to call. She hated to disturb the Jonases, and she was leaning on Jack far too much already. Finally, Charli just decided to do what she'd have done if she'd gotten a flat two weeks ago. She pulled her keys from the ignition, pocketed her cell phone, and got out.

There was a spare tire and hydraulic jack in her trunk. Charli had never changed her tire alone, but she'd never changed her own oil until this year either. *If I can change my oil, I can change my tire,* she thought.

After she manhandled the spare from the trunk, Charli had worked up a sweat and hoped the lug nuts weren't as difficult to extract as the tire had been. "Whoever put this baby in that trunk meant for it to *stay,*" she groused and rolled the tire to the car's side.

Charli felt her way through inserting the jack beneath the car and began the chore of pumping the lever when a familiar, male voice called her name, "Charli? Charli Friedmont?"

Straightening, Charli spotted a blue Lincoln stopped near the curb. When the driver stepped out, she recognized Mr. Harlings from work.

"Looks like you've got a flat," he stated. "Need some help?"

She dashed aside the perspiration trickling down her temple as her shoulders drooped. "Mr. Harlings!" Charli exclaimed. "Thank you so much! Do you mind?"

"Not in the least," he said through a broad smile. He was dressed in a taupe-colored suit with no tie and looked as cool as he usually did at the refrigerated bank. "We really miss you at work," he said and offered an encouraging touch on her shoulder.

"Oh really?" she squeaked.

"Yes. There's quite a few of us who don't believe what they've pinned on you."

"Really?" she repeated. "I—I haven't heard from anyone and just assumed—"

"No, oh no!" Harlings shook his head and leaned closer. "As a matter of fact," he whispered as if they were co-conspirators, "several have even started a fund for you."

"A fund?" Charli gasped and clutched at her knit shirt.

Harlings nodded, and his pale eyes now brimmed with the offer of friendship.

"Mr. Harlings, I—I don't know what to say!" Charli stammered.

He reached inside his suit and pulled out a money clip holding a hundred-dollar bill. "Tell you what," he said. "I was going to wait and put my part in at the office, but since I'm here with you now, I'll go ahead and give you my gift." He extracted the bill from the clip and extended it to her.

"Oh, I *couldn't*," Charli protested.

"Please do," Harlings insisted and tucked the money against her palm. "It's the least I can do.

You've worked so hard for so many years. It's all just a shame." He shook his head and looked down while a blasting horn from one block over punctuated his words.

Charli's mouth fell open. Her fingers flexed against the crisp bill. "Mr. Harlings, I never took a dime from anyone—let alone embezzled a hundred grand."

"Of course not," Mr. Harlings said and placed the money clip back into his pocket. "And we believe in you. Once we get the rest of the money together, someone from the bank will be over to deliver it. Probably me. Okay?"

"But . . . but . . . but . . ."

"No buts!" He lifted his hand. "We know you'll probably be having to pay a private eye and a lawyer before this is all over. And those guys can be *very expensive.*" He shook his finger at her like an older brother advising his wayward sister.

Mesmerized by Mr. Harlings's generosity, Charli merely nodded. She was on the verge of explaining that her private eye and lawyer were both free, but decided that really wasn't any of his business.

"Now, let's get this tire changed pronto so you can get on with the day!" he said.

Never one to hinder a man at work, Charli stepped aside and let him take care of business. Harlings removed his suit coat, laid it on the hood, then tackled the chore.

In all the years she'd worked at the bank, Mr.

Harlings had never been more than distantly polite. Why he'd suddenly become so friendly and approachable was open for debate. *Maybe he's really concerned and just wants to help,* she mused.

Nevertheless, Charli fumbled with the hundred-dollar bill and debated whether or not to keep it. Mr. Harlings had said several in the office were pitching in to help, so if she gave it back he'd probably re-give it when the rest of the money came in. Sighing, Charli slipped the money into her skirt pocket, beneath her cell phone and keys.

Her gaze meandered toward the nearby overpass that housed a good number of pigeons. With the intermittent cars passing over them, the birds fluttered here and yon and cooed and settled back on their perches before repeating the whole routine. Charli wished she could feel even half as peaceful as the birds looked.

Within a few minutes, the man had the flat changed and the bad tire loaded into her trunk. After slamming the trunk shut, he brushed his palms together and then extended his hand to Charli in the offer of a shake. Wanting to be polite, she shook his hand.

"It's so good to see you, Charli," he said and peered into her eyes. "I'll be sure to tell the rest of the gang that you look great." Something dark slithered through the depths of his soul. Despite the morning heat a mild shiver danced along her spine, and Charli wondered if Mr. Harlings wanted to make a pass at her. He certainly never struck her as the type . . . until now.

Stifling a cough, Charli removed her hand from his and stepped away. She crossed her arms and hoped he took the hint. "Uh, thank you so much, Mr. Harlings," she said, her tone firm. "It's great to hear of your and everyone else's interest in my welfare. Please tell everyone I said hello," she stated and couldn't deny that she sounded like she was reading some kind of script.

"I certainly will, m'dear," he said and patted her shoulder again.

Charli backed away and wondered if he'd totally missed her cues.

"I'll be by your house later this week with the rest of the money, okay?"

The money! Charli thought and now fully believed she shouldn't take his money now or ever. She dug beneath her cell phone and keys to extract the hundred-dollar bill, but in her fumbling attempts her cell phone slipped to the concrete and popped open.

"Oh, man," Charli grumbled and retrieved the phone. After a worried glance at the face, she affirmed that the thing was still working. Once she retrieved the money, Mr. Harlings was already climbing into his vehicle. Trying to get his attention, Charli stepped forward and waved. He responded with a jovial wave of his own and then pulled away from the curb.

Sigmund halted at the first stop sign and watched Charli through his side-view mirror until she climbed into her car. The meeting had gone just as he'd planned. Charli had been grateful to the point of being flustered. Sigmund pressed the accelerator and eased through the downtown intersection just as he'd eased past Charli's defenses. Today's meeting would make tomorrow's encounter all the more doable. Sigmund would simply arrive at her front door, claiming to bring her the money from her friends at work. Once inside her home, he'd make short work of injecting her with the succinylcholine. The rest would be history—or rather, it would make *Charli* history.

He smiled. The smell of death had never been so enticing.

CHAPTER EIGHTEEN

Charli extracted three hundred dollars from the bank envelope, dropped it into her fireproof safe, and closed the door. She then closed the safe's outer door—a panel on her closet's wall—and backed through the gap in the clothing. Charli scooted the row of clothes into place with the sound of hangers against metal. They swayed to a halt, and she closed the closet door.

After placing the money in her billfold and plopping her purse near the computer desk, Charli settled into the chair and booted up her computer to check her e-mail. On her way home, Pat had called and asked permission to take Bonnie to Tyler with her. Of course, Charli had agreed and now had the place to herself. Even though the house was locked tight, Charli's ears strained for any strange noises. The encounter with Mr. Harlings today had left her uneasy. In retrospect, she couldn't imagine why. Logic insisted the man was simply trying to help and that perhaps Charli had only imagined his odd behavior.

"I'm starting to get paranoid," she told herself and wondered if she'd overreacted to his placing his hand on her shoulder. *Maybe he was just trying to be nice,* she thought. Charli reached for the bottle of water she'd retrieved from the fridge and twisted off the cap. She idly sipped the cold liquid while watching the computer go through the upload before it was ready for her to log onto the Internet.

Yet the computer screen became a jumble of meaningless images as her mind trailed back to Jack Mansfield and their midnight encounter. From there, she relived the months since her mother passed away. After her cookout with Jack last week and the way he'd come to her rescue this weekend, Charli now realized he'd been gently wooing her since her mother's death. Like the gentleman he was, Jack had never rushed in or been pushy. As Pastor Jonas said, Jack Mansfield was a good man—probably one of the most decent men in the world.

"And I dumped Jack and married Vince," she mumbled.

Charli covered her face, rested her elbows on the desk, and relived the last twelve years of her life. She'd turned her back on a jewel and married a sick man who gave her little love and less respect. At the time she couldn't see what the years had eventually revealed.

"Vince was so much like my dad," she breathed, and Charli could clearly identify the same tendencies in her mother that she'd exhibited with Vince. *Neither of us stood up to our alcoholic husbands,* she thought. *We both took whatever they wanted to dish out until they walked out on us.*

She rose from her chair, paced toward the window, and lifted the blinds. "Oh, God help me!" she begged and gazed toward the pasture that stretched to the wooded acres. As the scenery blurred with the sting in her eyes, Charli wondered how many times her past had drowned out even the voice of God. Desperately, she wondered if she'd ever fully followed His promptings.

"If I had," she groaned, "I'd have never married Vince Friedmont. I'd have married Jack Mansfield."

Charli squeezed her eyes shut and pressed her fingertips against them. She bit down on her lips and trembled with the wretched truth. She didn't deserve Jack after all she'd put him through. The man had loved her with his whole soul, but Charli wiped her feet on that love and married an alcoholic.

Even though Jack had wooed Charli, it now appeared that he might be on the verge of something special with his redheaded neighbor. Pat Jonas knew it just as well as Charli did. That's the reason she'd insisted on Charli going over to Jack's house tomorrow night.

"She and Pastor Jonas want Jack for me."

Charli walked back to the computer desk and reached for the box of tissues near the keyboard. After dabbing at her eyes, she grabbed the bottle of water and downed a third of it. The cold liquid solidified her resolve.

Pacing to the closet, then back to the bed, Charli decided that Jack Mansfield deserved a happy life with a good wife. After all Charli had put him through, she couldn't bear to see him anguish over her another day. This Mary Ann was probably everything Jack deserved and then some.

"And I love him too much to let him get tangled up with me again. I'm broken. He deserves more." Charli set the bottled water back on the desk as her own words echoed through her mind. *I love him too much . . . I love him too much.*

"I love him." The realization unleashed a warm rush of passion through her spirit. *That's the reason I let him kiss me last night,* she reasoned, *because I love him. I need him.* Yet the understanding that should have brought joy only reaped more tears. For Charli knew that the depth of her love required that she release Jack. He'd be way better off with a woman who didn't have Charli's problems. The last thing he needed was to have to go through a trial with a lady who might be facing time in prison. Jack Mansfield deserved more, and Charli hoped Mary Ann was the "more" he needed.

Her cell phone's muffled ring slashed through her thoughts. After several disoriented seconds in which she tried to remember where the thing was, she fished it out of her pocket and noted the unfamiliar number. Shortly after her hello, a crisp, female voice came over the line.

"Hello, Mrs. Friedmont?"

"Yes."

"This is Beatrice Green, Ross Lavine's secretary—"

"Oh my word!" Charli gasped. "My appointment! I totally forgot." She snatched up her purse. "Oh my goodness! How could I have forgotten! I'm so—so sorry!"

Beatrice's chuckle mingled with her words. "That's quite all right. Sonny Mansfield is already in with Mr. Lavine. They'll be conferencing the rest of the hour if you'd like to go ahead and come."

"Yes, absolutely!" Charli agreed. "Of course I'll be there. Please tell him I'm *so sorry* for the delay.

Also, tell Sonny I'm sorry too. I just got, um, side-tracked." She gazed at the computer screen and realized she'd never checked her e-mail.

When Charli ended the call and fished her keys from her skirt's pocket, Mr. Harlings's hundred-dollar bill fluttered to the floor. Charli snatched up the money, stuffed it into her purse's outside pocket, and reminded herself of the night she thought her own kittens were an invader.

Mr. Harlings is probably as harmless as the kittens, she decided as she rushed to the restroom to repair her makeup. *I need to seriously chill out.*

After a productive meeting with Mr. Lavine and Sonny, Charli stood from her chair and shook hands with both. "Thank you both *so much,*" she breathed. "I feel so encouraged."

"And well you should," Ross said through a broad smile, "especially with this guy on your side." He jutted his thumb toward Sonny, whose eyebrows flexed as his lips quirked at the corners. A gold watch chain swayed from Lavine's vest pocket while he rounded the desk and sat on the corner. The man's graying hair and suspenders made him look like he belonged in the 1940s— right along with his antique desk and the ancient file cabinet in the corner. The musty smell that usually accompanied an old building only heightened the effect. Nevertheless, the sharp glint in his eyes suggested Ross Lavine was all the way in the present and ready to win every case he took on.

"From what I understand about you, Mr. Lavine," Sonny drawled and hiked up his baggy jeans, "you could probably win hands down without me."

"Hmmph." Lavine waved away the compliment as if it were an annoying fly. He crossed his arms and cut a sarcastic smirk toward the younger man. "You're just trying to butter me up. We'll figure out why later. Now—get back to work. I like what you've already started. Unearthing that petty theft charge on Rita Juarez was brilliant. And who knows what Gail Defore is up to when she's got that kind of credit card debt."

"My thoughts exactly," Sonny agreed and placed his leather briefcase on the desk. After slipping his notepad inside, he turned to Charli. At this angle, Sonny reminded Charli of Jack just a bit. The square chin and the shape of his nose couldn't be denied as the product of Mansfield genes. Other than that, the former basketball star was a force unto himself.

"By the way, I meant to ask you, Charli," he said, "what do you know about Sigmund Harlings?"

Charli blinked, shifted her purse strap to her shoulder, and slipped her hand into her skirt's pocket. "Why do you ask?"

"Don't know," Sonny said with a shrug. "I just saw him this morning in the bank and there was something odd about him somehow. I can't explain it. When I asked Rita who he was, she grimaced and told me his name. Said he was a vice president." He picked up the briefcase. "I asked her if he was always so brusque, and she confirmed. But I promise, I thought he went pale when he saw me. He left before I did."

"Oh, really?" Charli crossed her arms.

"Yeah. I haven't had time to do a *thorough* check on him yet, but so far I haven't found anything in his background to make him suspect. I was just wondering . . ."

"I had a flat this morning," Charli blurted, "and he helped me change it."

"Where?" Sonny questioned.

"At Austin Bank in Jacksonville." She scrunched her toes against her sandals.

"That's odd," Sonny said and narrowed his eyes. "What time was it?"

"Just after ten." She checked her Timex. "About three hours ago."

"Hhhmmm . . ." Sonny rested the briefcase on the edge of Lavine's desk and drummed his fingers against the side.

"What are you thinking?" Charli quizzed.

Lavine lifted his hand. "I'm thinking, what's a Bullard bank executive doing in Jacksonville at ten A.M.?" He swung his leg while chewing his bottom lip.

"Exactly," Sonny affirmed. "I saw him leaving the bank after nine. He rushed out, actually."

225

"Do you think he *followed* me there?" Charli croaked. Like a hunted fox, she gazed into the street but spotted no signs of Harlings.

"You had a flat?" Sonny questioned.

"Yes." She nodded and dragged her attention back to the private eye.

"Have you had it repaired?" Lavine asked.

"No." She shook her head. "Not yet."

"Might be good to see what caused it," Sonny mused and gazed past her. "When Harlings helped you fix it, did he in any way make you feel threatened?" He shifted his focus back to Charli.

"Noooo," she hedged. "Well, maybe a little uncomfortable." Charli fidgeted with the hem of her blouse. "He gave me a hundred dollars and—"

Lavine's boots thumped against the floor as he stood and rested his hands on his hips. "He gave you a *hundred dollars?* Whatever for?"

"He said the bank staff was taking up a collection for me and that he wanted to go ahead and give me his part."

"Okay, this is weird," Sonny said in a singsong voice.

"Could be the ol' let me get your trust built up routine," Lavine muttered and rubbed his chin.

"What do you mean?" Charli asked.

"You know," Sonny explained, "put the lady in a bad predicament and then rescue her so she'll trust you." He raised his brows.

"I had no idea men would—"

"Not *all* men," Sonny defended. "I'd never do that." He pressed his fingertips against his chest.

"Yeah, right," Lavine grumbled through a playful grin. "I wouldn't put anything past you."

"Hey, you!" Sonny protested. "I bet you pulled your own punches in your day."

"Let's not go there." Lavine settled into the chair behind his desk, and the thing squeaked with his weight. The playful exchange over, he picked up a pen and started tapping the desk's edge. "Charli, do you have anyone who'd be willing to stay with you as a bodyguard the next few days?" His sharp gaze sliced through every scrap of Charli's bravado.

"A bodyguard?" She gazed at Sonny who nodded.

"Might not be a bad idea," he said. "At least until I can figure out what's up with Harlings. I think that flat thing is very odd. Maybe I should follow him for a day or three."

"What if I just moved in with my pastor and his wife for a while?" Charli asked. "I'm sure they'd let me sleep at their place. Not that either of them is a bodyguard, but it's better than nothing."

"Sounds like a plan," Lavine agreed. "Pat's worried sick about you anyway."

"Maybe Jack would put a guy in your neck of the woods as well," Sonny mused and then huffed. "Probably already has."

"That would be him, I think," Charli admitted. "He slept on my couch last night."

"Well, well, well," Sonny drawled and crossed his arms.

"Don't even go there," Charli said before he could gain any ground. "Jack just said he had a *feeling* of sorts and couldn't shake it, so he came over." She shrugged.

"Yeah, he does that sometimes," Sonny admitted, his eyes still sparkling. "He knew something was up when I had my wreck a few years back. Came looking for me and everything."

"Well, we found my bedroom window unlocked," Charli explained, "and I didn't open it."

Ross Lavine whistled.

"Jack left a voice mail on my cell this morning," Sonny said. "I guess that's what it was about. He just said to call him, and I've been too busy. I'll call as soon as I leave here."

"Maybe you should get permission to leave the area for a while," Lavine suggested. "Do you have any friends in, say, Dallas or anywhere?"

Charli shook her head as her throat tightened. "Only a half sister in San Antonio. But we're"— she shrugged—"estranged, for lack of a better word. Her dad left her mom to marry my mom and well, it hasn't been good from the day I was born. I finally just quit trying."

"I've got a son who lives in Ft. Worth. He and his wife have a big place—no kids." Lavine stroked his forehead.

228

"I hate to intrude," Charli worried.

"Let me talk all this over with Jack," Sonny encouraged. "Then we can go from there. I'll trail Harlings for a while and see what I can come up with. He might be harmless, but you never know. I'll also see if I can find out if the bank really is taking up a collection for you."

"How?" Charli prompted.

Sonny smiled. "I have my ways."

"He's probably already charmed the socks off sixteen females and has his pick of which one to ask."

"Not quite sixteen," Sonny drawled, "just one. Rita Juarez was ready to tell her name, rank, and serial number. I don't think she'll mind letting me know about a collection underway for Charli."

Lavine laughed out loud.

Sonny pointed toward the window. "Well, speak of the devil," he said.

Charli glanced toward the street to see Jack crawling out of his patrol car. "What's *he* doing here?" she squeaked.

"Last I heard, bees always swarm where there's honey," Sonny said.

Lavine snickered.

Charli's face heated. She had no sass to shove back at Sonny Mansfield. All her sass was zapped . . . right along with the strength in her knees. As she watched Jack stroll toward the office's doorway, she reminded herself that he was better off with his Mary Ann.

He deserves someone stable, she recited. *Someone who can offer him a sure future.*

CHAPTER NINETEEN

Jack stepped into the law office and had barely glanced toward the matronly secretary when Lavine's door opened and Charli strolled out with Sonny and the lawyer on her heels.

"Mansfield!" Lavine boomed and rushed to pump his hand. "Good to see you."

"Mr. Lavine." Jack nodded at the portly lawyer and glanced toward Charli. "I saw your and Sonny's vehicles and thought I'd stop by. How's it going?"

"Great," Sonny enthused. "I'm turning stones, and Mr. Lavine's building arguments."

"Like, if Charli Friedmont took the money, why is there no evidence of where it was spent or how it was spent?" Lavine settled on his secretary's desk corner. "Charli has nothing to show for that hundred grand. She's got a pastor and his wife and a whole congregation who'll testify that she's been at church every Sunday and had a flawless work attendance record, so there's no way she's gone out of town and spent it at some exotic playground."

"Good point." Jack's lower lip protruded. "Very good point."

"Plus, we've got a few leads," Sonny crowed and glanced toward the secretary, whose attention was as riveted by the conversation as was Jack's.

The ringing phone cut her concentration. "Ross Lavine's office," she said into the receiver. "Yes. He's here. Just a moment." Beatrice Green pressed a button and gazed up at her boss. "Mr. Lavine, your conference call."

He stood. "Yes, of course." Lavine pointed toward Sonny. "Go to it, tiger!" he encouraged.

"I'm all over it," Sonny said with a broad wave. "I'll be in touch later."

Lavine extended a thumbs-up and disappeared into his office.

Jack eyed Charli, who averted her attention toward the road. *Okay,* he thought, *now what?* Once he saw Charli and Sonny's vehicles parked at Lavine's curb, Jack had pulled his car to a stop before he ever had a second thought. When it came to Charli Friedmont, he was like a zombie caught in her spell, and the effect was only increasing.

"Looks like we all need to get busy," Sonny explained and strolled toward the door with the gait of a graceful layup. He paused in front of the door, placed his hand on the knob, and jerked his head toward the sidewalk.

Jack took the hint and followed Charli and Sonny into the June heat. Once the door was closed, Sonny looked at Charli. "Tell him what happened this morning with Sigmund Harlings," he prompted.

His spine tensing, Jack rested his hand near his Glock 40 and said, "Who's Sigmund Harlings?"

Charli took a breath and then related a story of her flat tire, the hundred-dollar gift, and the supposed collection happening at the bank.

"I'm checking out the collection first thing and then going from there," Sonny explained. "Whatever the case, my gut tells me this Harlings cat needs to be followed."

"Absolutely," Jack agreed and gazed up and down the street. He saw no signs of anything unusual. While the line of aging buildings resembled Mayberry USA, the supposed peace seemed misleading . . . especially in the face of the haunted caution in Charli's big brown eyes. Jack's hackles began to rise.

"I'm going to spend the night with the Jonases," Charli explained.

"Good." Jack nodded. "That way, I can sleep in my own bed." He glanced toward Sonny. "I played watchdog last night and slept on Charli's couch."

"So I've heard," Sonny drawled, his lips twitching.

"I already told him." Charli rested her hands on her hips and decided the time had come to serve Sonny some of his own pudding. "And his mind went straight to the gutter."

"Yikes!" Sonny jumped away from Charli like she had the plague. "You're lethal this morning, sistah! What happened to that sweet little southern lady I met the other day."

"You *met* her," Charli shot back and wagged her head from side to side. "And she had to make a change or go down!"

Jack threw back his head and laughed out loud. "Looks like she's got you by the tail!" he cheered.

Sonny backed toward his truck at the curb and said, "Yeah, and I'm running before she grabs my ears too." He pointed at Charli. "I'll be in touch," he promised with a jovial wave.

Charli's chuckles mingled with Jack's.

But once Sonny was safely behind Charli's back, he mouthed, *Don't be so easy!* and pointed straight at Jack's nose.

Jack squinted as his brother's warning mingled with the leftover ire from Payton's prying. He focused on Charli's whimsical smile and tried to ignore the warnings. "You sure seem to be in good spirits today," Jack observed.

She glanced toward him, then cast her attention toward the street like she was as skittish as she was cheerful. "That meeting really raised my hopes, I guess. Now I'm thinking maybe I won't have to go to prison after all."

"You won't." Jack rocked back on his heels. "Not if I can help it."

Charli gazed toward the sidewalk and didn't reply.

"By the way," Jack began, "I called and talked with a locksmith out of Tyler. He can install deadbolts and also set up a complete security system, but he can't fit you in until tomorrow at nine. Does that work?"

"Sure." Charli fidgeted with her purse strap, then opened the flap and pulled out her car keys. "Like I said, I'll stay with the Jonases tonight, so I should be okay until tomorrow."

"Just be careful, okay?" Jack rested his hand on her shoulder.

She stepped toward her car at the curb and walked out of his reach. "I will," she said and avoided eye contact once more.

Finally, Jack realized that Charli was purposefully not looking at him, and he nearly shivered with her cold reception. Fact was, Charli Friedmont had been warmer last week when they had their cookout, and that was before he'd spent a whole weekend bending over backward to help her. Even though everything last night hadn't exactly been perfect, Jack had awakened with a wee bit of encouragement sitting on his shoulder. Bonnie's sweet reception of his help with her morning drink had only increased his hope.

Sonny's mouthing, *Don't be so easy!* now appeared before him like a beacon of wisdom from a heavenly messenger. Since Jack had never thought of Sonny as an angel sort, he barked out a laugh before he ever knew he'd released it.

And that got Charli's attention. Her brown gaze presented him with a silent question.

"Oh, it's nothing." Jack waved away his

laughter. "I just had a thought—something Sonny said."

"Oh." Charli rattled those keys, glanced toward her car, and then heaved out a breath.

A swoosh of wind whipped around the corner and lifted Charli's hair away from her face. Jack hardened his heart against his masculine reaction. Sonny was right. He'd been too easy for too long. Payton was right. He didn't need to set himself for a fall with a woman who was as wishy-washy as all get out.

Maybe she's not the only one who needs to work through some stuff, he thought. *If we're ever going to have a relationship, my being a dog on her chain is a loooong way from healthy. We've got to be equals, or it's not going to fly.*

As that understanding settled upon Jack, his spine straightened. He squared his shoulders and looked Charli in the eyes with a new determination he wasn't exactly sure he understood. Her eyes widened a fraction before she gazed past him.

"Well, I, uh, guess I'll go, then. Mr. Lavine and Sonny both wanted me to get my flat tire fixed and tell them what the guy says."

"Right. Sounds like a plan. We need to know if it looks like a real accident or foul play."

"Yes." Charli blessed him with a final glance, offered a hurried wave, and then strode toward her Taurus.

Jack watched her sway along the sidewalk and

wondered where the next few weeks might lead. As much as he loved Charli, he also knew it was time for him to get on with his life. While he doubted he'd ever love another woman as much as he did her, Jack also understood that he couldn't spend the rest of his life pining for the unattainable.

Father, he prayed as he turned for his patrol car, *I'm tired of trying to make this happen between her and me. I'm placing Charli in your hands. If you want us to be together, then please let it happen soon. And if not, then take away the love I have so I can get on with my life.*

"Sonny's right," Jack breathed. He unlocked his car and settled into the heated interior. "It's time for a change of direction."

His cell phone bleeped from his belt, announcing a text message. Never taking his attention off Charli's car, he pulled his phone from his belt and flipped it open. Only when she pulled from the curb did he read the text message: "What time tomorrow night? R."

Jack groaned as he recalled tomorrow night's events. The children's group at Charli's church was coming over. He'd even invited Ryan as an afterthought. Mary Ann would be there with her "portable petting zoo," and Charli just might be there with Bonnie. At the time he'd invited the church over, he'd thought it was a good idea. But now he saw the situation for what it was: a virtual pressure cooker waiting to happen! Jack's temperature increased just thinking about it.

He inserted his key into the ignition, cranked the car, and flipped the A.C. on high before typing in his reply to his brother. "Six. And don't forget . . . you're in charge of ice. J."

"You can bring an extra ton for me, while you're at it," he mumbled and snapped his phone shut. "I'll probably be sweating like a cow."

"That's ten seventy-eight," the serviceman said.

Charli pulled a twenty out of her purse and handed it to the man who stood behind a desk in the tiny office. The smell of stale coffee blended with the scent of oil and tires and fit the dingy room as much as the mound of desk clutter that looked like it had been there since 1970.

"So, you just think it was a screw or nail?" Charli repeated what the toothless man had told her before asking for her money.

"Yep," he said, his lined lips sinking around his gums. "Like I said, it's real common." He narrowed his watery eyes and extended the change. "Why you keep askin' anyway? You scared of somethin'?"

"Uh . . ." Charli took the change, tucked it into her side pocket. "I'm a single woman," she explained, "and I just don't think I can be too careful."

"Well, deary," he shook his head, "I wouldn't

waste any time worryin' none. I fix a dozen of those a week. Yur just one in a long line of folks that's done picked up a nail or screw. Don't give it another thought."

"Okay, thanks," Charli said and turned toward the glass door. The tarnished bells hanging from the door's handle released a tired jingle as she exited. With a sigh, Charli strode to her car and climbed in.

Once the car was cranked, she couldn't turn on the air conditioner soon enough. However, she also lowered the power windows to ventilate the baking interior until the A.C. was cool enough to reduce the temp. Charli cruised down the street, toward the country road that led her home. Thankful that the serviceman noticed no foul play, she planned to call Mr. Lavine and Sonny with the news but also thought, *What about Jack? He needs to know too.*

Turning onto her road, she relied on her subconscious knowledge of the route to steer her vehicle home while her mind pondered the recent encounter with Jack Mansfield. Her sacrificial desire to release him to find another love tasted sour in the face of their last encounter. Something seemed to snap during that conversation. What, Charli wasn't sure.

"He just seemed more . . . independent," she mused and wondered if he might be losing interest in her after all these years. She frowned and lowered the air conditioner's blast. Now that she was just a minute from home, the thing had finally reduced the temperature to the comfort level. She tugged at the neck of her knit shirt and wondered if there'd ever be a summer that didn't bring on the sweat the second you stepped outside.

But no amount of chilling sweat could distract Charli from the Jack Mansfield business for very long. *What if he doesn't want me after all,* she thought. When she'd decided he deserved better, Charli had done so with the belief that she was still Jack's first choice.

But what if I'm really not? she thought, her fingers tightening on the steering wheel. *What if he's finally decided he really* is *better off without me? What if he really does want Mary Ann more than me?* Her foot slipped off the accelerator.

CHAPTER TWENTY

The next evening, Charli turned beside a mailbox with "Mansfield" written on the side. The simple black box was perched atop a cedar post that was as rustic as the log cabin at the end of the paved driveway. Numerous familiar vehicles claimed spots near the cabin. The place hadn't changed at all since Charli and Jack shared their first kiss in the barn. The only difference was that the barn and cabin were a bit more weathered.

"There's Uncle Jack," Bonnie exclaimed as Jack

239

emerged from the barn and motioned for the group of kids and adults to come inside.

Charli glanced at her watch. The evening on the ranch was supposed to start at six. It was five after. "Yes, that's him," Charli said and glanced toward her daughter whose rapt attention rested upon Jack.

Only days ago, Bonnie had declared she hated Jack, but her childish fury had been extinguished. Several times, she'd mentioned Jack's helping her with her morning drink and Charli wondered what magic touch he'd put on the simple glass of water and the book he'd read. Since she didn't recall a lot of positive times with her father, Charli could only imagine the affect of a tender, masculine voice upon a thirsty girl early in the morning.

Whatever he did, Jack apparently won a conquest. Charli pulled her trusty Taurus next to a new Cadillac Escalade. *But then, I laid some groundwork on that as well,* she admitted. Charli had been the one who arranged for Jack to present the kittens and numerous times she'd told her daughter that "Uncle Jack" was there to help. *So maybe we worked together to win Bonnie over.* Charli turned off the engine.

The back door opened. Surprised, Charli glanced toward Bonnie to see her already scrambling out. When she whizzed past the passenger side, her features were fixed in a determination that reflected no fear. Charli opened her door, stepped out, and called, "Bonnie, wait!" but the child's jean-clad legs pumped all the harder while she surged straight into the barn.

Sighing, Charli locked the car and strode toward the barn. After a scorcher of a week, the east Texas heat and humidity had relinquished with a cool front. After a morning rain that resembled a spring shower, the thermometer had stopped climbing at eighty-five today. The evening breeze wafting off the bank of bluish clouds building in the west promised another shower that would close out the day.

Thankful for a day without "sweating like a sow," as her mom would have said, Charli reveled in the way the breeze fingered her ponytail and whipped at her loose-legged capri pants. As she neared the barn, Charli's spirits were lifted a bit, despite her misgivings over the neighbor factor.

After a year of his pursuing her, something had changed. Whatever that "something" was, Charli could almost feel it in the air. She'd expected him to call to at least confirm that her locks and security system were installed today. But when he didn't, she recalled the locksmith talking to someone on his cell phone as he was leaving. The conversation had been short and to the point; the locksmith simply confirmed that he'd completed the job. Since Jack hadn't called, Charli now wondered if the conversation had been with him.

She paused outside the barn's open doorway and

listened to the presentation that was happening inside. The smell of fresh hay mingled with the scent of the cattle in the pasture. While a woman's sweet, southern tone rose above the children's excited mumbling, Charli rested her hand on the barn's graying door and strained to glean every word.

"Goat's milk is very nutritious and it's the only milk, besides soy milk, that my son can drink. Cow's milk upsets his tummy. So, we have a couple of goats that we milk all the time. This goat's name is Fido."

The kids giggled.

"We call her that because she has fetched nearly since she was born. If you throw a Frisbee or an old hat or anything like that, she'll go get it and bring it back to you. We decided since she acts like a dog, we'd give her a dog's name."

The laughter escalated anew and Jack's low rumble rose above the crowd.

Charli opened the door a bit wider and slipped inside. The loft doors hung ajar, allowing the evening sun to blast the barn with ample illumination. Beams of hazy light also seeped through several gaps in the walls, and one beam christened the speaker in a glow that resembled a halo.

Her face stiffening, Charli gazed at the woman who must be Mary Ann. Her hair was every bit as vibrant as Charli imagined—especially in the evening sun. And Charli didn't have to ask if her blue eyes and peaches-and-cream complexion would snare a man's interest. That, coupled with her petite figure and demure demeanor was probably enough to discombobulate a whole army.

While the dozen or so kids pressed toward the makeshift stall's open doorway, Jack stood on the other side. With one boot braced on the stall's bottom rail and his arms resting along the top rail, he looked as good in his jeans and boots and cowboy hat as some country music star.

A movement near Jack's arm snatched Charli's attention from the man to the child dressed in a red-checked shirt who was crawling the bottom rung beside him. Bonnie smiled up at Jack as he circled his arms around her and lifted her to sit on the top rail. He said something through a smile, and Bonnie's reciprocal grin verified that it must have been the perfect comment for the moment.

"Fido is a very gentle lady," Mary Ann continued. "Once I show you how to milk her, I'll let each of you take a turn at milking her. Okay?"

"Okay . . . okay!" the children cheered.

"Ssshhhh," Pat Jonas admonished, along with several mommies who corralled their offspring.

When Charli glanced back toward Jack, he caught her eye. With a slight grin, he lifted his hand and waved. Charli wiggled her fingers and looked away.

After counting to ten, Charli stole another peek at Jack, only to confirm what she feared. Jack's admiring attention was solely fixed upon Mary Ann. Dressed in the typical jeans and boots, she now knelt beside the goat and talked her way through the milking process.

As splashes of creamy milk met the pail, Charli's stomach grew queasy.

Apparently, Jack Mansfield had made his choice, and it wasn't her. That would explain why he was more distant outside Mr. Lavine's office yesterday and why he hadn't called at all today. With that realization came a deeper recognition of what Charli was beginning to register on a conscious level. During the last year, she'd gradually begun to depend on Jack's encouraging smiles and small talk, and his presence had been a source of comfort after her mother died. Even though Charli had never called him for direct help until recently, she'd been subconsciously aware of his availability. Furthermore, Charli had taken for granted that he'd always be there . . . no matter what.

But Jack's got to want to get married at some point, she reasoned. *Most healthy people do. He's going to want a family . . . kids.*

Two boys broke away from the edge of the crowd, rounded the stall, and crawled onto the rungs on Jack's other side. He grinned toward the kids and roughed up their hair. The redhead needed a haircut, and his wavy hair had the texture of a dust mop. But it was the exact same shade as Mary Ann's. If that didn't peg him as hers, his freckled nose did. The other boy didn't resemble Mary Ann quite as much, but he did have her blue eyes. Both of them gazed toward Jack like the whole world revolved around him.

Charli's eyes stung. Her motives for coming tonight had been too complicated for her to sort. But now the confused jumble became exceedingly clear. Charli had wanted to see Mary Ann and to determine just how attached Jack might or might not be to her. Well, she'd found an answer. In her eyes, Jack was as smitten as all-get-out.

She edged back out of the door and into the evening breeze. Turning, Charli strode across the yard, toward a small cabin. She swallowed hard and blinked against the sting. While the resolve to sacrifice her love for Jack's betterment had tasted sour yesterday afternoon, this evening, it was all the way bitter.

Crossing her arms, Charli stopped in the middle of the backyard and grappled to control her emotions. This was no place . . . or time to cry. Although, she was tempted to go straight back home and ask Pat if Bonnie could ride home with her.

A movement in the pasture drew Charli's attention toward a sandy-haired man leading a saddled mare toward the barn. His graceful gait brought to mind a lean panther whose keen eyes missed no detail. Charli recalled the laughs she'd shared with Jack's brother, Ryan. The years hadn't changed him much . . . only added haunted shadows to his chiseled features.

Charli vaguely remembered Jack mentioning that Ryan was now divorced from his wife, Shelly. He'd been dating her when Jack and Charli dated. The news of a divorce always affected her more deeply since her own divorce, and she wondered if his haunted demeanor was the result of that pain.

Ryan's attention shifted toward Charli, and he caught her eye. He lifted his brows as a surprised light momentarily chased away the shadows. Waving, Ryan offered a friendly smile to round out the gesture. Charli returned the wave and broke into a huge grin.

Drawn by his easy manner and the chance of some friendly conversation, Charli was walking toward the gate before she realized it. If she could use one word to describe Ryan Mansfield it would be mellow. While Jack was more a force and Sonny could be a crazy man, Ryan always affected her like a cool drink on a hot summer day . . . relaxing and refreshing. And after getting a good look at Mary Ann Osborne, Charli could use a double dose of relaxing and refreshing. She'd left the barn feeling anything but mellow.

"Hey there, you!" he said through an easy smile. "Jack hinted that you might be here tonight, and I couldn't quite believe it."

"Well, believe it," she quipped and reached to stroke the mare's nose. She nuzzled Charli's hand as if searching for a treat, and Charli was enveloped by the pleasing aroma of leather and horsehair.

"She's such a beggar," Ryan said. "I brought my son, Sean, out here the other day, and we wound up giving her all the carrots in Jack's refrigerator."

"I'm sure he was blessed," Charli drawled.

"Yeah," Ryan admitted while tugging on the tail of his western shirt. "I promise, even with a cool spell on, I'm still working up a sweat."

"You know you're in Texas when you call eighty-five degrees a cool spell," Charli drawled.

"Right," Ryan said with a snicker.

Charli pulled at the neck of her linen blouse and gazed toward the bank of bluish clouds along the horizon. "Maybe it will rain again and give you a break," she said.

"I hear you have a little girl now?" he asked and shifted his baseball cap off his forehead.

"Yes. Her name's Bonnie. And your son is Sean?"

"Right. I usually just have him on weekends, but Jack invited me to bring him tonight, and Shelly was fine with it." He shrugged and barely winced. "You know we're divorced now?"

"Yeah. That's what I heard," Charli said. "Sorry."

"Me too." His smile was laced with sadness. "But I guess that's what you get when you act like an idiot."

Charli stroked the mare's neck and didn't press for details. She figured if Ryan wanted to give them he would. Otherwise, she'd give him the same respect she appreciated when her divorce was brought up. As always, an easy silence soon settled between them.

"Shelly and I adopted Sean, actually," he finally said.

"No way!" Charli enthused. "How neat is that. I've thought about adopting a few times."

"I couldn't ask for a better son," he said with a nod. "You may have seen him in the barn." He pointed toward the aged structure.

"If I did, I didn't realize he was yours," Charli admitted and didn't add that she'd been too distracted by the chemistry between Mary Ann and Jack to have noticed too much.

"Jack asked me to come out and help Bud get the mares saddled up," he said and glanced over his shoulder toward a dark-skinned man who was leading a larger mare from the pasture.

Charli gazed toward Bud and recalled his being Abe's right hand man. She'd been stricken twelve years ago with the character that shone from his demeanor. The same integrity glowed from the gentleman's eyes now. Like the barn and cabin, the only thing that had changed was that he was a bit more weathered.

Noticing her, Bud waved. Charli returned the gesture when the sound of hard-core country music thumped into the yard. She turned toward the cabin to see a Chevy pickup rolling up the driveway. The driver parked in the first spot he came to and bailed out.

His disheveled blond hair and carefree stride were all too familiar. Charli chuckled at the way Jack's brother swaggered across the yard like he owned the whole place. While Jack's gait certainly revealed a measured amount of confidence, Sonny's was more in line with a cocky strut. Fleetingly, Charli wondered what woman he might one day encounter who would take him down a few notches. If not for the stress of the Jack–Mary Ann business Charli could have laughed out loud.

"Uh-oh," Ryan said and grinned. "The hurricane is upon us."

"Isn't that the truth?" Charli said through a grin. "He's *so* wired."

"You should have tried growing up with him," Ryan said. "He was something else."

"But I like him," Charli admitted and cut Ryan a sideways glance.

"Good thing from what I hear." Ryan winked.

Charli's gaze faltered. She gazed down at her sandaled feet and tried to make sense of Ryan's cryptic remark.

"Hey, guys!" Sonny called and was now making a straight line for them. "I tried to call you, Charli, but didn't get an answer," he continued. "When I couldn't get Jack to answer either, I decided to come over here and see if I could track him down. But here you are. What's going on?" He waved toward the cars and then looked straight at Ryan. "Are you guys having a party without me?"

"We wouldn't even try," Ryan drawled and reached across the fence to fondly punch his younger brother in the arm.

"Our church children's group is here," Charli explained. "It's like a night on the ranch or something. I left my cell phone in the car, I guess."

"Oh, yeah, I think maybe Jack *did* mention that." Sonny gazed toward the barn where raucous laughter erupted. "Sounds like they're having a high old time."

"Yeah, I guess," Charli mumbled and observed the bank of clouds that grew larger with every minute.

"They're about to come out to ride the mares," Ryan explained, and the horse's soft whinny punctuated his claim.

"Mary Ann's showing them how to milk a goat right now," Charli mumbled and knew she sounded about as enthusiastic as a comatose turtle.

Sonny's mischievous snicker riveted her attention. "What's so funny?"

"Oh, nothing." He crossed his arms, rocked back on his heels, and gazed toward the sky.

Charli narrowed her eyes and scrutinized the guy. He'd always struck her as someone who had some sneaky secret hidden who-knew-where.

Once his humor had vanished, he made eye contact and said, "I have a little bit of info from the bank." His expression was as guileless as the cows' lowing from the far pasture. But Charli couldn't shake the impression that his mischievous humor had had something to do with her.

"Sorry to leave you," Ryan injected, "but Bud's needing me. I'm going to just tie this little lady up right here and leave you two with it."

"That's fine," Charli said. "Great to see you again."

"Same here." He waved. "We'll talk more later, okay?"

"Sure thing," she replied before turning back toward Sonny. "So, do you have any new info?" she asked while her mind clicked with possibilities.

"Of course," he said with an assured nod. "I followed Harlings to his home last night and sat down the block until way after dark. I was ready to leave when he exited. I trailed him to Tyler, where he met up with some hot mamma of the Latin persuasion, I'd say. She met him at the door. He went inside and didn't come out until three." Sonny yawned, and Charli noticed the dark circles under his eyes. "Today about four, I followed him again. This time, he drove straight to Tyler. Didn't even bother to go home. When he entered, he had some roses."

"So, you think he's having an affair?" she reasoned. Curling her toes against her sandals, she leaned forward.

"Looks that way," Sonny drawled. "Either that, or he was sleeping on the couch to protect her."

Charli crossed her arms and tapped her toe. "Somehow, I don't think so," she quipped and ignored his sarcasm. "Not this time anyway. Really, when he was changing my flat, he struck me as that sort for the first time."

"Did he make a pass at you or something?" Sonny asked.

"No." Charli shook her head. "Not exactly. He just seemed a little . . . warm."

A gust of wind tossed Sonny's hair and clawed at his loose T-shirt that read "Eat my grits!" and featured an old lady who was serving a large bowl of steaming grits. Charli dashed aside the bangs that had blown into her eyes and wondered if Harlings had been thinking toward a tryst when he offered his services.

"Maybe he's building a harem and wants you in it," Sonny stated.

Charli nodded. "That's what I was just thinking . . . or something like that anyway," she agreed. "And what about the collection at work?" she added.

"Believe it or not," Sonny replied, "there is one on. I talked with Rita this afternoon. She said that Harlings was discreetly making that happen. She acted like she thought it was strange. Apparently, the man isn't known for his humanitarian acts."

A dart of lightning skipped along the edge of the clouds as gooseflesh danced up Charli's spine. "Maybe Mr. Lavine was right," she suggested. "Maybe he's trying to get me to depend on him just so—"

"You'll fall into his arms in gratitude?" A distant rumble of thunder mingled with the concern in Sonny's voice.

"Yeah." Charli swallowed. More gooseflesh broke out, on her arms, and she wondered if there were any other darker motives in Harlings's mind.

"You know, a hundred grand is a lot of dough." Sonny rubbed his chin and gazed past Charli. "And that town house his mistress is living in ain't too shabby."

Charli gulped and wondered if she'd come face-to-face with the person who framed her yesterday morning.

"Jack said he was going to get you set up with an alarm system. Did he?" Sonny questioned.

"Y-yes." Charli shook her head and fidgeted with her collar.

The barn door clapped open, and the cheerful children scurried into the yard with a group of adults behind. Charli noted that Bonnie now held Pat's hand before she saw Mary Ann strolling beside Jack with her boys nearby. A man followed Mary Ann. He was nearly as tall as Sonny and favored Mary Ann's youngest son. Before he hurried off with the boys, he darted a look toward Jack that the dullest would interpret as unbridled jealousy. While Charli watched the guy head toward the horse pasture with a boy on each side, she experienced a high-level connection with him. Her emotions weren't too far removed from his.

She eyed Jack smiling down at Mary Ann and admitted the ugly truth. *I'm jealous!* she thought. *That's why I wanted to shave Mary Ann bald the other night.*

Sonny's laughter once again held a sly undertone, and Charli scowled straight at him—except he lost the impact because he was watching Jack and Mary Ann as well.

"Pretty isn't she?" Sonny observed.

"I hadn't noticed," Charli shot back. Even though she knew she sounded beyond petty, she was too keyed up to correct the impression.

Before Sonny could reply, Jack said something to Mary Ann, then waved toward them and strolled forward while she walked toward the children. "Hey, whazup, man?" he called to his brother.

"Not much." Sonny jutted his thumb toward Charli. "I was just talking with Charli about what I told you earlier. I was also checking to make sure you got the alarm system installed. I forgot to ask you."

"It's done, right Charli?" he gazed down at her with a kind concern that any conscientious brother might direct toward his sister.

"Yes," she replied, her legs rigid.

"Good." Jack rubbed his hands together. "But I still think it would be wise for you to stay with the Jonases awhile. They're not exactly armed and dangerous, but it's still safer than at your place."

"I agree," Sonny said.

"They told me I can stay as long as I want." Charli's gaze trailed toward Mary Ann leaning against the pasture's railing. The kids were surrounding Bud and Ryan while the tall, jealous guy helped Bonnie into the horse's saddle. The man reached for the harness and began leading the mare around the pasture. A huge smile dimpled Bonnie's face as she clung to the saddle horn.

"Bonnie says she wants to ride with me," Jack said.

Charli focused on him to find that he was watching the pasture as well.

"She told me you helped her with her drink yesterday morning, and it's like she's been taken with you ever sinse. What exactly did you do to her? Put charm juice in the water or something?"

"Exactly," Jack replied through a slow grin, "how'd you ever guess?"

The brotherly concern merged into something a bit warmer, and Charli's stomach responded accordingly. Charli examined her freshly painted toenails, and an eruption of confusion merged with a slow burning ire. She was too old to be one in a collection of Jack Mansfield's girlfriends. He was going to have to make a choice.

Jack cleared his throat and finally said, "Actually, I didn't put anything in her water."

"Who?" Charli raised her head.

"Bonnie. You asked me about the charm juice in her water." His lazy smile couldn't have been more satisfied, and that made Charli all the more exasperated.

"Oh, yeah," Charli replied.

"Anyway, after she got her drink, I saw one of her books on the counter. Before it was over, she read it to me and I read it to her."

"Let me guess," Charli said as she recalled the book that had been on the coffee table yesterday morning, "*Barney's Day at the Farm*?"

"Yep." He nodded.

"You lucked out. She'd let Godzilla read that book to her. She loves it."

"Ugh!" He clutched his chest. "I thought it was because she was loving *me*."

"Well, the way she looks tonight . . ." Charli encouraged him.

"I've been training Jack," Sonny explained. "He's much better with little girls and, uh," he glanced toward the pasture "*women* since he's been taking my classes."

Charli followed Sonny's gaze and made direct eye contact with Mary Ann. The woman's blue-eyed stare held a knowing intensity that nearly knocked Charli to the ground. A rush of mortification sent a hot wave up her neck, and she ducked her head to hide the inevitable flush to her cheeks.

Why did I even come? she fretted. *I should have known this was a bad idea!*

"Uh, I'm n-not feeling so—so well," she rasped and gazed toward the clouds that now threatened rain within the half hour. "If it's okay, I think I'll leave Bonnie with Pat and go on back home. I need to get packed for tonight at the Jonases anyway."

"Sure," Jack said, "I don't mind. Are you sure you'll be okay? You've gone kinda pale." He leaned a bit closer.

Charli stumbled back. "Yes," she croaked and gripped her throat. "I'll just go tell Pat I'll meet her at her place."

"Well, okay," Jack said, "but be careful. Keep your eyes peeled. And make sure your security system is engaged when you're in the house."

"Right. I won't be there long," she affirmed and began stepping away.

"I've got a patrolman cruising your neck of the woods some," he added.

"Thanks." Charli hastened away before she blurted something she'd regret. She and Jack certainly had a lot to talk about, and he had a choice to make. But Charli didn't have the presence of mind to make it through a logical conversation, and *now* was not the time anyway.

CHAPTER TWENTY-ONE

With Charli driving away, Jack meandered back to the pasture and helped Bonnie into the saddle again. As he settled behind her on the mare, Jack gazed after the silver Taurus zooming up the lane. He'd nearly gone after her, but Sonny insisted he stay put. Jack had. Now he wasn't so sure. Keeping his distance did seem to be opening Charli's eyes, if her blatant jealousy was any indicator that her eyes were opened. Nevertheless, Jack did not want to purposefully mislead her, and he was thinking that might be what was happening.

Bonnie's trusting grip on his forearms reminded him that she needed a daddy as much as Charli needed a husband. The horse picked up her pace, and Jack let her work out a little energy. The saddle squeaked with the cadence, and Bonnie's grip increased.

"Whoa!" she protested.

With a chuckle, Jack tugged on the mare's reins, and the horse responded accordingly. "Not too fast, huh, Bonnie girl?" Jack crooned.

"No, not too fast," she replied and leaned against him. They'd certainly bonded through Barney, and Jack was tempted to send a thank-you note to the creator.

When their ride was over, Jack dismounted first. Bonnie slid into his arms, and he deposited her on the ground. "Now tear out!" he encouraged. "Granny Pat's helping with the petting zoo over there. You need to take your turn before it rains!" After a glance toward the threatening clouds, Jack pointed toward a makeshift pen Bud had created for the rabbits and goats. The child dashed toward it without a backward glance seconds before another lady stepped to his side.

"Can we talk, Jack?" Mary Ann questioned. Her fresh-as-flowers cologne blended with the horse and leather "perfume" in an effect that stated exactly what Mary Ann Osborne was: a down-to-earth ranch owner with a touch of class.

"Sure," Jack agreed but wasn't really sure he wanted to talk to a woman with Mary Ann's troubled expression.

"Maybe we could go back into the barn," she suggested.

"All right." Jack handed the mare's reins to Ryan and followed the stiff-backed lady toward their destination.

This evening had been far from comfortable, to say the least. When Charli sped off, Jack sensed that her "feeling bad" had been linked to many other factors besides her physical health. Now Mary Ann looked nearly as upset as Charli had.

Oh brother, Jack groaned to himself, *I'm really tangled here.* He pointed a brief glare toward his brother who cheerfully chatted up Pat Jonas. The guy was oblivious to the predicament his advice had thrown Jack into. *He* was the one who encouraged Jack to take out Mary Ann. And *he* was the one who told him not to be easy with Charli. Now Jack was sandwiched between Charli and Mary Ann at a church children's social, for cryin' out loud, and Sonny was charming the pastor's wife without a care in the world.

Jack was on the verge of punching his brother—in Christian love, of course—when he noticed Zeke Osborne glaring at him like he was the anti-Christ. Tonight when Mary Ann had introduced her brother-in-law, Jack recalled briefly meeting him at Zane's funeral. He also remembered Mary Ann saying Zeke was coming over Sunday night to tend her broken water heater and that the guy helped her quite a bit. Soon after their arrival, Jack's assumption that he was the only man in Brett and Brad's life had been annihilated when the boys repeatedly called for Uncle Zeke and clung to his every word. Now the guy looked like he wanted to punch Jack as much as Jack wanted to punch Sonny.

And this whole ordeal was about to wear Jack out.

As of last week, his life had been uncomplicated. His desires had been straightforward: to serve the Lord, to fulfill his job with dignity, and to gradually woo Charli Friedmont. Now he had two disgruntled women on his hands and a guy named Zeke who was ready for all-out war.

What is your deal, man? Jack followed Mary Ann into the barn. When he closed the door, she crossed her arms and faced him.

Sigmund Harlings trailed Charli from Mansfield's ranch. The farther west they went, the darker the clouds grew until finally, a few fat drops crashed into the windshield like watery bullets. Sigmund cursed and turned on the wipers. The last thing he needed tonight was to get drenched. His plan was the same as it had been two nights ago. He'd park in the clump of trees across the road from Charli's house, inject her and savor her death, and then sit with the body until the rain stopped and darkness fell.

He'd already been watching her place around six when she pulled from her driveway. Sigmund had trailed her to Mansfield's place and waited. When she left without her daughter, Sigmund had been convinced that the wait was worth it. Now he'd have her alone and wouldn't have to deal with the child. The rain presented the only flaw to his plan. The longer the delay, the tighter Sigmund's nerves stretched . . . the more ready he was to inject Charli and be done with it.

He turned on the radio and allowed the classical music to ease his tension. Taking several deep breaths, he forced his rapid heart rate to slow. The last thing he needed was to get too hurried, nervous, and worked up. In that state, Sigmund would stand the chance of blowing the whole operation.

"And I can't do that." He ground his teeth together.

The windshield wipers slapped in sequence with the rush of new resolve that overtook his mind and hardened his face. The distant rumble of thunder became one with the beat of his heart. The smell of rain pouring through the vents became the opium of courage.

He recalled the night when he was fifteen and his mother had started beating him with one of her high-heeled shoes. For the first time in his life, he'd dared to stop her. He ripped the shoe from her hand and twisted her wrist until she yelped and begged for release. He'd watched with little feeling as her eyes pleaded for him to stop the pain . . . just as the eyes of the deer pleaded to live. Finally, Sigmund had released her. Later that week, he noticed the bruises on her wrists. That was the last time his mother attacked him.

And this would be the last day Charli would have the chance to attack him as well. Sigmund vowed nothing could stop him now. "I will kill her," he hissed and narrowed his eyes as the countryside took on the surreal aura of those hazy dreams when he relived Brenda's death.

As determined as Mary Ann looked when she turned to face Jack, her gaze now faltered. She uncrossed her arms, fidgeted with the button on her western shirt, and finally graced Jack with her focus once more. He rested his hands on his hips and wished he were in west Texas eating cactus . . . or dead armadillo. Anything would be better than sorting through all this mess.

"Are you *seeing* Charli Friedmont?" Mary Ann questioned. The light now spilling in from the loft doors was as gray as the clouds blotting out the sun, and the shadows only deepened her reddening cheeks.

"Uh, well, n-not exactly," Jack hedged. He pushed at his hat and wondered if kissing her at midnight counted as officially "seeing" her.

"If you and her are," Mary Ann waved her hand, "then it would mean a lot if you wouldn't get my hopes up. Am I just a diversion for you?" she rushed. "Or—"

Out of desperation, Jack lifted his gaze toward the heavens, and the heavens responded with a rumble that shook the rafters.

"It's going to rain us out," Mary Ann grumbled.

"What's the deal with Zeke?" Jack asked and wondered if he'd really blurted the question or if he'd just imagined it. "Are you and he—"

"What do you mean?" Mary Ann wrinkled her brow.

"Well . . . he's looking at me like he's ready to filet my liver and feed it to the crows."

"Zeke is?" she squeaked. "You mean my brother-in-law?"

"Yes," Jack insisted.

"Zeke?" Mary Ann repeated and peered past Jack.

"I take it he isn't married?"

"No." She shook her head and inserted her fingers into her jeans pockets. "He never has been. He and Zane were twins—not identical, though. Zeke just never found the right woman."

"I don't think so." Jack shook his head and let his hint sink past Mary Ann's blindness.

"You mean?" She rested her hand on her chest.

"Yeah." Jack nodded.

Mary Ann stared at him like he'd just told her it was about to rain turtles. "Oh my word," she finally breathed and pressed her fingertips between her brows. "He's been so helpful ever since Zane died, but in the last few months . . ." She covered her lips with her fingertips, and memories Jack couldn't read played through her eyes. "Yes, I believe you might be right," she finally admitted and a tiny smile replaced the shock.

The smile grew, and Mary Ann gazed up at Jack with a candid friendship that had characterized their relationship before Zane passed away.

"And how long have you known Charli?" she prompted.

"How do you even know her name?" Jack questioned.

"I asked Pat Jonas."

Sighing, Jack shook his head and mumbled, "I

wonder if I've been set up by that woman?" He recalled her accepting his open-house-at-the-ranch offer with a speed that would rival a Texas twister. That plus the hints that her husband had dropped when Jack delivered the bond money all gelled into a probable case.

"Jack?" Mary Ann prompted.

"Oh!" Jack refocused on the question at hand. "I've known her since before she dumped me eleven years ago and married a jerk who left her," he blurted.

"So, I guess I really wasn't imagining things?" she gently prompted.

Jack raised his brows and waited for her to expound.

"You really do love her a lot, don't you?"

He blinked. His heart thudded in his throat. And Jack scrounged around for any way to make this conversation easier. Apparently, he was wearing his feelings all over both sleeves and the whole world knew he was in love with Charli Friedmont. That explained Payton's warning. The guy was probably just a concerned friend and nothing else.

Finally, he said, "Look, Mary Ann, I didn't mean for all this to happen this way. I asked you out because I thought maybe it was time for me to move on. I've pined after Charli all these years, and she doesn't seem to do anything but keep me at arm's length. I guess I just got tired of being shoved away."

"You're kidding, right?" Mary Ann prodded.

Jack silently waited for her to expound.

"The way she looked at you tonight . . . and then she was looking at *me* like you're saying Zeke was looking at you," Mary Ann insisted in a tone that underscored Jack's observations. "And she really has been shoving you away?"

"Well, yes." Jack nodded.

Mary Ann crossed her arms and shook her head like some expert on female behavior. "I didn't see any intent to push tonight."

"You didn't?" Jack leaned closer.

"No way! Look, I'm a woman, right?" Mary Ann laid her hand on her chest.

"Uh, right."

"I should know. And I say, you need to go after your lady."

"Well, thanks," Jack said. "That's the first time in my life my latest date has encouraged me to go after another woman."

Mary Ann laughed. "Ah well, Jack." She stepped forward and punched his arm. "We've known each other forever. We were friends before, and we'll be friends again, no matter what."

"Thanks, Mary Ann." Jack pulled her hand into his for a brief squeeze. "You're a real trooper."

She sighed. "That's what Zane always used to say," she admitted, a hollow loneliness in her voice.

The barn door creaked open, and Jack pivoted to face the topic of their conversation. Zeke gazed through the gathering shadows with at least a tinge of civility. "It's about to rain," he said, "Mizz Pat asked me to find you and see what you want us to do. She said they can just all go home, or—"

"No. That won't do," Jack hurried.

"Why don't we just put all the animals in here, and they can at least keep enjoying the petting zoo awhile," Mary Ann suggested.

"Works," Jack said. "Plus, I think Bud has grilled a bunch of wienies for some hot dogs and the ladies were supposed to bring chips and fixin's."

"I'll help," Zeke offered and held the door open for Mary Ann to pass through.

"Thanks," she said and smiled up at her brother-in-law with a new awareness in her expression.

Zeke eyed Jack anew, and Jack gave the guy a thumbs-up. A surprised smile flitted across Zeke's features before Jack followed the pair outside. As intermittent sprinkles penetrated his scalp, Jack realized he might have just done Zeke Osborne the favor of the century.

Well great, he groused and wondered when someone would do the same for him.

CHAPTER TWENTY-TWO

By the time the horse was stabled, the last rabbit caged, and the wayward goats were in the barn, Bud and the ladies had spread the food all over a wooden table covered in white paper. As if the heavens were awaiting their safety, another thunderous boom ushered in the downpour.

"We made it just in time!" Sonny crowed. He turned from lighting the final lantern, among several now glowing from their hooks along the wall. The flaming lanterns cast a cozy flicker across the barn and baptized faces in a warm glow. That plus the rain's rhythm and the smell of hot dogs made Jack want to settle on one of the bales of hay and indulge in some of the hot cider Bud had come up with. The guy was all over this event, and Jack wondered if he'd enjoyed it more than the kids.

Satisfied with the group's progress, Jack strode toward the back of the barn and pulled his cell phone from his belt. The phone testified that nearly thirty minutes had lapsed since Charli left. He didn't like the idea of her being out in this weather alone and debated whether or not to call and check on her. Sonny's "back-off" advice warred against Mary Ann's encouraging him to go for his lady.

Finally, Mary Ann won. Jack scrolled through his phone book and pressed Charli's name. He lifted the cell phone to his ear and counted the rings while gazing at the rain through the loft doors. Just when he figured he'd get her voice mail, she picked up.

"Hello, this is Charli," she said, her voice stiff.

Jack winced. Her caller ID screen would have indicated he was the caller, and her chilly greeting wasn't very encouraging. "Hey, Charli," Jack said, his voice as hesitant as his heart. "I was just checking to see if everything was all right. I'm concerned about you over there by yourself. Is it raining there? It's flooding here." A swoosh of wind blew moisture through the loft's opening, and the kids squealed as all gazed upward.

"Yes, it's raining cats and dogs," Charli replied like she'd rather eat grub worms than talk to him.

Jack's frown deepened. His fingers tightened on the phone.

"I've got all my things together, but I was just waiting to see if it might let up before I go on over to Pat's." By the final syllable, her words were stilted.

"All right," Jack drawled and debated whether or not to say any more. "Uh, are you feeling any better?" he asked.

"Well, what do *you* think," she snapped.

Jack blinked, strained for something to say, and wished he'd taken Sonny's advice rather than Mary Ann's. "Charli, have I done something—"

"Have you *done* something?" she repeated. "Look, I was going to save this for later, but since you brought it up—"

"Brought *what* up?" Jack shook his head, turned for the corner, and hunched his shoulders. The last thing he wanted was for the group to realize he was in a spat with Charli.

"We need to talk about—about—it's time for you to make a choice, Jack," she finally blurted.

"A choice?" he echoed and picked at a splinter in the barn's wall.

"Yes, between me and Mary Ann."

Jack's eyes widened as astonishment mixed with joy. "So *that's* what this is about?"

"You better believe it!" Charli replied. "I am *not* interested in being part of the Jack Mansfield girlfriend collection. It's either got to be me or her, but it can't be both of us."

His laugh bounced off the back wall, and the whole group went silent. Jack glanced over his shoulder and made direct eye contact with Ryan, whose rapt attention reflected that of the whole group.

"This is *not funny!*" Charli fumed.

"Look . . ." He moved closer to the wall, lowered his head, and hoped the group took the hint. The renewal of chatter indicated they did. "I'm in the barn, and I have an audience here, okay?"

Silence permeated the line. Jack checked to see if they were still connected and noted the Call Ended message. He sighed and didn't know if she'd hung up on him or the bad weather had interfered with their reception. Whatever the case, Jack weighed his choices. He could either drive over to her place immediately or let her stew awhile longer. Jack pivoted toward the crowd and spotted Sonny, helping a little girl with her hot dog. He knew what his brother would say.

Charli looked at the cell phone and whispered, "Call ended." She pressed her lips together and wondered if Jack had hung up on her. "Oh shoot!" she fretted and flopped onto the couch before her trembling legs betrayed her.

"I cannot believe I just said all that," she croaked. Resting her head on the back of the couch, Charli stared at the whirling ceiling fan and shivered against the breeze. Her mind spun as swiftly as the fan while she tried to comprehend what she'd just done. In so many words, Charli told Jack that he needed to make a commitment to her or they were through. Problem was, they'd never been an official item. She'd allowed her emotions to overrule her mouth, and Charli had forced the issue of their relationship because she'd been overcome with jealousy.

"Good grief," she groaned. *After the way I've jerked him around, he probably thinks this is just another jerk.*

But Charli knew there was nothing further from the truth. She sighed, eyed the phone, and debated whether or not to call him again. A tiny voice nibbling at her mind suggested she might have been too hard on the guy. After all, she'd implied that there was no chance for them to have a relationship. Therefore, he'd been perfectly free to pursue Mary Ann. Now Charli was telling him he had to make a choice or they were done.

She chuckled and shook her head. "Oh, brother," she mumbled, hoping that their stormy conversation just might catapult them into a deeper relationship.

She flipped open the phone and prepared to press his speed-dial number when her doorbell rang. Charli glanced toward the door and realized the rain had finally diminished. Her hopes flew to the ceiling. She was sure Jack had come straight over to wrap her in his arms and tell her he was choosing her . . . forever her.

Charli laid her phone on the coffee table, bounded toward the door, and flung it open before she ever thought to check the yard for Jack's vehicle. She regretted that decision the second she encountered Sigmund Harlings.

"Hello, Charli," he drawled and lowered his black umbrella. "I came by to give you the money we collected at work."

Charli's internal alarm clanged with a force so strong it nearly made her dizzy. Her crazed gaze searched the yard for any signs of Jack, but she saw only her car in the driveway. Why Harlings's Town Car wasn't in the drive became an enigma Charli couldn't fathom.

"Mr.—Mr. Harlings," she stammered and began fumbling to lock the screen door. "This is not a good—"

Before Charli could secure the lock, he whipped open the door and shoved his way inside. Charli stumbled backward. He slammed the door, locked it, and turned to face her. The grin that stretched his lips was nothing short of demonic.

"Now," he said and tossed the umbrella aside. "I have a little"—his eyebrow lifted—"surprise for you."

Her heart hammering, Charli backed toward her cell phone on the coffee table. Only one thought screamed through her mind, *Call Jack! Call Jack! Call Jack!*

The fiendish glint in Harlings's eyes affirmed that he was everything they'd suspected him to be . . . and then some.

"Mr. Harlings," Charli panted. "I don't know what's going on, but—" She bumped into the coffee table as he whipped a capped syringe from his sport coat pocket.

Charli's throat constricted. "Wh-what are you doing?" she demanded.

"I'm going to kill you," he replied as if he were reciting a simple verse of poetry. "You're threatening me, and now you must pay," he chanted. With a wicked snicker, he removed the cap, tucked it into his pocket, and stepped toward her. A tiny bead of moisture formed on the end of the silver needle like a glistening portent of death.

"H-how am I threatening you?" Charli wheezed while blindly fumbling for her cell phone.

"You hired a private eye, of course," he said, his eyes taking on a surreal intensity. "You and Brenda and mother are all the same," he continued.

"Brenda?" Charli breathed and grappled for any scrap of a memory about someone named Brenda.

"Yes, Brenda Downey." His smile was slow and twisted. "Remember? She just vanished." He swept his opened hand through the air like a crazed magician.

And Charli remembered the bank employee that had disappeared last year. Even though she hadn't been close to Brenda, Charli had been as dismayed as the rest of the employees. "You killed her?" she croaked. "You killed your own secretary?"

"Of course." His snicker merged into maniacal laughter.

"You're crazy!" Charli blurted.

His smile wilted, and his eyes took on a sadistic gloss that sent rigid terror through Charli.

"No, you're crazy," he snarled, "for thinking you can ever get away from me." He lunged forward.

Whimpering, Charli stumbled backward, crashed into the coffee table, and tumbled to the floor. The table turned onto its side and sent her cell phone spinning across the wooden floor toward the dining table.

Sigmund hovered over her and held the syringe with his thumb propped against the top, ready to mercilessly ram the needle into her body.

"You'll never get away with this!" Charli screamed before shifting to all fours and scrambling for the cell phone.

Sigmund grabbed her leg and jerked her back

toward him. Charli grappled for anything that would stop the easy slide across the polished floor, but to no avail.

"Oh, yes, I'll get away with it," he crowed. "Yarborough will make sure of it!"

Sweat erupting from every pore, Charli kicked against her captor while the name reverberated through her mind. But the fight for her life proved too taxing for her to remember who Yarborough was and why the name was so familiar. In a blur of twisting and sweating and calling out to God, Charli finally realized she was losing the battle. Now on his knees, Sigmund wrestled her leg into a vice grip and held the needle inches from her calf.

In a last effort for her life, Charli delivered a final, desperate kick at his chin that sent him sprawling backward midst a long stream of expletives. He released her leg. The syringe toppled to the floor.

Charli crawled to her cell phone and snatched it while stumbling to her feet. A frantic glance over her shoulder proved that Sigmund was recovering as swiftly as she. With a primal roar, he gripped the syringe and lunged toward her. On her way past the dining table, Charli grabbed a chair and hurled it over. The bumping and cursing that followed suggested the move had been successful.

However, Charli didn't take the time to even look. Instead, she focused on her goal: the utility room. The doorknob had an inside lock that might not be the sturdiest but it would at least buy Charli enough time to call Jack.

By the time Charli whipped open the door, Sigmund's footfalls sounded on the tile. When she tried to step inside, the cats darted out, and Charli lurched into two giant steps to keep from squishing them. The momentum flung her into the room, and she crashed against the washing machine. The door banged the wall. Her cell phone spun toward the litter box with as much velocity as the air swooshing from Charli's lungs.

She collapsed to the floor at the same time Sigmund's cursing began anew. "Stupid cats!" he hollered. A crash followed.

Charli crawled to the door, slammed it, and locked the knob. Whimpering, she eyed the closed door while reaching for the phone. Expecting the knob to rattle, she held her breath and blindly tried to flip open her cell phone. But her hands shook so fiercely she dropped the phone. As it clattered to the floor, Charli realized the kitchen had gone strangely silent. There was no indication that Harlings was even standing up.

Nevertheless, Charli pressed Jack's speed-dial number and held her breath. He answered immediately.

"Jack," she cried.

"Charli! Charli! What's wrong?"

"Come quick! It's Harlings! He's here! He's trying to kill me!"

"I'm only a minute out," he replied.

"He's in the kitchen!" she screamed and scooted toward the washer. "He's after me with a syringe full of something deadly!"

"I'm coming!" Jack declared.

"He locked the front door," she hurried. "The key—I put the new key under the rock! Oh, Jack, he killed Brenda Downey too! He told me! And somehow—somehow somebody named Yarborough is involved."

"Dan Yarborough?" Jack echoed. "You mean, my Dan."

"He just said Yarborough would cover for him."

Jack groaned. After a pause, he demanded, "Just stay put."

"I am!" Charli exclaimed.

"I'm pulling up. No matter what you hear, don't come out. Understand?"

"Y-yes," Charli agreed and strained for any sound of Sigmund.

Panting, Charli waited what felt like an hour before the front door opened. Jack's heavy footfalls pounded through the living room and stopped in the kitchen. Charli held her breath and expected the inevitable fight, but was only met with more silence.

Swallowing against a whimper, she resisted the urge to call out to Jack. But soon, a soft knock vibrated against the door. "Charli? Open up," he said. "The coast is clear."

Fully trusting Jack's judgment, Charli struggled to her feet and stumbled for the door. Once opened, she looked up into Jack's grim face. Without a word, he pointed to a still figure lying facedown in the middle of the kitchen.

"He's dead," Jack stated with a peculiar twist to his words. "I checked his pulse, but I didn't move the body. What happened?"

A movement near the doorway drew Charli's attention to the two wide-eyed cats who skulked into the kitchen like they didn't know whether to give in to curiosity or fear.

"He must have tripped over them," she deduced, "and fallen on his own syringe."

She met Jack's gaze. And this time, when Charli wrapped her arms around him, she had no intentions of pulling back. "Oh, Jack," she said and sobbed against his shirt. "He's the one who set me up! And he killed Brenda Downey," she repeated.

"Come on," Jack crooned and ushered her toward the garage door. "Let's get you outside. I'll call an ambulance. You don't have to even look at him again."

Averting her gaze, Charli allowed Jack to lead her outside. After the shower, fragrant rain dripped from the house's eaves around the opened garage in a peaceful cadence that belied the recent upheaval. Quivering, Charli covered her face and blindly followed Jack's lead.

Jack tucked the coverlet tighter around Charli and draped his arm across her shoulders. After the ambulance departed, the police report had been filed, and he'd assigned Payton to question Yarborough, he'd helped Charli gather her things and then brought her home with him long enough for her to calm down. Even though he was highly distracted over Yarborough's connection to all this twisted mess, Jack decided he was more needed here than at the station right now. Payton would take care of business as well as Jack ever could, and Jack would pick it all up tomorrow.

He and Charli had both decided Bonnie didn't need to know anything. Pat had gladly taken the child home with her, as planned. The church group had long departed, and Bud was banging around in the kitchen.

Charli leaned against Jack and rested her head against his shoulder. She hadn't said much after giving her official report, and Jack sensed the shock was just now wearing off.

"Thank you *so much,*" she breathed. "You saved my life!"

"Looks to me like the cats slew that giant," he said through an odd chuckle. "That was the weirdest thing I ever saw—a grown man lying dead in the floor and two cats looking guilty as all-get-out."

"Yes," she lifted her head, and her eyes were

now liquid pools of love, "and you gave me the cats."

"Yeah, I guess I did, didn't I?" Jack stroked her cheek.

"I'm *so sorry* for everything," Charli whispered. "All these years . . . all the pain. I'm sorry I jerked you around and then told you you had to make a choice. It's only the grace of God you even came over when you did."

Jack laughed and stretched out his legs. "I loved it when you told me I had to make a choice." He smiled. "It meant *you'd* finally made your choice, and it was all for me." He laid his hand on his chest, and she relaxed against him once more.

His eyelids drooping, Jack observed the rustic pine walls and wished Bud would hurry with the warm apple cider he'd promised. If the smell was anything to go by, the stuff should be done.

"If there's any way I can ever make it up to you, Jack—"

"You can," he said with a slight nod and wondered if he should push his luck. Deciding he had nothing to lose, Jack finally added, "If you'll promise to spend the next few months getting seriously reacquainted."

Her silence left Jack wondering, but when she lifted her head and observed him with eyes full of wonder, Jack already had his answer.

"Are you asking me to . . ." she wrinkled her forehead.

"Just that we hit the rewind button, I guess, and start over where we left off eleven years ago."

"So you really *have* made your choice?"

Jack rested his head on the back of the couch, closed his eyes, and let the laughter rumble through him. "Oh, Charli," he finally said, "you're so funny. Mary Ann and I only ever went out once. I barely even held her hand. You *so* overreacted to her."

"Well, the way you started acting made me think—"

"I just backed off to give myself some space," he admitted and didn't add that Sonny had been his coach. Reminding himself to kiss Sonny's feet, Jack added, "I guess I had to get to a point where I placed it all in God's hands and just let him make it happen or not. I was tired of trying to force it."

"I've wondered why God allowed me to be arrested, and now I know," Charli admitted. "I guess we'd still be just small-talking here and there if you hadn't arrested me."

"Yeah. I think the Lord allowed this to bring the you-me thing to a head. Looks like it worked, huh? And by the way, you still haven't answered my question."

"Oh, you know the answer." She playfully slapped at his chest. "Yes, of course." Her triumphant smile reminded him of Bonnie's when she slid from the horse. Then her eyes took on an anguished light. "I've realized the reason I married Vince," she admitted.

"Oh?"

"I was sick, and it drove me to marry someone else who was sick. But I guess I learned from a pro." Her focus rested across the room, upon a memory Jack couldn't see. "I've realized my mom was just as sick as I was. All I did was follow the pattern she set for me with Dad."

"Yeah." Jack took her hand and stroked the palm with his thumb.

"You already know that?"

Jack nodded. "I pieced some of it together, but didn't exactly know how to tell you."

"I was so blind to it. I had *no idea,*" Charli said on a sigh before her gaze trailed to his lips, and she leaned toward him in silent invitation.

Jack settled for a light brush of their lips and then tugged her head back to his shoulder.

"Thanks for letting me lean on you," she said.

"Lean on me all you want," he encouraged. "That's what these big shoulders are for."

Dear Friend,

I hope you enjoyed reading *Texas Heat* as much as I enjoyed writing it. I set the book in Bullard, Texas, which is a small town just north of where I live in Jacksonville, Texas. Many of the references to street names and the countryside are all factual, as is the down-home, cozy feel of a small, east Texas town. Small Texas towns are my favorite setting for my novels because I'm a small-town Texas gal who enjoys the simple pleasures of life, including pine-covered hills, breath-taking sunsets, the beauty of country churches, and fishing in our family's pond. I hope you enjoyed the picture of my world painted within this book.

My even greater hope is that the deeper themes of this book will encourage you in your faith as well as empower you to be all you can be for Christ. I always try to feature thought-provoking messages in my novels that will give my readers something to take away. This time, I created a heroine who had issues with co-dependency, as does both the heroine and hero's mothers. Co-dependency can manifest itself in a variety of ways but always boils down to the tendency to need approval and the willingness to enable even abuse due to the fear of not receiving approval. It can lead to a lot of different coping mechanisms, including creating situations where others depend upon the co-dependent as well as workaholism—

even church workaholism. Co-dependency can be subtle or more blatant—especially when enabling drug or alcohol addiction. Whatever the case, co-dependents can't and don't draw boundaries on unhealthy behavior in others.

My own deliverance from subtle co-dependency played a role in my ability to create this theme in *Texas Heat*. Once my deliverance was complete, my eyes were opened to the vast number of people in churches who are co-dependent. No, they may not be enabling drug or alcohol addiction, but they do manifest other co-dependent tendencies, such as using positions as a means to having control over others by making others depend upon them. True Christian service is about empowering others to be all they can be for Christ. It's not about control or co-dependency. The answer to breaking free requires honesty, not denial.

If you'd like to read more on this subject, please visit my Web site where you can contact me for references:

www.debrawhitesmith.com

or write me at:
Debra White Smith
P.O. Box 1482
Jacksonville, TX 75766

RealLifeMinistries@suddenlink.net

DISCUSSION QUESTIONS

1. Charli didn't quit her job when she felt that she should because she was afraid of displeasing her employer and of not being able to find another job. How does fear paralyze us from doing what we sense God is telling us to do?

2. 2 Timothy 1:7 states, "God has not given us a spirit of fear, but of power and of love and of a sound mind" (NKJV). How many sins can you think of that are related to or driven by fear?

3. Many times, people get the patterns of their issues mixed up with the promptings of God. Dialogue about how Charli did this.

4. Jack was frustrated that his mother was in denial about their family having issues that needed to be dealt with. How does denial perpetuate dysfunction?

5. Jack reflects that his mom equated forgiveness with enabling bad behavior or sin in others. In her eyes, the more dysfunction you allow people to unleash upon you, the more forgiving you are. Discuss how you can place healthy boundaries on bad behavior, sin, or abuse while still manifesting a forgiving spirit.

6. Jack believes that his father's neglect of his family due to workaholism contributed to

Sonny's drinking problem. Parents often pass their issues on to their children. How can a child of a dysfunctional parent break the patterns of generational sin?

7. What suggestions would you make to Charli and Jack in raising Bonnie so that she won't perpetuate Charli's co-dependent tendencies?

8. Sometimes God communicates with us in an urgent and direct way—as with Jack when he awoke in the night and went over to Charli's. It's up to us to listen to the voice of God and act upon it. How would the story have been different if Jack had ignored God's promptings that night?

9. How would "your story" be different if you chose to ignore God's urgent promptings?

10. When Jack finally got to the point of releasing his relationship with Charli to the Lord, God completed the work of bringing them together. Discuss how our totally releasing all control to God often precedes his answering our prayers.

DEBRA WHITE SMITH is a seasoned Christian author, speaker, and media personality who has been regularly publishing books for a decade. She has written over fifty books with over one million books in print. Her titles include such life-changing books as *Romancing Your Husband*, *Romancing Your Wife*, *It's a Jungle at Home; Survival Strategies for Overwhelmed Moms*, the Sister Suspense fiction series, and the Jane Austen fiction series.

Along with Debra's being voted a fiction-reader favorite several times, her book *Romancing Your Husband* was a finalist in the 2003 Gold Medallion Awards. And her Austen series novel *First Impressions* was a finalist in the 2005 Retailers Choice Awards. Debra has been a popular media guest across the nation, including Fox TV, The 700 Club, ABC Radio, USA Radio Network, and Moody Broadcasting. Her favorite hobbies include fishing, bargain-hunting, and swimming with her family. Debra also vows she would walk fifty miles for a scoop of German chocolate ice cream.

Center Point Publishing
600 Brooks Road ● PO Box 1
Thorndike ME 04986-0001 USA

(207) 568-3717

**US & Canada:
1 800 929-9108**
www.centerpointlargeprint.com